Dream a Little Death

Also by Susan Kandel

Dial H for Hitchcock

Christietown

Shamus in the Green Room

Not a Girl Detective

I Dreamed I Married Perry Mason

Dream a Little Death

A Dreama Black Mystery

SUSAN KANDEL

WITNESS
IMPULSE

An Imprint of HarperCollinsPublishers

This is a work of fiction. Names, characters, places, and incidents are products of the author's imagination or are used fictitiously and are not to be construed as real. Any resemblance to actual events, locales, organizations, or persons, living or dead, is entirely coincidental.

HarperCollins books may be purchased for educational, business, or sales pro-motional use. For information, please email the Special Markets Department at SPsales@harpercollins.com.

Digital Edition MAY 2017 ISBN: 978-0-06-267499-9

Print Edition ISBN: 978-0-06-267500-2

Map designed by LSD (Louise Sandhaus Design)

WITNESS logo and WITNESS are trademarks of HarperCollins Publishers in the United States of America.

HarperCollins is a registered trademark of HarperCollins Publishers in the United States of America and other countries.

FIRST EDITION

17 18 19 20 21   LSC   10 9 8 7 6 5 4 3 2 1

For my father, who taught me to love Los Angeles

DREAMA BLACK'S NOIR L.A.

west hollywood & the hills

19. Sheats-Goldstein House

17. Villa Primavera

18. Greystone Manor

16. Formosa Café

hollywood

15. The Dietrichson Residence

14. High Tower Court

9. Sowden House

11. Musso & Frank

12. Alto Nido Apartments

13. Crossroads of the World

10. Philip Marlowe Office

glendale

1. Mildred Pierce House

2. Glendale Train Station

mid-city

7. MacARTHUR PARK

8. Black Dahlia Death Site

downtown l.a.

3. Union Station

5. The Varnish

4. Far East Cafe

6. Eastern Columbia Building

Chapter 1

THE FIRST TIME I set eyes on Miles McCoy, I worried he might try to eat me. He was the size and girth of a North American grizzly bear, with long silver-tipped hair, a long silver-tipped beard, and small dark eyes that bore into me like I was a particularly fine specimen of Chinook salmon. It couldn't have helped that I'd used a honey scrub the morning we met. I should've known better. Not just about the scrub, but about a lot of things.

Like braving the freeway during rush hour.

Like thinking you can't get a ticket for parking at a broken meter.

Like racing up to his penthouse in Balenciaga gladiator sandals, and expecting not to twist an ankle.

Like watching his fiancée shoot herself, and assuming it was suicide, instead of murder.

But I'm getting ahead of myself, which is another thing I should know better about. Because if I've learned anything at all from my study of film noir (which got me into the whole sordid Miles McCoy mess to begin with), it is to tell the story *in the precise order* in which it happened.

The trouble started the day before, which was Valentine's Day, a pagan holiday named after the Roman priest who defied Claudius II by marrying Christian couples. After being hauled off in shackles, the soft-hearted cleric was beaten with clubs, stoned, and when that didn't finish him off, publicly beheaded. Makes you think.

It had poured rain for eight days running, which isn't what you sign on for when you live in Los Angeles. But that morning, as I stepped outside for a run, the sun was blinding—so blinding, in fact, that I didn't see the fragrant valentine my neighbor's dog, Engelbart, had left on the stoop for me. Not that I minded spending the next twenty minutes cleaning the grooves of my running shoe with a chopstick. It was a beautiful day. The rollerbladers were cruising the Venice boardwalk. The scent of medical marijuana was wafting through the air. Engelbart's gastrointestinal tract was sound.

An hour later, I hopped into my mint green 1975 Mercedes convertible, and made my way up Lincoln to the freeway. I was headed to Larchmont, an incongruous stretch of Main Street, USA, sandwiched between Hollywood and Koreatown. This was where studio executives' wives and their private school daughters came for green juice, yoga pants, and the occasional wrench from the general store that had served Hancock Park since the 1930s. It was also where my mother and grandmother ran Cellar Door, known for its chia seed porridge and life-positive service. I helped out whenever my coffers were running low. Which was most of the time.

You are probably frowning right about now. Surely a young woman who owns a classic convertible—as well as Balenciaga gladiators—should not be perennially low on funds. But it's true.

The car came from my grandmother, who received it as part of her third (fourth?) divorce settlement and gave it to me as a gift when I strong-armed my mother into rehab for the fourth (fifth?)

time. The sandals I purchased online in a frenzy of self-loathing shortly after watching my ex-boyfriend the rock god serenading his current girlfriend the supermodel on an otherwise uneventful episode of *Ellen*. I'd tried to return the sandals, but one of the studs had fallen off, making them damaged goods. Like their owner. Not that I'm hard on myself. It's just that my career—I take clients on custom-designed, private tours of my hometown of L.A.—wasn't exactly *thriving*, which is why I was easy prey for the likes of Miles McCoy. But I'm getting ahead of myself again. Here comes the good part. The part where I'm driving like the wind and almost don't notice the flashing lights in my mirror. I *knew* I should have fixed that taillight.

I pulled over, cut the motor, handed the cop my license and registration. He looked down, then did a double take. *"Dreama Black?"*

That would be me.

"*The* Dreama Black?" he continued. "As in 'Dreama, Little Dreama'?"

Perhaps I should explain.

I am a twenty-eight-year-old, third-generation rock 'n' roll groupie—or "muse," as the women in my family like to put it.

My grandmother, a fine-boned blonde who never met a gossamer shawl or Victorian boot she didn't like, spent the sixties sleeping her way through Laurel Canyon, winding up in a house on Rothdell Trail (a.k.a. "Love Street") purchased for her by a certain lead singer of a certain iconic band whose name is the plural of the thing that hits you on the way out.

My mother, blessed with thick, dark tresses and a way with mousse, was consort to many of the pseudo-androgynous alpha males of American hair metal, her chief claim to fame an MTV video in which she writhed across the hood of a Porsche wearing a white leotard and black, thigh-high boots. She also bought Axl Rose his first kilt.

As for me, well, I was on my way to freshman orientation when this guy I'd been seeing, who'd played a couple of no-name clubs with some friends from summer camp, intercepted me at LAX, put his lips to my ear, and hummed the opening bars of a new song I'd apparently inspired. Instead of boarding the plane for Berkeley, I boarded the tour bus with Luke Cutt and the other skinny, pimply members of Rocket Science. Four world tours, three hit albums, two Grammys, and one breakup later, "Dreama, Little Dreama"—an emo pop anthem that went gold in seven days and has sold eleven million copies to date—had made me *almost famous* forever.

"Step out of the car, please."

The cop removed his sunglasses. Peach fuzz. Straight out of the academy. "So."

He wanted to get a picture with me.

"I'd love to get a picture with you," he said.

I smoothed down my cut-offs and striped T-shirt, removed my red Ray-Bans, ran my fingers through my long, straight, freshly balayaged auburn hair . The cop put his arm around me, leaned in close, took a couple of snaps on his phone. Let me guess. He'd had a crush on me since tenth grade, when he saw me in a white tank and no bra on the cover of Rocket Science's debut C.D., and now he was going to post the pictures on Instagram to show all his buddies.

"Awesome." He gave me a brotherly punch on the arm. "No way is my wife going to believe this. She's crazy about Luke Cutt. Hey, is he really dating that Victoria's Secret Angel? She is *smoking hot*."

At least I didn't get the ticket.

I arrived at Cellar Door just in time for the staff affirmation, a daily ritual in which the servers, line cooks, busboys, and dishwashers all sit in a circle on the sustainably harvested bamboo floor and pass the talking stick. Today, after the group hug, my grandmother passed out napkins and small, odoriferous pellets which everyone nibbled at politely, then tossed surreptitiously into the trash.

I set to work wiping down the fir slab that constituted the communal table. Next I watered the herb wall and ironed the hemp tablecloths. Then I ducked into the kitchen. Gram was at the stove, testing the curry of the day.

"How are you?" I gave her a kiss on the cheek.

She whipped around, chiffon skirt flying, batwing sleeves fluttering. "Actually, I'm in a bit of a state."

"It's the Night of 1,000 Stevies, isn't it?" Gram always got upset when the annual Stevie Nicks tribute-cum-drag show, now into its third decade, rolled around.

She shook her head. "I'm so over that. Everybody knows full well that she-who-we-shall-not-name stole her so-called 'look' from me. No, it's Uncle Ray. He's back in my life. And he's in trouble."

"Uncle" is the generic term I've given to the unending parade of my mother's and grandmother's lovers. Uncle Ray stood out. He was high up in the L.A.P.D., for one thing. For another, he'd broken Gram's heart.

She took off her apron. "I don't want you to worry about it. I want to hear about you." She gave me a wink. "Anything special planned for tonight?"

The woman could not comprehend a life without romantic

intrigue, and I hated disappointing her. "The usual. Soft music, candles."

"Cruelty-free, promise?"

"You're mixing me up with my mother." Whose use of handcuffs and floggers has been well-documented elsewhere.

"I'm talking about the candles," said Gram. "Are you aware that beeswax is stolen from hives, tallow is a slaughterhouse product, and paraffin is carcinogenic?"

"You're a fine one to talk about cruelty-free," I answered. "What were those pellets you gave everyone earlier?"

Gram narrowed her lids. "Carob-dipped goji berries."

I rest my case.

My shift ended at four, and I took off soon afterward. I was driving against traffic so I made it home in under an hour. Home would be a tiny, bougainvillea-draped bungalow off Abbott Kinney, not far from the Venice canals, that I'd purchased with my unused college fund. The listing called it a "character house" in a "newly gentrifying area," which means a teardown plastered with gang graffiti. After I signed the papers, the broker suggested I get a Doberman. But I'm not easily intimidated. Too bad. Maybe if I'd gotten the Doberman, I wouldn't have gone for that gun. But I'm getting ahead of myself yet again.

After opening my mail, I uncorked a bottle of Pinot Grigio and decided on a B.L.T. As I was pulling out the bacon, however, I remembered next month's food tour for a group of Jewish singles from Milwaukee. I'd locked in the Kibitz Room at Canter's Deli and a meet-and-greet with a fermentation evangelist in Van Nuys who makes artisanal sauerkraut (certified kosher-pareve). Beyond that, however, I had nothing. Suddenly verklempt, I took to my bed with a third glass of wine.

The next thing I knew it was pitch-black and the doorbell was ringing. I looked down at my phone. Nine-thirty. I'd been asleep for hours. I pulled my cut-offs back on and stumbled out of the bedroom.

"Who is it?" I called out.

"Pizza delivery."

I looked through the peephole. Standing there was a hot guy in a Voidoids T-shirt. I let him in. His schnauzer, the aforementioned Engelbart, followed.

"You look like you were asleep." He scanned the room. "Alone, I hope."

When it comes to friends with benefits, geographical proximity can be a fine thing. Take the case of my next-door neighbor, Teddy. He's there when the urge strikes. The walk of shame is only a few steps long. And once in a while he shows up with an extra-large pizza.

"Sit down," I said. "Pour yourself some wine while I freshen up."

I hustled into my bedroom, looking for something fetching but not trashy. And then there was my mother's black leather catsuit, which I kept forgetting to drop off for her at the specialty dry cleaners on Sepulveda the exotic dancers all swore by. Oh, why not? After yanking out the shoulder pads, I have to say I looked pretty good. More like Scarlett Johansson in *The Avengers* than Tawny Kitaen in that Whitesnake video. Scarlett, if she were the waif type, that is. And wore a smaller cup size.

"Freeze!" I whipped around at top speed.

Teddy strode into the bedroom and put up his hands. "I surrender."

"Maybe we should eat first." I'd never gotten to that B.L.T.

"Not hungry." He reached for the zipper running down the front of the catsuit.

"Let me." I tugged, but it didn't budge.

Teddy kissed me long and hard, then pulled back. "I have an idea." There was a glint in his eyes. "Just like in the movies."

"No!" I backed away. "You can't rip it! It's *vintage!*"

He raised an eyebrow.

"I'm sorry, Teddy, but my mother wore it to Heather Locklear's wedding to Tommy Lee. Where are you going?"

He came back from the kitchen with a can of WD-40. "Hold still."

"You're kidding, right?" I closed my eyes.

"Fisherman spray it on their lures. The fish love it."

He pressed down on the nozzle. As the noxious scent filled the room I doubled over coughing. Plus, the zipper was still stuck.

Teddy disappeared into the kitchen again, coming out this time with a slice of pepperoni and some scissors. "I'm cutting the thing."

"Can you get me a piece, too?" After he left the room, I called my mother.

When she heard it was me, she dispensed with the usual niceties. "It's Valentine's Day, and you're home alone on your computer. And drinking. Sad."

Leos are caring, but lacking in tact. "Actually, I'm with someone."

"Then what are you doing calling me?" Muffled laughter. "Stop that! Bad boy!"

Teddy had returned and was waving a slice of pizza under my nose. I shooed him away. "What's going on over there, Mom? Is that the guy who makes the savory seitan pies? Has he actually graduated from high school?"

"He's twenty-one, which was legal last time I checked. What about you? Please don't tell me it's your next-door neighbor. That is not how the women in our family do things. Love is not supposed to be *convenient*." More laughter, then gulping sounds. "Ooh. Pineapple?"

I was feeling vaguely ill now, so I cut to the chase. "The zipper on your catsuit is stuck and Teddy wants to cut me out of it."

"Grease the pig!" my mother commanded.

"What pig? Mother, what is going on?"

"I'm talking to you," she said. "Do you have any Crisco?"

"Crisco? Why would I have Crisco?"

Teddy looked up from his phone. "Crisco? That sounds *awesome*."

"If you shove some down the front of the catsuit," my mother said, "your body heat will warm it up enough to allow you to wriggle out. Remember, leather gives."

I walked Teddy and Engelbart to the front door with a full market list. Might as well kill two birds with one stone. After they left, I found the savory seitan pie dude on Facebook. He was eighteen. Then the phone rang.

"Well, that was *quick*," I said to my mother, trying not to sound superior. Only it wasn't her. It was a man whose voice I didn't recognize. He told me his name, but I wasn't sure if I'd heard right. It couldn't be.

"*The* Miles McCoy?" I asked. "Miles McCoy, the *record producer*?" His story was legendary. A burly white guy from Detroit, he started a rap label in his college dorm room back in the nineties and won eight Grammys before graduation. After a split with his partners, he went into seclusion at a Tibetan monastery, only to emerge as a master of the turnaround, resurrecting the careers of washed-up crooners by getting them to record heavy-metal ballads, or engineering collaborations between country stars and faded hip-hop divas. He had four ex-wives, didn't touch alcohol, and always carried prayer beads and a miniature legal pad.

"Yes," Miles said. "But don't believe everything you hear. People lie."

People lie.

It wasn't like I'd had to read between the lines. The man had come right out and said it. But apparently, I hadn't been paying attention. And what a pity that was. Maybe if I had been no one would've died.

"You're quite the cynic," I said.

"Not really," Miles replied. "It's just that I keep falling for smooth, shiny girls, hard-boiled, and loaded with sin."

"Wait," I said. "Don't tell me. *Double Indemnity*? No, *The Big Sleep*?" The other thing everybody knew about Miles McCoy was that he was obsessed with film noir. Me, too. Growing up, Gram, Uncle Ray, and I spent a lot of time on her couch, watching old movies on cable while my mother was AWOL.

"You'll have to look it up to be sure," Miles said.

"I will," I said. "In the meantime, how can I help you?"

He said he'd like to go over it in person. Was I available Thursday—tomorrow—at 9 a.m.?

I hesitated only a minute before agreeing to make room in my busy schedule. Maybe Miles McCoy wanted to resurrect *my* moribund career.

Later in the evening, I learned just how versatile Crisco can be. Soon after I would learn there are things out there a lot more slippery.

I don't mean rain-slicked pavements in a classic film noir.

I mean music moguls who can quote Raymond Chandler's *Farewell, My Lovely* by heart.

Chapter 2

MILES McCOY LIVED in the penthouse of the Eastern Columbia Building, which I'd always admired from my car while stuck on the 10 heading downtown. Clad in turquoise terra cotta, ornamented with zigzags and chevrons, and capped with a four-sided clock tower, it's the most beautiful Art Deco building in L.A., and—even more important—the site of the climactic scene in the pilot episode of *Moonlighting*, where Cybill Shepherd hangs by her fingernails from one of clock faces until she's saved by Bruce Willis, when he still had hair.

(Yes. Bruce is one of my uncles.)

The neighborhood was, as they say, in transition. I found a metered spot in front of a check-cashing store, then jogged across the street, past a cold-pressed-juice bar and a boutique selling dresses for *quinceañeras*, and through the building's front entrance, with its recessed two-story vestibule adorned with a blue and gold terra cotta sunburst. Inside the lobby were some plush armchairs, one of which was occupied by a homeless man holding up a piece of cardboard that read, "Let's Do Lunch: You Buy." Sign of the times.

Like the brochures fanned out on the front desk advertising two-bedroom, two-bathroom loft-style condos affordably priced at just under $2 million.

The concierge directed me to Miles's private elevator, which was playing a Muzak version of "Que Sera, Sera." I hummed along. Then the doors slid open.

The woman standing in front of me was a cross between Jessica Rabbit and a Maori shaman. Between the boobs and the tattoos, it was hard not to stare.

"Hi!" I focused on a spot just above her left shoulder. "Sorry I'm late." I pointed to my sandals. "I twisted my ankle running in these stupid things."

The woman looked me up and down, pausing at the small picnic basket slung over my arm. "We don't do sandwiches. We're gluten-free."

"Do you mean *this*? It's my purse." I'd stolen the idea from Jane Birkin, whom I've been told I resemble. She's the British model from the sixties they'd named the handbag after, though only a lunatic would buy a Birkin at Hermès when you could buy one of these at Bed Bath & Beyond. Plus, no waiting list.

"Oh, my *god*," she said. "Do you *not get* that we're busy here? *Mookie!*"

Mookie was a XXXL easy. As he approached, the windows shook, the floor vibrated, the crystals on the chandelier trilled.

"Can you please remove this person?" The woman studied her nails.

"Excuse me, but I have an appointment. Dreama Black?"

"How nice of you to make an effort," she snapped.

In L.A., skinny jeans, a black tank, and designer footwear usually counts as business casual.

"It's not like anybody could compete with *your* outfit," I said. Which would be a green sequined corset worn with cream-colored gauchos and matching platform clogs. "Or your hair, which is *so* great." Did I mention it was the precise color and texture of Flamin' Hot Cheetos?

"It isn't natural," she said.

"Mine either."

She slapped her forehead. "No kidding."

Enough was enough. "I believe Miles is expecting me?"

"Miles and his expectations," she muttered under her breath. "This way."

The living room was enormous and lined with bookshelves. I caught a glimpse of *Little Women, The Hindu Book of Astrology,* and a biography of Steve McQueen. A large sandstone Buddha sat crossed-legged in the middle of the space, a bowl of oranges at his feet. At the far end was a baby grand piano, flooded in natural light. Outside the window were gray clouds and a vintage neon sign reading, "JESUS SAVES."

The two of us approached a black leather couch. There was a leg hanging over the edge, and a bare foot buried in a furry white rug.

The woman cleared her throat. "Miles? Your nine o'clock is here."

We waited.

"Earth to Miles," she intoned.

No response.

"Miles!" She shook his shoulder. *"Get the fuck up!"*

He whipped off his earphones. "No echo, no slap-back, no overdubbing, no mixing. It's brilliant. But the bridge." His eyes were closed. "I'm, like, *dismayed* with the bridge."

The woman wrinkled her brow. "I knew you were going to say that."

Miles wiggled his toes, then opened his eyes like he was coming out of a trance. "Dreama Black?"

"Hey," I replied. "Nice to meet you."

He padded around to the other side of the couch. Miles wasn't as enormous as Mookie, but he was still larger than life. If he'd been garbed in flowing robes instead of an oversized white T-shirt and khakis you could totally imagine him pairing up goats and wildebeests on the Ark.

"The pleasure is all mine," he said. "You keep popping up on my radar these days. Great article in the *Times*."

The tenth anniversary of "Dreama, Little Dreama." They ran a photo of me holding up the C.D. with the photo of me on the cover. Humiliating. As a small business owner, however, you do what you have to.

"And then," Miles said, "a buddy tells me about this cool chick who ran a deathrock tour a few weeks back. Heard it was awesome."

Marilyn Manson types from Chicago. They wanted B-horror movie locations, taxidermy shops, and the Museum of Death. After we finished up at Hollywood Forever Cemetery, I threw in a stop at La Guanaquita because after a long day, even Goths need *pupusas*.

"I see you've met my right-hand woman," Miles said.

I glanced her way. "Unofficially."

Miles shot her a warning look. "Pee Chee."

"That's your name?" I asked.

Her smile was as warm as liquid nitrogen. "P-E-E space C-H-E-E. As in the school folders."

"They come in multiple colors now," Miles said. "But I'm partial to the original goldenrod."

"Flatterer." Pee Chee walked over to the door, spun around. "I'll be in the study, if you need anything."

Miles turned to me. "Let's sit. I want to get right to the point."

I sat. He remained standing.

"You've heard a lot about me," Miles said. "We established that in our previous conversation."

"Right," I said. "Also, that I shouldn't believe everything I hear."

"True that," said Miles. "Anyway, one of the things you might have heard is I'm getting married in two weeks."

I got it. "And you're not."

"Are you crazy? Fuck, *yeah*, I'm getting married." He lowered himself onto a white leather chaise. "Her name is Maya Duran. She is *incredible*. My green-eyed goddess. Not that anybody knows. She's had issues with stalkers, so she's militant about her privacy. No red carpet. No social media. Nothing out there for pervs to pin up in their weird-ass storage spaces, if you know what I'm saying. Maya's, like, my little secret."

Strange comment. I should have called him on it. First mistake.

"We met in the summer." His eyes misted over. "I don't know how I got so lucky. She's a dancer. Burlesque. Like Dita Von Teese, but younger. I'd introduce you, but she's locked in her studio all week rehearsing, and swears she'll beat the shit out of me if I so much as knock on the door. You'll meet her on Sunday. That's the night of her big debut. So much for privacy after that, am I right? Hey, Dreama? I want to show you something."

Miles bolted upright. Attention deficit disorder. Increasingly common in adults. He pulled me down the hall. "We're going to the inner sanctum."

The inner sanctum was his bedroom, judging by the king-sized bed. He saw me square my shoulders.

"Now don't go worrying about ol' Miles." He squeezed my arm. "I'm kind of a monk these days."

He walked me over to a revolving magazine rack in the corner of the room, right by his nightstand. I knew it was his nightstand because the other one had a vase of red roses on it. His had the remotes. Also, a pair of handcuffs. Some monk.

"These look like junky old magazines, right?" he asked.

"Actually—"

"Wrong. These are the original *Black Masks*, with the original stories by every important hard-boiled and noir writer. Along with filler by hacks nobody's heard of. All in all, the crème de la crème of pulp fiction. And I've got the full run."

He pulled out an issue. "This one's my pride and joy." The cover featured an illustration of a Chinese gangster holding a smoking gun. "December 1933. Raymond Chandler's first appearance in print. 'Blackmailers Don't Shoot.' The story's got it all. The chivalrous detective, a modern-day knight in shining armor. The fucked-up damsel in distress. Melancholy. Corruption. Murder. And Los Angeles, great and gaudy and neon-lit. Which is where you come in."

At last.

Miles started pacing. "Couples should share interests, am I right? Unfortunately, Maya doesn't exactly *get* my stuff. Dusty old pulps. Bad prints of black and white movies. I get it. She's a young girl. But there is one thing we both like, and that's driving around and looking at cool shit. So Pee Chee had this, like, *vision*: the whole wedding party, dressed to kill in a fleet of cherry forties Plymouths, gunning down dark alleys and ducking into cheap hotel rooms and low-rent apartments on this fucking amazing, one-of-a-kind noir-themed tour of L.A. that you will organize as my wedding present to my fiancée."

I sucked in some air. "Wow. This is quite an honor. But—"

"With craft mocktails. In an historically appropriate setting. Followed by dinner. Vegan preferred. And dancing. No floor show. We can skip that part."

Let's see if I had it right. He was looking for a tour guide. Who was also a location scout, art director, local history buff, film scholar, event coordinator, plant-based nutritionist, sober minder, and couples counselor. "Miles, I—"

"And it's got to happen next Thursday."

In one week, that would be. I was about to ask for aspirin when he said he'd be paying me in cash. Apparently, his accountant didn't approve of his extravagant gestures. Then he threw out a number. An *insane* number. I'm talking *five figures* insane. I could pay off my credit cards. Pay down my mortgage. Invest in my business. Buy my mother and Gram some decent restaurant equipment.

"I'm in," I said breathlessly.

"Before we shake," Miles said, "there is one thing."

There's always one thing.

Miles said, "Your website promises 'satisfaction guaranteed.'"

My mother's idea. Also, the name of her unpublished autobiography.

"I just want to be clear that I'm going to hold you to that." Miles looked at me. "I mean, Maya's kind of hard to please. And if she's not happy . . ." He shook his head. "Well, *I'm* sure as fuck not going to be happy. So are we cool?" He stuck out his hand.

I shook it. "We're cool."

"Boss." Mookie lumbered into the room, knocking over a lamp. "Sorry to interrupt." He picked up the lamp. "But you got an appointment with Destiny."

"Destiny D-Low," Miles explained. "The rapper."

"You know she doesn't like that word," Mookie chided. "She's an *artist*."

Miles took a deep, cleansing breath and pulled out his prayer beads. "Like *I'm* a fucking artist. She's just pissed because I'm on her to tighten up the structure. Everybody thinks all the problems can be worked out in the mix, but like I keep saying, I'm not a god-damn knob-turner. Is the car ready?"

Mookie said, "Yeah, boss."

Miles turned to me. "Wait for me in the living room, then I'll walk you out."

In the living room I took a seat on the white chaise. Something hard pressed into my back. It was a wallet. I looked up for a minute. No one around. No harm in flipping the thing open. Interesting. Miles's Wikipedia page said he was forty-five, but according to his driver's license, he was fifty. And what was this? Opposite his license was a photo of a beautiful girl. Twentyish, with pale skin, red lips, a cap of dark, glossy hair, and huge, green eyes. The fiancée. Maya Duran. Talk about smooth, shiny, and loaded with sin. Jesus. I hoped I hadn't just sold my soul to a she-devil for financial security and a walk-in refrigerator.

"Dreama?"

I shoved the wallet back into the chaise, and snatched up my basket. "Ready!"

While we were waiting for the elevator, Pee Chee came clomping out in her platform clogs. "You almost forgot this." As she handed Miles his wallet, she cast a baleful glance my way.

"What would I do without you?" Miles pecked her on the cheek.

She turned her face up to his. "I think we both know."

I thought it was harmless banter.

Second mistake.

By the time Miles and I stepped out onto Broadway, the air was warm and the sky a cloudless blue. Mookie was at the curb, holding open the door of a shiny black stretch Bentley, but Miles signaled that he'd be a minute. We walked down the block in companionable silence. Then he pointed to a building. "You know what that is?"

I looked up. Samsung. Sony. Toshiba. Sanyo. "A place to buy a camera?"

Miles shook his head. "When that building went up in 1910, it was one of the finest motion picture houses in the country. Now it's a swap meet. But if you go into the storage room and wade through the cardboard boxes and counterfeit crap there's the original screen. The original projection booth. The original decorative walls. And nobody knows a thing about it."

Another one of Miles's little secrets.

We stopped at my car. "Figures." I plucked a parking ticket off of my windshield. "That's the last time I'm parking at a broken meter."

"Let me take care of it." Miles pulled out his wallet and handed me a hundred-dollar bill. "You're on the payroll now."

As I pulled away from the curb, I caught a glimpse of a frowning Miles, thumbing through his wallet, like he was looking for something.

His snapshot of his fiancée, Maya Duran.

Which I'd apparently just stolen.

Chapter 3

"Yesterday you did *what*?" My best friend, Cat, put down her tattoo liner and peeled off her gloves. Who knew that a girl who spent her formative years swallowing fire at the Coney Island Freak Show could be so easily shocked?

Her second-in-command, Tigertail—nine months pregnant and ready to pop—yelled from across the room, "I never figured you for a klepto, Dreama!"

"Excuse me, but are we done yet?" The half-naked man spread-eagled in front of Cat mopped his forehead with his flannel shirt. "I need to throw up."

"I still have to put the wash in the background," Cat said. "Stay strong."

Five years ago, Cat had opened a tattoo shop, Cat House, with the money she'd gotten after divorcing Max the Human Pin Cushion, who turned out to have a sizable trust fund. Since then, Cat had expanded twice, turned down three reality shows, and been voted president of the board of the West Hollywood Chamber of Commerce. Some people have a gift.

"Our shit-for-brains intern didn't restock the candy machine," grumbled Cat's third-in-command, Rory, who also happened to be Tigertail's babydaddy. "And I can't find the release forms. And the hordes are descending."

As Cat liked to say, Friday night is Monday morning in the tattoo business. True enough, there were already a dozen customers lined up outside, anxious to get a tribal marking, religious icon, or flower inked onto their skin for eternity before they changed their minds and bolted.

And koi. For some reason, everybody always wanted koi.

"It was the stupidest thing," I said to Cat.

"I get you," the half-naked man said. "My girlfriend kept saying, do you *really* want a six-pack of Pabst Blue Ribbon tattooed on your stomach?"

Ignoring him, Cat pressed the foot pedal and her shader started whirring. "You really need to work on impulse control, Dreama."

"It's not like I *meant* to steal it," I said over the din. "But then Miles came back and there was no time to slip it back into his wallet. What was I supposed to do? And how am I supposed to get it back to him?"

Cat sighed. "I think the real question is why do you keep getting yourself into these kinds of situations?"

"I was just trying to do my job," I said. "Which apparently entails figuring out this mystery woman Miles is besotted with so that I can somehow make her *happy*."

That was part of it, at least.

"You?" Rory snorted. "How are *you* supposed to make a total stranger happy when you couldn't even make your ex Luke Cutt happy?"

That was the other part.

I wanted to know what Maya Duran had that I didn't.

"*Luke Cutt* is your ex?" The young woman at Tigertail's station, who was getting the outline of a tiny butterfly inked onto her shoulder, sat straight up. "Are you *Dreama*? Oh, my god!"

Before I could answer, she and the two friends she'd brought with her started harmonizing on the chorus of "Dreama, Little Dreama." After posing with them, and answering their many queries about Luke, like whether or not he waxed his chest (yes) and whether or not he'd been high at his Bar Mitzvah (no), I was desperate to change the subject.

"Have you decided on a name for the baby?" I asked Tigertail.

She looked over at Rory. He stroked his goatee, then nodded.

"Sprite." Tigertail patted her tummy.

"That's so cute," said the girl getting the butterfly tattoo. "Like the soda?"

Rory looked appalled. "Sprite, as in fairy, elf, pixie, *gnome*?"

"I should go," I said. "It's a long drive back to Venice. And I still have a lot of work to do on this tour."

Cat glared at Rory, then turned to me. "It's going to be incredible. I feel like this is your moment. Don't you?"

I had to admit I did. Yesterday, after leaving Miles's, I'd gone straight to the library, and by the end of the day I'd come up with an amazing itinerary. Among the highlights were visits to the High Tower Court, a Streamline Moderne complex in the Hollywood Hills with a five-story private elevator, described in Chandler's *The High Window* as P.I. Phillip Marlowe's residence; the crumbling Alto Nido apartments on Sunset and Ivar, immortalized in Billy Wilder's *Sunset Boulevard* as the home of the suicidal screenwriter played by William Holden; and the Formosa Cafe, founded in 1925 inside a defunct Red Car trolley, where gangsters

Bugsy Siegel and Mickey Cohen would drink, smoke, and order hits, hiding the spoils in a safe still visible under one of the curved red leather booths. After seitan "ribs" and virgin Mai Tais, we were going to drive south to Leimert Park, where on the morning of January 15, 1947, a local resident discovered the body of twenty-two-year-old Elizabeth Short—naked, mutilated, and drained of blood. Like so many before and after her, Short came out West to seek her fame and fortune. Who could've predicted she'd find it as the Black Dahlia, pin-up girl of L.A. noir? And how ironic was it that if you stood on the very spot where she was found and cast your eyes due north, you could see the Hollywood sign, forever icon of the fatal lure of Los Angeles?

It was everything Miles had asked for.

That's the thing about us groupies.

We are good at fulfilling other people's fantasies.

"You're done!" Cat taped a bandage over the half-naked guy's six-pack. "Leave it there for at least two hours, then consult the aftercare sheet. Remember, no Neosporin. It pulls the color." She took my hand. "Come with me."

I followed her into the bathroom. "You okay?"

"I'm fine." Cat lathered her hands. "I just wanted to make sure Rory hadn't offended you. Tigertail is pregnant, but he's the one who's impossible."

Tigertail and Rory were old friends from Coney Island. They'd held Cat's hand on the historic day she got her first tattoo, a cat-o'-nine-tails.

"Me? Offended?" I smiled. "I was serious about getting back to work. Satisfaction guaranteed, remember?"

Cat dried her hands, then looked into the mirror and fluffed her nimbus of blond hair. "Hey, can I see her picture?"

I reached into my purse and handed it over.

Cat studied it for a moment, then turned on her heel.

"What?" I followed her out of the bathroom.

Cat marched straight over to Tigertail. "You know I never forget a face. This girl. Don't we know her?"

"You *know* Maya Duran?" I asked, incredulous.

Tigertail looked at the picture, then said she didn't think so. She handed the picture to Rory, who didn't think so either. Then he returned the picture to Cat, who suddenly blurted out, "The lotus flower!"

"Let me see that again." Rory peered at the picture. "The *goddamn lotus flower!*" He slapped his thigh. "I *knew* I should have gone with her to the ATM."

Apparently, Maya Duran had come in three or four years ago wanting an entire sleeve consecrated to her spiritual path: a mandala, a Bodhi tree, the eternal knot, the circle of Zen, a couple of mantras. All she got was one large pink lotus on her arm. And without paying so much as a dime.

"I'm getting that girl back in here." Cat started thumbing through the receipt book. "If she's marrying Miles McCoy, who's richer than God, then she can pay me for the lotus flower, and we can finish the rest of the Buddhist cosmology while we're at it. We have Sprite's college fund to think about!"

"I don't know," I said nervously.

"Come on," said Cat. "While she's here, I'll even let you hide in the corner and spy on her."

"Miles says she's obsessive about her privacy. You can't find her on the internet." Believe me, I'd tried.

"Yeah, well, I'm obsessive about not getting stiffed. Aha!" Cat pulled out the receipt. "Here it is." She frowned.

"What now?" I asked.

"This makes no sense. The name on the receipt isn't *Maya Duran*." Cat picked up her cell phone and started dialing. "It's *Carmen Luz*."

Carmen Luz? I grabbed the piece of paper and studied it. Carmen Luz didn't live with Miles downtown in the Eastern Columbia Building. She lived somewhere in Glendale. Whoever Carmen Luz might be.

"The number's disconnected." Cat tossed the phone across the desk. "Just my luck."

The one whose luck I worried about wasn't Cat.

It was Miles McCoy.

Chapter 4

Carmen Luz."

THAT NIGHT I slept badly.

What kept me up wasn't the wind blowing through the fallen
palm fronds in my front yard, the gangbangers partying after
hours at the Oakwood rec center, or the feral cats prowling the
alleyways off the boardwalk.

It was the girl in the picture.

Cat, Rory, and Tigertail all agreed her name was Carmen Luz.
Were she and Maya Duran the same person? If so, why did Carmen
Luz change her name to Maya Duran? Was the green-eyed goddess Miles was in thrall to more hard-boiled and loaded with sin
than he knew? Was I duty-bound to tell him? I mean, I *was* on
the payroll, not to mention I actually *liked* the man. There was
something else. If Carmen wasn't Maya, why did Miles—a man
purportedly in love—carry her picture in his wallet?

I had lots of questions.

Too bad they weren't the right ones.

After a short run and a long shower, I got dressed, shoveled
some cereal into my mouth, and was out the door. Then I dou-

bled back and set the alarm. A girl on her own can never be too careful.

Teddy and Engelbart were taking the morning air. I took mental inventory of my outfit: red kitten-heel mules, white knit mini-dress. Then I started fussing with my bangs. They never blended into my hair as perfectly as Jane Birkin's.

"Leave it!" Teddy said.

He was talking to the dog, who was sniffing something that looked like a broken glass pipe. In Venice, you never know. About the people. Or the dogs.

Teddy turned to me. "Where are you off to at this ungodly hour?"

It was 11 a.m. "Work."

"Cool." He gave me a wolfish grin. "Say hi to your mom."

"I'm not going to the café," I said. "I'm off on a research expedition."

"Oh."

Teddy didn't say much. His abs did most of the talking.

"Okay, then." I got into my car. "Have a good one." I realized I had no idea what he did all day. Something with computers, possibly.

"Dreama. Wait." Was he blushing? "We should hang out later."

"Are you asking me out? On a *date*? I think we're kind of past that."

Teddy leaned into the window. He smelled good, like pine needles and campfire smoke and other manly things. "Is that a no?"

Luke Cutt never stopped talking. Even in his sleep.

I smiled at Teddy. "It's a maybe."

Things were in good shape for the noir tour. I'd planned on eleven sites, concluding with a late supper at the Varnish, which was hidden speakeasy-style behind an unmarked door in the back of Cole's, the legendary downtown restaurant. All that remained was to scout one last location. Which just happened to be in Glendale. Which just happened to be where Carmen Luz lived. Not that I had any plans where Carmen was concerned. Absolutely not. I was going to be far too busy checking out the neighborhood where Mildred Pierce lives in the classic hard-boiled novel to engage in those kinds of shenanigans.

Poor, long-suffering Mildred Pierce.

After her husband leaves, she hits it big with a chain of fried chicken and pie restaurants, but no matter how much she sacrifices—and how well she rocks a fur coat with padded shoulders—she can't win the approval of her narcissistic daughter, Veda, who's repulsed by the smell of grease Mildred wears like perfume. Glendale plays a big part in the story. The author, James M. Cain, portrays it as a symbol of working-class aspiration, a suburban hell with endless rows of cookie-cutter Spanish bungalows. Wouldn't he have been shocked to learn that according to Zillow, 1143 North Jackson Street—the house where they filmed the Joan Crawford movie—was currently worth a cool million?

The first thing I noticed when I got there was that the Canary palm on the front lawn had shot up maybe fifty feet since 1945. The second was that there was a pocket park nearby. Perfect. That was where I was going to take our little tour group for a boxed lunch of fried chicken and pie.

After taking a few notes, I pulled out the receipt that I may have inadvertently dropped into my purse when I was at Cat's, and typed Carmen Luz's address into my phone. Turned out she lived in the foothills, a mere ten minutes away.

It was weird.

The car just sort of drove itself.

I pulled up in front of a standard post-war bungalow, one story, pinkish stucco, gray slate roof, shielded from the street by some overgrown bushes. I cut the motor, then grabbed my clipboard. If Carmen opened the door, I could pretend I was taking a survey.

Nobody answered.

I peered through the windows on either side of the front door. The place looked deserted. Maybe I could just tiptoe around the back and see if there was an open door.

No such luck.

I did, however, find a key under a potted succulent.

Yes, reader, it's a slippery slope. You start by stealing from people's wallets, and before you know it you're breaking and entering. Actually, trespassing. Which is barely a misdemeanor in the state of California. Like giving out plastic bags at supermarkets.

The lock was a little rusty, but I jiggled it a couple of times, then pushed so hard I nearly lost my footing as the door gave way.

From the looks of it, Carmen had cleared out in a hurry. In the living room there were hangers scattered on the floor. In the kitchen, dirty cups in the sink. The bedroom was equally atmospheric, with cabbage rose wallpaper, stained couch cushions, and an overturned peacock chair, like Morticia's in *The Addams Family*. Before leaving, I took a couple of pictures and posted them to Instagram, the beast that must be fed. Then I tweeted about it. #hauntedhouse, #ghostsofglendale, #DreamaDoesLA. After that, most people would have called it a day. But I'm not most people. Regrettably.

The house next door to Carmen's looked like it'd been built by tweaking elves. I'm talking trippy stained glass, sharply pitched gables, a fish-scale roof. A small sign read, "Psychic Readings by Madame Anna." I knocked.

The woman who opened the door was thirtyish, wearing a tight pink velour tracksuit and a diamond stud in her nose. She was holding a small dog, who gave me the evil eye.

"Hello," she said in a thick accent. Russian? Romanian? Some-place with castle ruins and a diet heavy on cabbage.

"Sorry to disturb you." I reached into my purse for the picture.

"Nothing disturb me. Come in. Do not be shy. I do not bite. The dog, maybe." She set him down and shooed him away.

The inside matched the outside—wood beams stenciled with flowers, iron sconces straight out of a medieval banquet hall. On the mantel, above a vintage tiled fireplace, was a bonsai tree and a Beanie Baby. Patti the Platypus.

"You are prepared to hear good and bad?" the woman demanded.

Before I could answer, she said, "I start with bad. You are open wound attracting negative energy."

She'd obviously been talking to my mother. "I'm not here for a reading."

"That is what they all say," she sniffed.

I showed her the picture. "Do you recognize this girl? She lived in the house next door. Her name is Carmen."

"Sixty dollar for reading. After, I make chit-chat."

I was doing this for the benefit of my client, wasn't I? And business expenses are tax-deductible. I handed the woman three twenties. She tucked them into a crystal bowl filled with pot-pourri and batteries. Then she closed her eyes.

"Wait!" Her eyes flew open. "You hear that?"

Jerry Springer was chiding somebody's mud-slinging mistress. The vacuum cleaner was on. The dog was barking.

"Is terrible! I cannot think!" The woman tossed her tarot cards onto the table, then bellowed down the hall, *"Quiet!"*

"I get it," I said. "It's hard running a business from home. By the way, can I get a receipt?"

She looked at me uncomprehendingly, then studied the card

that had flipped over. A hand holding a sword. "Bah!" She turned the card facedown.

"What is it?" I asked.

"Nothing," she said ominously. "We try something else. Think of two wishes, and tell me one."

The first wish was the same one I always made. I never said it out loud. The second wish would get me out of here. I wanted the dirt on Carmen.

"Carmen this, Carmen that." The woman made a face. "Why you are so obsessed with this girl? You are *snoop*. You live precariously."

"Do you mean *vicariously*?"

She nodded. "Self-awareness is encouraging sign."

"Can you just look at the picture?"

She glanced at it, handed it back. "Sorry. I do not know her."

Sixty bucks down the drain. "You never saw her next door?"

The woman said, "I am here only two months. I house-sit while owner is, how you say, *detained*. Do not mess with IRS."

"So you're not Madame Anna?"

She turned frosty. "This is America. I can be anyone I want."

Apparently. "I've got to run."

"Is better for pert bosoms to walk." She grabbed my phone and typed in her number. "I make house calls. In meantime, be careful. The card that turned over? Ace of Swords. This is card of persons who have desire for truth and justice. But Ace of Swords is double-edged. Your quest can bring misery and pain to others."

Cheering words from a post-Soviet imposter.

As I walked down the path, I saw a thin woman dragging the trash cans in from the curb. The housekeeper.

"Excuse me?"

She looked up, wiped her hands on her faded jeans. "Yes?"

I introduced myself. She said her name was Lizeth. I asked her if she'd worked here long.

"I've worked for Madame Anna for four years," she said.

Now I was getting somewhere. "I was wondering if you knew the girl who used to live next door. It would've been a couple of years ago."

As she looked at the picture, something passed across her face. "This is Carmen."

"That's right," I said. "Carmen Luz."

Lizeth peered at me. "You're her friend?"

This wasn't the time to get bogged down in technicalities.

"Yes," I said.

"Oh, Carmen," Lizeth sighed. "I miss her. She was so happy with her life, her house. For a girl like her, she said, it was a dream come true. Until—"

"Until what?"

She paused. "She showed up one day with a black eye."

Jesus.

"After that—" Lizeth shook her head. "*Que pesadilla. Nadie merece ese trato.*"

"I'm sorry, I don't speak Spanish," I said. "What happened after that?"

Lizeth looked puzzled, then said she thought I was Carmen's friend. When I didn't answer, she said she couldn't talk to me anymore. She was busy. She had work to do.

Driving home I remembered something James M. Cain said about *Mildred Pierce.*

Cain said that a dream come true is the worst possible thing that can happen.

Chapter 5

ABOUT FIVE MINUTES after I got home, the doorbell rang.

It was my uncle Ray.

It may not surprise you that my mother was sleeping with more than one person when she found out she was pregnant with me. Many more, in fact, not one of whom ever bothered to step up. And then there was my grandmother's on-again, off-again boyfriend, Ray, who was the closest thing to a father I'd ever had. It was Ray who bought me my first Pokémon card. Ray who took me to the eighth-grade father-daughter dance. Ray who taught me to drive. And even though we hadn't seen each other much lately, Ray was family. I knew that if I ever needed anything, he'd be there in a heartbeat.

"Hey, princess." He wrapped me up in a hug. "I've missed you."

"I've missed you, too." I put my hands on his shoulders, gave him the once-over. "You look good." The man was Denzel Washington's doppelgänger. "For an old man."

Ray tugged on a strand of my hair, then handed me a box.

Inside was my favorite, a cherry pie from Du-par's in the old Farmer's Market. I put on a pot of coffee and when it was done we took our cups and slices of pie into the living room.

"So." I sat down on the couch. "What's wrong?"

He sat down next to me. "What makes you think something's wrong? Can't I drop by because I haven't seen you in a while?"

I shot him a look.

"I like the new rug," he said. "It really complements the décor. What do you call that color? Mauve?"

I rolled my eyes. "Uncle Ray."

"Fine. There is something I wanted to tell you. It's going to be all over the news tomorrow, and I thought you should hear about it from me first."

Ray had been suspended from the force. Internal Affairs was investigating. They had an informant who said he'd shaken some-body down for $40,000, then laundered the money. Or hidden it offshore. They hadn't found it yet, but they would. And then he was going away for a long time.

"That is the *craziest* thing I've ever heard," I said.

"Crazy is right." He started pacing. "I'm not going to pretend that after twenty-three years on the job I haven't made enemies. But this I never expected."

"You think it's some guy you put into prison? Maybe the informant is doing the guy's dirty work for him. No, no! I'll bet it's someone on the force whose toes you've stepped on. A classic frame job."

This time Ray shot *me* a look.

"Sorry," I said. "Go on."

"The worst part is the timing. I'm up for a huge promotion.

Deputy Chief. I've worked my ass off to get it, but the announcement is going to be made next Thursday, and if this garbage doesn't get cleaned up by then, I'm out of the running."

I took his hand. "Is there anything I can do?"

"Yeah, there is. Did your grandmother mention that she and I were talking again?"

"'Talking'?" I smiled. "Is that what the kids call it these days?"

"Listen," he said, "the last thing I ever wanted to do was to come back into her life and cause more problems. She's already worked herself into a frenzy. Can you calm her down? Tell her not to worry? I could really use your help, Dreama."

I told him I would do that. And that he shouldn't worry either.

"What, me worry?" Uncle Ray stood up. "I've got to go. They're coming over this afternoon with a warrant to search the house."

I shook my head. "Do they really think they're going to find the money under your mattress? Who could get a decent night's sleep like that?"

Roy gave me a rueful smile. "$40,000 doesn't take up that much room. You could fit it in a manila envelope."

One minute after he left the doorbell rang again.

I ducked into the bathroom to check my teeth for pie, then went to open the door.

No one was there.

There was something on the stoop, however.

A manila envelope.

I looked up and caught the tail end of Miles McCoy's black stretch Bentley.

After the car disappeared from view, I went inside, sat down on the couch, and opened it up.

There was cash inside.

The five figures I'd been promised.

$40,000, to be exact.

Chapter 6

I BELIEVE IN certain laws of the universe. Cold hands, warm heart. Objects in the mirror are closer than they appear. There is no such thing as a coincidence—much less forty thousand of them. Which meant it was time to talk to Miles. About the money he'd just left on my doorstep, and what it might and might not have to do with my uncle. And about Carmen Luz, and who exactly she was or was not to him. Today, however, was not going to be the day.

Today was Maya Duran's debut.

My invitation had been dropped into the mailbox sometime this morning, while Teddy and I were otherwise engaged. It came with a souvenir flip book in which a dark-haired girl in her birthday suit performs a series of acrobatic maneuvers while dangling from the swing of a birdcage. The girl's face was so small I couldn't tell if she and the green-eyed girl in the photo I'd stolen from Miles's wallet were one and the same. Neither could Teddy, who was gracious enough to go through the flip book for me at least a dozen times. Not that it mattered anymore. I was about to see Maya Duran in the flesh. Which was only one of the reasons I'd decided against bringing Teddy as my date.

Sundays were slow at Cat House, so tonight was going to be girls' night. It was just after eight when I pulled up in front of Cat's West Hollywood condo. She was waiting outside in a midnight blue sequined mini-romper and thigh-high black boots, her short blond curls tucked inside a floppy, seventies-style hat. "Go big, or go home" is her mantra. For me, this was a work event, so I dressed accordingly: low-cut silk top, narrow black leather pants, leopard-skin ankle boots, a fluffy, cream-colored faux-fur jacket.

We made it downtown in record time. Maybe I'd been reading too much Raymond Chandler, but that evening L.A. looked exactly like he'd described it back in the thirties, the lights an endlessly glittering sheet, neon signs glowing and flashing, the languid ray of a searchlight prodding the high, faint clouds. Chandler also wrote that L.A. had the personality of a paper cup, proving you can't expect consistency from romantics with drinking problems.

No street parking, so we pulled into the lot next door to the Mayan Theater, whose spectacular pink façade—embellished with carved stone serpents and stout warriors in ceremonial headdress—looked like a Mesoamerican wedding cake.

Cat snapped a couple of pictures on her phone, then said, "Bet you didn't know this is the place that Whitney Houston and Kevin Costner go clubbing in *The Bodyguard*."

Of course I did.

Kevin was another one of my uncles.

The lobby looked like a set designer's Aztec fever dream, every surface ornamented with hieroglyphics and animal-sacrifice-themed bas-reliefs. A motley crew of dudes in snap-backs, skinny girls with statement glasses, and Williamsburg types sporting Dust Bowl workboots wandered about with neon yellow cocktails as waiters passed hors d'oeuvres.

While Cat went to check her hair, I inhaled half a dozen pigs in a blanket. My mother had canceled our usual Sunday brunch, and I hadn't eaten all day.

"Try saving some for the rest of us," I heard someone say.

I spun around. "Pee Chee." I finished swallowing. "Nice to see you again."

She looked almost chaste in a chartreuse satin slip dress, fishnets, and a crystal eagle necklace that took up most of the real estate on her ample chest.

"Don't bother," she said. "Miles is impressed with you, but I'm not buying."

"What makes you think I'm selling?" I asked.

"Cheeky." She reapplied her vermillion lipstick. "I'm going backstage to give Maya some moral support."

"I didn't know you two were close," I said.

"The things you don't know," she sighed.

"Who was *that*?" Cat handed me one of the signature cocktails.

"Miles's enforcer," I said.

"Phyllis," said Cat.

"Pee Chee," I said, taking a sip of my cocktail.

Cat tried her drink, then wrinkled her nose. "Nope. That's definitely Meyer lemon."

I shook my head. "The woman's *name* is Pee Chee. Like the folders."

"If her name is Pee Chee," Cat asked, "why does she have an ankle tattoo that says 'Phyllis'?"

Excellent question.

Just then they removed the velvet ropes, and everybody filed past the dwarf palms into the auditorium, which was filled with dozens of round tables covered with white cloths and flickering candles. We cruised around for a while trying to find Miles, then hemmed and hawed about the best place to sit.

"Excuse me?"

I turned around. It was the infamous Destiny D-Low. I recognized her by the vertiginous headwrap and razor-sharp cheekbones. "Y'all are welcome to join me over here."

The man sitting next to her—a dead ringer for Harry Potter, if he were gay and black—exclaimed, "Sweet Jesus! You're *Dreama*!" Then he broke into a rousing a cappella rendition of the song that had stolen my life.

Cat patted my hand, then gave the man a nudge. "Sh. It's starting."

The curtain parted to reveal a Rockefeller Center–sized Christmas tree strung with silvery tinsel and flickering white lights. Instead of an angel on top, however, there was Sam-I-Am holding a plate of green eggs and ham. Then the music came up: "You're a Mean One, Mr. Grinch."

Maya Duran tiptoed onto the stage. She was dressed as a foxy Cindy Lou Who in a skin-tight pink onesie and blond wig with red bows, and in her arms was a large red ornament ball, which she used to excellent effect as she stripped off her garments to the wailing horns of the beloved Christmas classic, now ruined for me forever, by the way.

Cat whispered, "Where's Miles?"

Another excellent question.

Next up was "Cherries in the Snow," a sexy homage to the classic Revlon shade. The climax consisted of Maya slithering to the top of a twelve-foot tube of lipstick, rubbing herself against it, then shimmying down wearing nothing but a smeared kiss on her inner thigh.

"Girl's a professional," said Destiny. "That shit isn't easy."

I signaled the waiter for another drink, then turned to Cat. "Luke bought me a Lil' Mynx for my twenty-first birthday."

Cat nodded. "The Cadillac of stripper poles."

Destiny said, "I met Luke Cutt at the VMAs once. He was a pussy."

I said, "Yeah, he couldn't get it up."

Cat nearly spit out her drink.

"I'm talking about *installing the pole*," I said. "It's ten feet long."

Destiny raised an eyebrow. "Size matters, honey."

In the next number, Maya was done up like a silver-screen goddess. She preened in front of a heart-shaped mirror, then dropped her white satin robe and sashayed over to a glass tub. As it filled with water she traced imaginary lines over her breasts, popped bubbles with her nails, and shed her marabou-trimmed panties and bra. Then she got in and lathered her X-rated bits. When she was done, she played peek-a-boo with her towel. As she exited stage left, the crowd erupted in catcalls.

I turned to Cat. "So? Is Maya the girl you tattooed? The stripper formerly known as Carmen Luz?" I handed her my opera glasses and she peered through them.

"Same hair, same skin, same body type," Cat said. "The face looks about right. But there's no way to be sure from this distance."

So much for that idea.

Suddenly, there was a commotion as two people made their way up to a table in the front.

Miles and Pee Chee, just in time for Maya's closing number.

Which was called—pithily—"Suicide."

First came a home movie of a little girl projected on a screen. Then, the haunting vocals of Lana Del Rey's "Young and Beautiful." Finally Maya appeared, hair pulled back, face scrubbed, wearing jeans and a white T-shirt. As the flickering image of the little girl gave way to increasingly quick cuts of burns, flashes, and scratches on the reel, Maya paced the stage, taking picture after picture of herself in a doomed attempt to catch the attention of an unseen lover. As the minutes passed, she began to move more and more frenetically, shedding more and more clothing until, stark naked and breathing hard, she crawled across the floor, picked up a gun, and shot herself in the chest.

You could have heard a pin drop.

Then the audience burst into applause.

"She has it," Cat said. "That thing. That juju."

Destiny nodded. "You can't buy that shit, you can't learn it, and you sure as hell can't fake it."

It was true. Everyone knew it. Maya was going to be a star. But then, something strange happened.

Maya didn't get up.

Then "Young and Beautiful" started to play again.

Lana Del Rey sang about cake and diamonds and having seen the world, and Maya just lay there.

Lana Del Rey sang about pretty faces and aching souls, and Maya still wasn't moving.

Then the song broke off, the lights came on, and the audience rose to its feet.

And that was when we all knew.

Because under the bright lights there was no mistaking Maya's unblinking eyes.

It was real.

The gun, the bullet, the blood.

Maya Duran was dead.

Chapter 7

OR WOULD HAVE been dead if the bullet hadn't missed her heart by half a centimeter. I didn't think I believed in miracles, but when I woke up the next morning and checked Daily Mail, then TMZ, then E! Online, I wasn't so sure. Maya had made it through the night. But what a night it had been.

The bullet had shattered into fragments, one of which struck a major vessel, causing her to lose massive quantities of blood. On the way to the hospital, she went into shock. They gave her four transfusions, then patched up her insides during a grueling five-hour operation, and when it finally started to look like she was out of the woods, she'd gone into cardiac arrest. Twice. But time after time, Maya came back from the dead.

Everyone said she must have had a lot to live for.

A few days later, she was moved out of intensive care and into a room on a private floor, with no access to guns, knives, sharp objects, chemicals, ropes, or cords. Not that she was in any condition to do herself further harm. For the time being she was being kept under total sedation. The doctors were guarded about her prognosis, but Miles was hopeful. He'd called me after she was settled and asked if I'd come visit. He'd consulted with a specialist in Eastern medicine who'd said it was essential to cultivate the qi field around Maya through motivation, stimulation, and affirmation. How could I say no? He'd just described my genetic legacy.

The entrance to the hospital was thronged with news vans, reporters, and seedy-looking paparazzi. So much for Maya's private life. A member of the hospital staff validated my parking ticket, then escorted me up to the sixteenth floor, where Miles was waiting.

He looked like hell. Noah after the flood.

"Thanks for coming," he said. "Nobody else could find the time."

"What about Pee Chee?"

"She doesn't do hospitals."

"Sorry you've been here all alone."

"People are assholes. They think bad luck is contagious."

"I thought you weren't cynical," I said.

"Maybe I've changed."

Or maybe we don't know who we are until the proverbial shit hits the fan.

Miles shook his head. "Listen, this whole thing is so fucked up. I have no idea why she did it."

"She didn't leave a note?" I asked.

He shook his head.

"Look, she's alive," I said. "That's all that matters."

Miles led me down the hallway to room 111. He knocked once, then pushed open the door.

It wasn't exactly your ordinary hospital room. The walls were the color of champagne. The carpet was seashell pink. Cut brass lanterns cast shimmering nets of light. In one corner was an antique vanity draped with a coral and white botanical print, and in another, a slipper chair upholstered in a fluffy white flokati. And in the very center of the room was a huge gilded bed in the shape of a gondola. That was where Maya lay, pale and fragile, her eyes closed, her arms by her sides.

"I don't want her to feel confused when she wakes up," Miles explained. "So I moved all her stuff from home. Including a god-damn *mountain* of clothes she bought at Neiman Marcus the day before her show and never even had a chance to take out of the bags. That gown she's wearing? The nurse had to remind me to cut off the tags."

"You don't do things halfway, do you?" I pointed to the open window, which looked onto the palm-fringed Hollywood Hills and the blue sky beyond. "That's some view."

"Yeah," he said bitterly. "It's like we won the fucking lottery."

"Knock, knock." A woman in a white uniform appeared. "I need to get a pulse."

I froze in place. Waited. Listened. To Maya's ragged breaths, the muted beep of the heart monitor, Miles cracking his knuckles, the nurse's pen scratching on paper.

"All done." The nurse left the room.

I let out a sigh.

"Good thing I'm a Buddhist," Miles said, pulling out his prayer beads, "or I'd be raging like an animal. I want to kill someone."

"Miles—"

"Don't say it. I just want you look at her." Miles fixed his gaze on his fiancée. "She's so young." He shook his head. "And so beautiful."

I pulled a chair up to the other side of the bed, sat down, looked at her. Even with her eyes closed, she was lovely, her short dark hair thick and glossy, her features tiny and perfect.

And then I saw it, beneath the fluttery sleeve of her gown.

A large tattoo of a pink lotus flower.

Well, that pretty much made it official.

Maya Duran and Carmen Luz were the same person.

This was the obvious moment to return the photo I'd stolen from Miles's wallet. And to tell him what I'd found out about the woman he was planning to marry. But what had I found out, really? That she'd changed her name from Carmen Luz to Maya Duran? So what? That she had a past? Who didn't? That a couple of years ago someone had given her a black eye? Maybe she'd walked into a door.

"She looks like Sleeping Beauty," I said.

"Too bad I'm not fucking Prince Charming," Miles answered. "I kissed her, and she's still out cold. Joke's on me, I guess."

I stared at him.

"Sorry," he said. "I don't mean to lay my personal shit on you. You're just easy to talk to."

Like I said, it's in the D.N.A.

Miles took a seat on the edge of the bed. "This thing's cursed. I should have never bought it for her."

Apparently, the gondola bed had a long and checkered history. Originally, it belonged to a French dancer who died of Spanish flu because she wouldn't allow the surgeons to perform a tracheotomy and scar her neck. After her death, it was purchased by Paramount Studios, who used it as the centerpiece of Norma Desmond's boudoir in *Sunset Boulevard*. One year later, it made it to the collection of Lili St. Cyr, the last queen of striptease, the "Anatomic Bomb" who seduced millions of strangers while barely surviving ten abortions, six marriages, obscenity charges, a heroin addiction, and multiple attempted suicides.

Maya Duran idolized Lili St. Cyr.

"Maya's bubble bath dance the other night was vintage Lili," Miles explained. "So was that damned suicide dance. In Lili's version, the girl jumps off a ledge. Maya wanted to use a gun. I didn't like it, but she never listens to me. Still, I watched her pull the trigger a thousand times. There was a muzzle flash, but she didn't *die*! She got up and we went out to dinner! Who wouldn't have assumed the thing was a goddamn replica? I'm telling you, somebody's got to pay for this, but I don't know who to blame. Toxic parents? A fucked-up exotic dancer from the 1950s? Fate?"

Seems to me he'd left a couple of names off of his list.

Mine, for starters.

I mean, I show up at a house in Glendale where Maya Duran once lived, ask a couple questions about her alter ego, Carmen Luz, and the very next day the woman tries to kill herself?

And what about Miles? Why wasn't his own name at the top of the list? If the person you loved had just attempted suicide, would you give yourself a pass? I don't think so.

I think you would take a long, hard look in the mirror.

I think you would struggle over what you could have done differently.

I think you would rend your clothing and tear your hair and curse the very day you were born.

Miles wasn't doing anything of the sort.

Suddenly, the door opened, and a woman stepped into the room.

Miles pawed anxiously at his beard. "Doctor."

"Could I have a few minutes with our patient?" she asked.

He went pale. "Something wrong?"

The doctor walked over to check one of the bags hanging from the IV pole. "Exactly the opposite. We're going to give it the weekend, then we're going to ease up on the sedation. I'm thinking Wednesday, Thursday at the latest, Maya should be talking and walking. And if all goes well, she'll be going home soon after that."

It sounded like a happy ending.

But for some reason, it didn't feel like one.

After the doctor left, Miles pulled out his phone and started typing.

"Sharing the good news?" I asked.

He put his phone back into his pocket. "Yeah. I'm so relieved." He didn't look relieved. There was sweat beading on his upper lip.

"Listen," I said, "if you want to go home for a while and clean up, you know, eat something, rest, whatever, I can stay with her."

"Not to worry." Miles opened the door. "I've got people for that. Thanks for everything, though. Really." He literally pushed me out of the room.

On the way back to the valet station, I checked my messages, and nearly collided with a woman also staring down at her phone. A beat later, I spun around and watched her disappear into the hospital. It was odd. I had a feeling that I knew her. But it wasn't until later that it came to me.

The day we'd met she'd looked thin and faded.

Today she'd looked bright and shiny as a new penny.

Lizeth the housekeeper, all the way from Glendale.

Chapter 8

A BLACK BUG with a pink head and pink spots crawled across the top of the big, wooden desk. He was moving pretty fast, for a bug. I watched him traverse a mountain of neatly stacked files, poke at a paper clip with his feelers, sidestep some folders, then plunge off the edge to an uncertain fate.

I empathized.

Shortly after I'd gotten home from the hospital I'd received a call from a Lieutenant Doug Hepworth of the L.A.P.D. He was hoping I could come downtown for a talk. It wouldn't take long, he'd promised. I'd assumed he was interested in what had happened at the Mayan Theater Sunday night, but I couldn't have been more wrong.

Lieutenant Hepworth led me into his small, windowless office, sat me down in a chair, then disappeared to get us a couple of coffees. The room was sparsely furnished. A bookcase, a filing cabinet, two framed photographs of a couple posed in front of a Hawaiian sunset, the desk and the black spotted bug. While I waited for him to return I scanned the books on the shelf. *The*

Meditations by Marcus Aurelius. *The 48 Laws of Power,* a perennial favorite in American prison libraries. A DVD of *300.* I fidgeted a little in my chair, unsticking my thighs from the cracked vinyl seat.

"Sorry to keep you waiting, Miss Black."

Lieutenant Hepworth had ten-day stubble and a lazy eye that I found disconcerting. He kicked the door closed, then set two Styrofoam cups down on the desk.

"I'm not going to beat around the bush," he said. "I understand that this must be very difficult for you. Because it's personal. And you're probably harboring some guilt about your part in all of it."

That was taking it a bit too far. "Look, I'm not trying to let myself off the hook. But the more I think about it, the less certain I am that it was a suicide attempt."

"Excuse me?"

His left eyeball had wandered over to the outer corner of his eye, which made it look like he could see behind his head. I imagined it would be an effective tool in interrogations, but right now I was the one looking for answers.

"Why would Maya stage such an elaborate suicide," I asked, "and not leave behind a note explaining herself?"

I'd thought it was a good question, but Lieutenant Hepworth didn't look particularly impressed.

"Okay," I said, "here's something else. Maya had just gone to Neiman Marcus and bought herself a ton of clothes. I'm talking an entire trousseau! Does that sound like someone planning to shoot herself through the heart?"

Lieutenant Hepworth pulled a pen out of his drawer and placed it on top of a blank sheet of paper. "In my experience, shooters, much like jumpers, have a markedly lower history of depression, bipolar disorder, or substance abuse than we would find in suicides who use other methods, such as pills. Offsetting that, however, is an unfortunate tendency toward impulsivity. You might also consider the fact that men shoot themselves in the head for maximum expediency, while women shoot themselves in the chest in order to leave behind a pretty corpse."

Misogynist.

"In any case," he concluded, "we really need to move on now, Miss Black."

Move on? I hadn't even gotten to the part about the mysterious stalkers Miles had mentioned. "But Maya—"

"We're not here to talk about *Maya*," he interrupted. "Whoever that person might be."

"I don't understand," I said, confused. "If we're not here to talk about Maya, why are we here?"

He passed something across the desk.

A black and white photograph of Uncle Ray standing outside my front door.

It took me a minute to clear my head. "This is about *my uncle*? You have him under *surveillance*?" I pushed the photo away. "This is absurd. Ray is a twenty-three-year veteran of this force and the most honest man I know. Please don't tell me you're from Internal Affairs."

He said, "I'm just helping out some friends."

"Well, you can tell your *friends* that someone is setting Ray up. And they're not going to get away with it. *You* are not going to get away with it."

The lieutenant raised an eyebrow. "Interesting, you threatening me. I'm going to ignore it for now. Just answer the question. Do you or do you not recognize this photograph?"

I pursed my lips. "It's Captain Ray Laffitte. He came to see me on Saturday."

"Family is everything," he said. "Here's another photo." This one was a shot of Ray giving me a hug as he left my house. "Notice that the box your uncle had in his hand when he arrived is no longer in his hand."

"Oh, my god," I said. "It was a *pie*."

"Do you think this is a joke, Miss Black?"

"Of course not. But I really don't know what you want me to say."

"I'd like you to look at the time stamp on that last picture."

It read 5:25 p.m.

I looked up. "So?"

He passed another photo over to me. This one was a shot of me opening the door just after Ray had left.

"Look at the time stamp, please."

Five twenty-six p.m.

"Call me crazy," he said, "but I find it odd that exactly one minute after your uncle leaves your house a manila envelope magically appears on your doorstep."

To be perfectly honest, that made two of us.

"Well?" He tapped his pen on the desk.

"Well, what?" I asked. "I like to shop online. I get deliveries all day long. It was probably something from Amazon."

"Funny," he said. "I don't have any pictures of FedEx or UPS or the US Postal Service showing up at your house between five twenty-five and five twenty-six. Which suggests not only that the envelope in question did not contain something you purchased online, but that the person or persons who dropped it off had some experience with surveillance countermeasures."

Surveillance countermeasures? That did not sound good.

"Hello? Miss Black?" He glanced up at the clock. "I don't have all day."

My throat was starting to close. I was feeling lightheaded. But there was no way I'd give him the satisfaction of putting my head between my knees. Instead, I took a deep breath, then let it out slowly.

"Miss Black? You have nothing at all to say?" Lieutenant Hepworth jotted something down on his paper. "Well, then, I'll keep talking. Because what seems pretty obvious to me is that that manila envelope and whatever was inside it was intended for your uncle Ray."

I swallowed hard. "That isn't possible."

Lieutenant Hepworth leaned forward and looked me in the eye. "I'm thinking that it is. And I'm also thinking that your uncle will be picking it up sometime very soon."

It seems so obvious in retrospect. That right there was the moment I should have told Lieutenant Hepworth that the manila envelope contained a cash payment for my services—which I was planning to declare, by the way. And that it had nothing whatsoever to do with my uncle. And that sometimes a cigar is just a cigar. But as I sat there, my cheeks growing hotter, my palms getting stickier, I wasn't sure about anything. And the last thing I wanted to do was give someone I didn't trust something he might be able to use as ammunition. Against me. Or worse yet, my uncle.

"Am I free to go?" I asked. "Unless you're going to be charging me with something, in which case I'd like to make a phone call."

He rose from his chair. "You're free to go, Miss Black. Before you do, however, I want to be sure you understand the severity of the situation. When we prove what Ray's been doing—and we *will* prove it, that I promise you—your uncle's going down. Are you familiar with the Rampart scandal? Back in the nineties, a handful of bad cops nearly destroyed this department. Because of their criminal misconduct, a hundred convictions were overturned and dozens of lawsuits were filed. Do you get it now? Every single arrest Ray Laffitte made during the course of his long and allegedly distinguished career is going to be called into question. Every single time he's been called to testify against some criminal, well, that's fucked, too, pardon my French. Because your uncle's dirty. And the taxpayers of this city are going to pay the price."

I stood. Lieutenant Hepworth did the same. He knew I wasn't going to shake his hand, so he didn't put it out. He just met my gaze with his lazy eye.

"Oh." He grabbed the edge of the door. "One more thing."

I should have seen it coming.

"I'm going after you, too." He smiled broadly. "I'm thinking accessory before the fact, accessory after the fact, co-conspirator— hey, maybe I'll get lucky and have enough to put you away as a joint principal. So I'd watch my back if I were you. And you might want to tell your mother and grandmother to watch their backs, too. People get judged by the company they keep."

This man had no idea what he was talking about. I knew that. I also knew that I was in the middle of something ugly. And that it was Miles McCoy and his crazy noir tour and his crazy five figures who'd put me there. Which meant maybe I was the only one in the position to make things right. But there wasn't much time for my uncle.

Maybe even less for Maya Duran.

I reached down to grab my purse and jacket. And there he was again. The black bug with the pink head and pink spots. Against all odds he'd made it up to the eighteenth floor and survived a perilous fall. He deserved another chance.

I scooped him up in a tissue, and carried him down in the elevator with me. Just past a homeless encampment I found some shrubs, and I put him down next to the star jasmine. He burrowed into the dirt, and then he was gone.

Chapter 9

I RACED HOME. That $40,000 was a ticking time bomb. How could I have been so *stupid*? The second I saw what was inside that manila envelope I should've gone straight to the closest bank and opened a safety deposit box. Even petty criminals know not to leave a paper trail. But it was Saturday night, and the bank was closed. And the next day was Sunday. And after that, well, I guess I kind of liked the feeling of having all that money at my fingertips. It felt illicit. Sexy. Crazy. Fun. The party, however, was clearly over. I'd canceled the cars, canceled the picnic boxes, canceled the private room at the Varnish. Now I had to get rid of the cash before the cops showed up at my door with a warrant, and Uncle Ray's life went up in smoke.

My hand was trembling as I punched in the alarm code. As soon as I was inside I ran into the bedroom, slid my hand between the box spring and mattress, and when my fingers brushed against the envelope, I let out a huge sigh of relief. Which turned out to be somewhat premature. On account of the envelope being empty.

Shit. Shit. Shit.

This made no sense whatsoever.

I'd put the envelope under the mattress myself. I'd counted the money beforehand, and it was all there. Forty *thousand* dollars. And no one had been in and out of the house since then except me. And Teddy, of course.

Impossible.

Teddy wouldn't steal my money. He didn't even know there *was* any money. Plus, he'd been glued to my side the entire time he was over.

There was one other possibility. I'd been robbed by professionals. That had to be it. I'd obviously rushed in too quickly to notice that the place had been ransacked.

But no such luck.

My laptop was on the coffee table, exactly where I'd left it. And there was my flatscreen T.V., my Bluetooth speakers, my antique opera glasses, and my faux-fur jacket, which was by Alexander McQueen and worth a pretty penny. What kind of amateur leaves all that stuff behind? No kind. Meaning no one had broken in. I'd set the alarm before I'd left this morning, and no one knew the code except me.

And Uncle Ray.

Who'd installed a state-of-the-art security system for me, right after I'd moved into the house.

A girl on her own, he'd insisted, can never be too careful.

Suddenly, I felt cold all over. I had to get out of there and think. I grabbed my purse, and as I was shutting the door, Teddy and Engelbart came out.

"Hey," Teddy said.

"Hey! Actually, I'm really glad to see you."

He smiled. "I'm glad to see you, too. I wanted to—"

"Stop talking," I said. "I need to ask you a question."

Teddy's smile crumpled.

"I didn't mean—"

"Forget it." He shook me off. "What's the question?"

I didn't have time to soothe anybody's ego right now. "I was wondering if you saw anything strange around here today. After I left. Like anyone at my door. Peeking in the windows, maybe. Or trying to get around the back." Actually, who said it had to have happened today? It could have been any time in the last few days. The thought made me physically ill.

"Are you okay?" Teddy asked. "What is going on?" Engelbart had spied a corgi on the other side of the street and was pulling on his leash. "Stop it, boy!"

"So is that a no?" I asked sharply.

"I didn't see anything," he said.

"Great." I made a beeline for my car.

Teddy stood by as I slammed the door shut. "Sorry, but I wasn't paying attention. I was on my computer."

"That's fine," I said. "It's not your responsibility."

"Don't be like that. Where are you going in such a hurry anyway?"

I had no idea. I couldn't go to Ray. It would break his heart. How could I ask him why he'd turned up out of the blue at my house? And what he knew about the $40,000 that had been dropped at my door a minute after he'd left? And was now inexplicably missing?

Gram.

Gram would have some insight into this situation. I could drive over to her house, choke down some kombucha tea, and see what I could find out. But the truth is, I'm not the subtlest of inquisitors. And I'd promised Ray I wouldn't add to Gram's stress. Which, unfortunately, left me with only one other source of misinformation—sorry, *information*.

I sighed.

A Freudian slip is when you say one thing, but mean your mother.

Chapter 10

I can't say I was surprised when my car didn't start. It had been that kind of day. Week. Life? At least I could rely on Venice Tow. They showed up when they said they would, jacked up the car, and took off for North Hollywood, where my longtime mechanic, Vlad the Impaler, was on standby. In the meantime, I had to get to my mother's. Teddy offered me a ride, but it seemed tacky to accept after I'd been so rude. Thank goodness for Uber.

Five minutes later, a red Maserati pulled up in front of my house. Only in L.A. I gave the address to the driver, who was working on his broker's license and bursting with information about Trousdale, the hilly subdivision at the northeast end of Beverly Hills that my mother called home. Who knew, for example, that in 1977 Realtor-to-the-stars Mike Silverman had taken out a ten-page ad in a Tehran magazine, singlehandedly making Trousdale the number one destination for Persians fleeing the revolution, including my Uber driver's entire extended family? What I did know was that Elvis and Frank Sinatra had once lived there, and that these days celebrities were flooding back in to reclaim the pristine examples of mid-century modern chic, which I'd venture to say did not include my mother's faded pink neo-Hawaiian abode, with its lava rock walls and chipped Easter Island–esque lawn statuary.

My Uber driver dropped me at the curb. "Looks like your mom hasn't made any upgrades. And there's no privacy." His voice was heavy with regret. "She'd be lucky to get $500 a square foot."

It probably didn't help that the woman was holding yet another one of the impromptu lawn sales that so endeared her to her neighbors. This time there was more crap than usual: fraying towels, novelty picture frames, a hat rack, sequined separates of unknown vintage.

"Thank god you're here." My mother, relaxing on a lawn chair under a plastic umbrella, peered at me from beneath her visor. "Can you see what that man over there wants? I'm trying to price this item." Which looked to be a curling iron, but could easily have been a vibrator.

The man, who had a pompadour and carried a man-bag, wanted to know if my mother was willing to sell the astrology-themed leggings she was wearing, which to my mind constituted the key element of her porn-star-meets-yoga-mommy ensemble, along with her signature water bottle fanny pack. I distracted him with a Big Mouth Billy Bass, still in its original packaging.

"So?" My mother pulled up another chair for me.

"So." I sat down. "I wanted to talk about Ray."

"Oh, *Ray.*"

"What's that supposed to mean?"

"Now don't get defensive on me. I know you think the man walks on water, but trust me. He's not perfect."

I glowered at her. "Who is?"

"Thanks a lot. I did the best I could, considering."

"Considering what? That you couldn't help with my homework because you were too busy stocking the condom bowl and lugging cases of Aqua Net backstage?"

"You should let go of your anger." She handed me a bottle of water. "Are you drinking eight of these a day? I don't think so. Your skin looks off."

"You have another customer." I pointed to a man in dark sunglasses holding up an inflatable Care Bears pool toy.

"How much?" he asked.

My mother gave him a withering stare. "$1,000."

"*Excuse me?*" he said.

"Fine. Ten percent off for seniors."

I shook my head.

"Cheapskate," she muttered as the man walked away. "That highly coveted item was used by Whitesnake and the assorted members of their entourage during the pivotal 1990–1991 Liquor and Poker World Tour."

"Mother."

"I'm listening."

"I just want to know what Gram has told you about Ray's situation."

She took a slug of water. "As you know, Ray has been accused of being on the take, which is, of course, bullshit."

"Of course it is. Right?"

"*Dreama!* You know better than that."

"I know, it's just that this is all so incredibly—"

"Fucked up?"

"Exactly."

"And of course Ray is especially upset that whoever's out to get him has chosen this particular moment in time, when he's up for Deputy Chief."

On Thursday. A week from now. When Maya was going to be walking and talking. And I was betting she was going to have plenty to say.

"On top of that," my mother continued, "there's some kind of hearing next week where Ray's supposed to testify, but the judge who's presiding is the same person who signed the search warrant on his house so he's worried that that's yet another thing going down in flames because of this ridiculous witch hunt. Oh, hello!"

Mom paused to pose for duckface selfies with a woman wearing a Grumpy Cat sweatshirt.

"One of my many fans from the lesbian community," she explained. "*Anyway*, adding fuel to the fire, after all these years, Ray is trying to quit smoking. For Gram, which is totally adorable. He swears by nicotine gum, but I told him to try self-massage—"

"You would."

She gave me a dirty look.

"I guess what I'm really asking," I said, "is about Uncle Ray's state of mind. Do you think he's okay? I mean, has this whole thing driven him over the edge? To the point where he's not really acting like himself?"

My mother raised her chin in defiance. "What is *the self*, Dreama? I don't like to put limits on people. I'm all about fluidity."

Just then, another car pulled up in front of Mom's house.

A black stretch Bentley.

Miles McCoy.

Was he *following* me?

The back window went down. Miles was absently stroking his beard. "Hey, Dreama. How's tricks?"

"What are you doing here?" I asked.

Miles held up his phone. "Hate to be the bearer of bad news, but you're all over social media. E! Online, among others, is wondering if your mother is bankrupt, and if not, what percentage of today's proceeds is being donated to charity. When Teri Hatcher had a yard sale, she raised thousands of dollars for local food banks."

My mother said, "Miles! It's been a long time."

Miles took off his dark glasses. "Good to see you, Desirée. You're looking well."

My head swiveled. "You *know* him?"

My mother smiled enigmatically.

"Did you guys ever—you know?" I whispered.

She mouthed, "Not my type."

Thank god.

"Good timing, by the way," my mother said to Miles. "Dreama's car isn't working. She needs a ride."

I shot a glance at her. "It's fine, Mom. I've already called Uber."

"Don't be ridiculous." Miles feigned nonchalance. "Why spend a penny of your hard-earned money?"

"Speaking of money," my mother said.

She made her way over to her stuff and came back waving a dog-eared photograph of herself draped across the laps of the visibly addled members of Guns N' Roses.

"For you," she said to Miles. "A souvenir of the night the boys played a fraternity basement at UCLA for beers and thirty bucks. It was 1985, right before they were signed by Geffen Records. A must for any collection at the bargain price of $2,500."

"Mom."

"Okay, $3,000. All of it going to local food banks," she added.

The front window of the Bentley went down with a whoosh and Mookie handed my mother a check, which she promptly tucked into her sports bra.

"Take that, Teri Hatcher." She looked like the cat who ate the canary. "*Now*, dear Miles, you can have my daughter."

I wish I could say it was the first time the woman had sold me down the river.

Chapter 11

THE INSIDE OF the car smelled like late nights and cold sweat. Miles shoved aside some newspapers and a couple of empty Starbucks cups.

"This isn't necessary," I said, climbing in.

"Not a problem." He rapped on the glass and Mookie pulled away from the curb.

I immediately started snapping pictures and posting them to Instagram. It never hurts to establish a timeline.

"Now where'd I put my detox tea?" Miles murmured. "Ah. There's the little sucker." He popped open a plastic bottle and took a long swig of his beverage, which happened to be the exact same color as bourbon—his drink, when he was still drinking. Just saying.

"There's something I wanted to talk to you about," Miles said.

"Me, too." I wasn't sure how to begin. I wasn't even sure if I *should* begin. But Uncle Ray's neck was on the line. I *had* to ask about the $40,000. "It's kind of awkward."

"It's the money, right?" Miles shook his head. "Yeah, I feel really bad about it. You must think I'm a total shit."

Well, that was easy. "What I need is an explanation. Other people are involved. People I care deeply about."

Miles started fingering his prayer beads. "The thing is, I'm having a bit of trouble right now. It's a personnel thing. Which is kind of fucked up because as you know I already have my hands full with the whole Maya commotion."

That was an interesting way to describe it. "Any changes in the last few hours?"

His face brightened. "Still out like a light, but I'm starting to see some color in her cheeks. Hey! Mookie!"

The glass went down.

"Don't you think Maya looks better?"

Mookie's hair was gelled into spikes. He looked like Sid Vicious on steroids. "Yeah, boss."

Miles nodded. "Mookie's not a yes man, so if he says she looks good, she looks good."

But people lie.

People lie.

"The police completed their investigation," Miles offered.

"That was quick. What was the verdict?"

"Attempted suicide. Not surprising given there were over two hundred eyewitnesses."

Only a fool trusts an eyewitness. "And you never found a suicide note?"

He shook his head. "Nope. Never found the gun either."

"That's kind of *odd*, isn't it?"

"Yeah, I guess. Cops said in all the commotion, all those people rushing the stage, it must've gotten lost."

Just then Miles got a text.

"Excuse me." He looked down at his phone, then said, "*Goddamn it!* I can't believe this shit."

I raised an eyebrow. "Bad news?"

He pulled a mini legal pad from his back pocket and flipped through the pages. "Fucking Destiny D-Low. *Yesterday* she's pissed about having to go on tour. Goddamn One Direction goes on tour! Goddamn Christina Aguilera! *Today* she's pissed about the title of the album. I take it personally, actually. Destiny's career was nothing. In the toilet. Have you heard anybody say a word about her in *years*? Who pulled her up, hosed off the shit, and gave her one last chance? Me. Because I believed in her. Fat lot of good it's done me." He took another swig of his "detox tea," then said, "Maybe I should go back to being a hit man instead of a goddamn white knight."

Good line.

I recognized it from one of the articles I'd read about him.

Miles scrawled something on the pad, then tucked it into the seat pocket in front of him. "Anyway, back to the money. Sorry. Even though we had to postpone the noir tour, you should have been paid by now. We'll get things straightened out."

"Wait, *what*?" Now I was *totally* confused. "But you already—"

"Look, the tour's going to happen as soon as Maya's better, which means you are still on the payroll. You have my word on that. I've done a lot of shitty things, but my word still means something in this town." Miles unzipped his backpack and pulled out some headphones.

This situation was getting stranger by the minute. Hadn't I seen a black stretch Bentley driving away from my house? Was it possible that I was mistaken? And that Miles *hadn't* left that

$40,000 on my doorstep? But if he hadn't, who had? And why? And who'd broken into my house and taken it back?

Just then my phone started to ring.

Unknown caller.

"I'd better take this," I said.

Miles put on the headphones and closed his eyes.

It was Uncle Ray. "I saw your Instagram and Twitter."

Just as I'd suspected. Following me on the internet was as good as following me in real life. Better, actually, because it saved gas.

"Cool car, right?" I snuck a glance at Miles, who was absorbed in his music. "Did you get it?" I whispered. "The license plate is '25 A DAY.'"

Miles said, "I can hear everything you're saying."

I turned to him. "I'm just telling my uncle I finally figured what the name of your company, 25-A-Day, refers to. It's what Philip Marlowe charged his clients. Plus expenses."

"I knew you were smart." Miles's phone started ringing. He ripped off his headphones. "This better be good," he snarled into the phone.

Ray said, "Dreama. Can I get you to focus? I'm not talking about a car."

I didn't get it. "You're not?"

"No. I'm talking about something you posted last week. A picture of a house in Glendale. A small house in the foothills. One story, pink stucco, gray roof. Inside there's some faded flowered wallpaper and a peacock chair. Ring any bells? #hauntedhouse? #ghostsofglendale? #DreamaDoesLA?"

Busted.

"What the hell were you doing there?" Ray yelled.

"Yeah, well, fuck you, too!" Miles tossed his phone onto the seat.

"Me?" I was trying not to get distracted. "I don't know why you're getting so upset."

Miles roared, "Because the fucking doctor isn't calling me back with the results of the lab work, and fucking Destiny is a psycho, and fucking Pee Chee isn't taking care of the shit I pay her to take care of, that's why I'm upset!"

"Sorry, Miles, but I wasn't actually talking to you." I scooted away from him, cupped my hand over my mouth. "Uncle Ray. Why are *you* so upset?"

"I'm going to ask you one more time." Ray was struggling to control his voice. I'd never heard him so angry. "What were you doing in that house?"

"I was doing research." Which was true. "For my noir tour." Which was not.

Then he lost it. "So you found an old *crime scene* to photograph? What are you, *crazy*? How did you even get inside? Please don't tell me you *broke in*. Jesus Christ, do not tell me that."

I dropped my voice to a whisper. "The door was unlocked. I thought the place was abandoned. What do you mean it was a crime scene? What are you talking about?"

Ray was quiet for a minute. Then he cleared his throat. "You do this job long enough, you see a lot of bad things. You see the dark places people go, and the devastation they leave in their wake. You want to know what I'm talking about, Dreama? I'm talking about the photos the techs took of that goddamn house in Glendale. As long as I'm breathing I'm never going to forget them. The guys working the case pinned them up in the squad room and everybody going in and out had no choice but to stare at them for weeks on end. Broken bottles, broken plates, overturned couch, blood all over the cushions, that goddamn flowered wallpaper, that poor girl."

Oh, god.

The poor girl he was talking about was the same poor girl I'd just seen in the hospital.

Maya Duran, a.k.a. Carmen Luz.

"What happened to her?" I whispered.

He was quiet for a minute. Then he said, "She was raped, beaten to a pulp, and left for dead."

"Did she—? Ray? Ray? Are you still there? Hello?"

Ray was gone. The phone had died. Or maybe he'd hung up on me.

"Dead men weigh more than broken hearts," said Miles, reading from his mini yellow pad.

"Excuse me?"

He looked up. "What do you think? As the title of Destiny D-Low's album? Nobody's gotta know I stole it from Raymond Chandler."

More secrets. More lies.

"Dreama!" Miles grabbed me by the shoulder, harder than he should have. I could feel his nails digging into my flesh. "I asked you a question. What do you think? Isn't it *fucking perfect*?"

I waited for him to take his hands off of me. Then I looked at this person and suddenly realized I had no idea who he was, much less what he was capable of.

"Yeah," I said. "Fucking perfect."

Miles and I drove down the hill to Sunset, then all the way back to Venice without either of us saying another word.

Chapter 12

IT HAPPENED THREE years ago.

Friday night, late winter, full moon.

Everybody remembered the moon. It looked like a ball of fire floating over the Hollywood Hills.

Everybody also remembered the girl. She was drinking. She was smoking. She was twenty-one years old.

That night she'd left her house at eight and met up with three men. They were in the music industry, and she had dreams of becoming a star. After stopping for gas, they went to a bar on the Sunset Strip. They flashed some cash and got a table. They invited two blondes visiting from New York to join them for a second bottle of Grey Goose, but the blondes weren't interested so they finished it off themselves. They paid for the drinks with a credit card, but left the tip in cash. They were excellent tippers.

It was ten-thirty when they left the bar. The red moon was rising. They pulled over on Mulholland, opened the sunroof, studied the night sky. Someone pointed out the brightest of the stars. Jupiter, fifth planet from the sun, traveling in sync with the moon.

After a quick detour for cigars, they made a stop in Highland Park, then drove back to the girl's house in Glendale. Things got hazy after that.

The girl wasn't sure which of the men came home with her. She thought she'd blacked out at some point. What she did remember was listening to music with her head on someone's lap. Dropping a dozen eggs on the kitchen floor. Somebody yelling about a phone. Waking up in the hospital, one eye crusted shut, bandages on her legs, wrists bruised, her arm in a sling.

She remembered the nurse refusing to give her a mirror.

They arrested one of the men. His name was Freddy Sims. He was a rapper who went by the name Big Fatty. His D.N.A. was everywhere: on the girl's underwear, on the bloody couch cushions, on the ropes he used to tie her hands to the bed, on the shards of glass the nurse had painstakingly picked out of her thighs. Big Fatty confessed after a twenty-two-hour closed-door interrogation. But that was hardly the end of it.

An internal review of the crime lab revealed significant errors. Sixteen pieces of evidence were initially placed in the wrong rape kit and were deemed unusable because of cross-contamination. An inexperienced lab tech failed to upload fingerprint evidence in a timely manner. And then there was the girl.

She'd been drinking. They'd found two hits of Ecstasy in her purse. She didn't remember the struggle. She couldn't identify her attacker. She was not a perfect victim.

The D.A. dismissed the rape, criminal deviate, and confinement charges, and talked Big Fatty into pleading guilty to battery, a class C felony. The judge sentenced the latter to two years in prison.

Two years, and Big Fatty's nightmare would be over.

What about the girl's nightmare?

The newspapers never identified her by name. It was the one and only courtesy they'd granted her. But I knew who she was. First a black eye, and then a brutal rape. No wonder Carmen Luz had changed her name to Maya Duran. Who wouldn't want to start over?

"Excuse me? Mrs. Dreama?" My gardener, Jovani, was rapping on the kitchen window. "Can you come outside for a minute?"

It was time to stretch my legs. I'd been on the computer for a while.

Jovani was in the backyard fussing with the sprinkler timer.

"Don't get mad," I said. "I forgot to reset it after it stopped raining."

"Do you think I care if you let everything die?" he asked. "It's your garden." He brushed past me, grabbed the hose and aimed it at the glorious thicket of angel's trumpet I'd inherited from the previous owner. "Although I would congratulate you if you killed this terrible plant, the Brugmansia. My friend told me about a young man who amputated his own penis and tongue after half of a cup of Brugmansia tea."

Jovani was full of garden horror stories. Infected plants sold by big-box stores, blight spores run rampant, fellow gardeners being overtaken by the toxic fumes of laurel leaves, toddlers sucking on oleander.

"Please look under the deck." Now he was spraying the bougainvillea, in hopes of getting rid of the long-tailed mealybugs he'd pointed out to me last week. "Do you see the holes in the ground?"

I squatted down. There they were. Nothing good, I was guessing.

"Rats." He nodded. "The holes lead to their nests. One more thing, Mrs. Dreama."

Could it get any worse?

He led me around to the side of the house, stopped under my bedroom window, looked up.

The screen.

It was hanging off of its frame.

"You should fix it," he said. "Before somebody breaks in."

It was a little late for that.

And it was hardly like I could call the cops.

After he left, I got out the toolbox Uncle Ray had given me for my sixteenth birthday, and reinstalled the screen. Then I sat in my backyard with a peanut butter sandwich and some Syrah and watched the sun go down. Nothing more spectacular than an L.A. sunset. When the mosquitoes started pricking at my legs I went back inside and called him. No answer. No answer at my grandmother's either.

I spent the rest of the evening searching the internet for anything—any image, any shred of information, any reference—I could find on Maya Duran or Carmen Luz.

There was nothing.

There was plenty, however, on Big Fatty.

Born in South L.A. to African-American and Salvadoran parents, he'd gotten mixed up with gangs at the age of thirteen. Before long he was stealing cars and dealing drugs. His cousin Floyd da Gangsta introduced him to rap. The two teamed up and, under the name Cuz Til Death, were signed to Hoo-Bangin' Records. Their debut album was *Thugstylin*. The second single, "Batshit in da Nite," featuring C-Murder and D.J. Quik, peaked at number eleven on the Billboard Hot Rap Songs chart.

Before long Freddy split with his cousin, and signed with Death Row Records as a solo artist named Big Fatty. He broke out with "Kill the Fatted Calf." The multi-layered track, with its slow hypnotic grooves and lazy delivery, is still considered one of the defining G-funk tunes. Fatty's fourth album featured the hit single "DissReputaBull," a diss track aimed at 50 Cent, who had earlier accused Fatty of plagiarism. Despite the controversy, the album was certified platinum. While out celebrating in Miami Beach, Big Fatty and his then-girlfriend were the targets of a drive-by shooting. Big Fatty accused his cousin Floyd of being involved. Floyd retaliated by releasing bootlegged Cuz Til Death tapes, which suggested 50 Cent's insinuations about Fatty were not unfounded. Big Fatty's career never recovered.

He released an underground single, but it failed to chart. He was accused of stealing beats from Nas. Soon afterward, he was arrested on assault charges for hitting a man with a baseball bat, though the charges were dropped. A year later, during a routine traffic stop, police discovered a loaded handgun in his car. He pleaded it down and served four months. Not long after he got out, his younger brother was killed during the course of a home invasion robbery. In the aftermath of that tragedy, Fatty tried to resurrect his career a couple of times, but with little success. I found a few paparazzi shots here and there, but nothing else until the third anniversary of his brother's death, when the family gathered to toss the young man's ashes off the Long Beach pier.

It was a shaky, hand-held video on YouTube.

74,675 views.

657 likes and 11,008 dislikes.

The second time I watched the video I stopped it smack in the middle.

A weeping Big Fatty—former rapper, future rapist—was embracing a woman whose acquaintance I had recently made.

A woman with razor-sharp cheekbones and a vertiginous headwrap.

Who would be the rapper—excuse me, *artist*—Destiny D-Low.

Chapter 13

THE WAIL OF a distant car alarm jolted me awake. I glanced at my phone. Seven a.m. Three calls from my good friend Lieutenant Hepworth. No messages. I staggered to the kitchen, made a pot of coffee, sucked it down, and wondered if it was bedtime yet.

The good news was my car was ready. This morning's Uber driver arrived in a Camry and didn't speak all the way to North Hollywood. Vlad the Impaler was more loquacious. He said the problem was a broken flywheel tooth, which he'd caught just in the nick of time. I paid him what seemed like a staggering sum, and remembered to look grateful for his expertise. From there, I headed off to see Destiny D-Low.

I'd checked her Twitter feed and discovered she was in Mac Arthur Park, shooting a video for her remix of Donna Summer's disco anthem of the same name. I figured I'd catch her between costume changes and ask a couple of questions. Like how long she'd known Miles. And if she was still close to Big Fatty. And how exactly that was working for her, considering that the latter had raped and nearly killed the former's fiancée. Not that I expected any clear-cut answers. Given that Maya Duran was going by the name Carmen Luz at the time. And that she'd just tried to commit suicide. Or been the victim of someone who'd tried to make it look that way.

While I was getting dressed, I'd noticed five small bruises on my shoulder. In the exact spot where Miles McCoy's fingernails had dug into my skin.

Could he have been the one who tried to kill Maya?

I didn't want to believe it.

But maybe.

Maybe he hadn't known about her past. Maybe he'd never so much as heard the name Carmen Luz. Finding out that the woman he loved had a secret life would've felt like a slap in the face. He lived by a code and she'd turned out to be a liar. Miles had a temper. He could have lost it. That day in the hospital, hadn't he told me he wanted to kill someone?

The sky had turned dark, like my mood. I put the top up, then turned on the radio, hoping for something equally grim, but all I found was Katy Perry, Selena Gomez, and other such peddlers of good cheer. At least traffic was light.

MacArthur Park was located in the Westlake area, just south of historic Filipinotown and west of downtown L.A. At the close of the nineteenth century, when the park was built, the area was swampland, but by the 1920s, it had been transformed into a veritable Champs-Élysées, with fancy restaurants, hotels, and boutiques. These days, not so much.

I parked my car on the northernmost end of the park. Ducking the abandoned shopping carts, *chicharron* vendors, and a steady stream of Spanish-speaking men offering me something I was pretty sure was illegal, I made my way down to the man-made lake, where you'd be more likely to catch a dirty needle than a fish.

The shoot was underway. People were rushing in every direction. Some were pushing racks of sparkly clothing. Others were shouting into mouthpieces, balancing boom mikes, or ferrying cups of coffee. I tried to blend in, but two youngish guys—one in gold Nikes, the other in silver Pumas—were on me within seconds.

"Excuse me," Nikes said, "but you can't be here."

"This is a closed set," said Pumas.

"Oh, shit." Nikes broke out in a sweat. "She's back."

Destiny D-Low, looking every inch the disco Cleopatra, was drifting toward us in an inflatable barge. When she finally bumped up against the shore, she started shouting.

"Your turn," said Pumas.

Nikes said, "Actually, it's your turn."

I put my hands on my hips. "Well, one of you better go."

Nikes rolled up his pants and waded into the water to help Destiny out, but wound up stepping on the hem of her white hooded pantsuit, tripping her, and tearing off a bronze epaulet.

"We're interns," said Pumas, quaking. "She's going to cut off our dicks."

No time for that, however, because the instant Destiny saw me she flew at me like a bat out of hell.

"Paying Pee Chee to harass me isn't enough for y'all?" she shouted. "Now Miles is sending *you*? Look, I'm not taking shit from *anybody*, not some holier-than-thou Buddhist who doesn't *understand* me, and certainly not some skinny little skank like yourself."

"Miles didn't send me," I said. "In fact, he and I are kind of on the outs."

"Why is that?" Destiny narrowed her eyes.

Because things weren't adding up.

Because Miles had a mean streak.

Because you always hurt the one you love.

"Money," I said.

She nodded. "He's got a Bentley, but he's *cheap*." She pointed to her ruined outfit. "This piece of shit came from Topshop."

"That's outrageous," I said.

"You're telling me," she replied. "Yo!" She was waving her arms at the intern in the wet pants and now-ruined Nikes. "You already fucked up the sweet green icing! What the hell are you doing with the hose?"

"Cleaning the grasshoppers off the barge," he called out.

"Stop! Those are *papyrus leaves*!" Destiny turned to me. "I gotta go."

I'd lost focus. I'd come here for a reason. "You know that I organize custom tours of L.A., right? Well, I have one coming up on rap music. And the guy who hired me is a huge fan of one of your old friends."

"Stupid glue doesn't work for shit." She yanked off her false eyelashes, then blinked a few times. "Who would that be?"

"Big Fatty."

Now I had her full attention.

"I was doing some research on Fatty," I said, "and came across your name. Coincidence, right?"

Destiny looked like she believed in coincidences about as much as I did.

"I've been listening to his music," I went on. "'Kill the Fatted Calf' blew me away."

She looked me straight in the eye. "Of course it did. Freddy's an *artist*."

"Totally. The song's about his brother, isn't it? So sad." I shook my head. "You must've been close to him."

She looked down, started fidgeting with her rings. "Yeah, we used to party. Me, Freddy, his brother, his whole posse—Lucius Ramsay, you heard about him? Loco Loverboy, those guys?"

No. "Of course. Those guys are *legendary*. I'll bet you've got some stories about Miles, too. Heard he wrecked a few hotel rooms back in the day."

Destiny shook her head. "Miles didn't have anything to do with that group. They were West Coast, he was East Coast. I only met Miles a year ago, give or take. It's all about the work with him. Now, *those guys*, we were close. We were *friends*. But friends can screw you, too, if you know what I'm saying."

Like mothers. Like fathers. Like lovers. "I know what you're saying."

"Excuse me, Destiny?" It was Nikes again. He was pointing at half a dozen hunks with oiled chests and loincloths. "The Nubian slaves have arrived."

Destiny didn't budge. She was lost in thought. And I knew exactly what she was thinking about. I didn't say a word. I just stood there, radiating calm. I learned it from my mother, who learned it from her mother. If you know how and when to be quiet, people will eventually tell you everything you want to know.

"That was some fucked-up night," Destiny finally said.

Works every time.

"I really don't know what happened," she went on. "Freddy was crazy, but I didn't think he was *that* crazy. He was good to his mother, his brother, you know what I'm saying?"

"I think so."

She gave me a sad smile, then reached into her pocket and pulled out some breadcrumbs, which she tossed to the ducks quacking at her feet.

"You and Fatty still friends?" I asked.

She shook her head. "I heard after he got out he went up into the mountains. He bought some kind of fancy house. He stays up there and doesn't bother anybody. He served his time. Let him be."

"Let him *be*?" My eyes widened. "He didn't let that girl *be*. He *raped* her."

Now she looked offended. "Are you stupid or what? You think black men in this country get any justice?"

"What are you saying?" I asked. "That Fatty *didn't* do it?"

She pursed her lips. "I'm not saying shit. Only that the evidence was tainted. The cops screwed it up. They should've thrown out the case. But they didn't because they had a fat thug to pin it on."

"Come on, Destiny. Fatty's D.N.A. was all over the house. And all over her."

Destiny threw up her hands. "All I'm saying is maybe the cops needed to work a little harder. It's like that gun they found in Fatty's car years ago. Somebody planted it. Fatty told them, and told them, but did they listen? No. They didn't care. What they should've done was follow that gun. Find out who it was registered to, how it got into Fatty's car, whose prints were on it, who it was supposed to jam up." She looked at me, exasperated. "Everybody damn well knows. If you want to find out shit, you have to follow the gun."

The gun.

Maya's gun.

I'd forgotten all about it.

And—as everybody damn well knows—if you want to find out shit, you have to follow the gun.

Chapter 14

UNFORTUNATELY, THE GUN was missing.

To my mind, there were only two possible scenarios.

Scenario #1: It was chaos that night. With the crush of people it had been kicked under the stage, or fallen between some loose floorboards, or been accidentally swept into a corner by the cleaning crew. Which meant maybe it was still there.

Scenario #2: Someone had taken it.

Either way, the answer was back at the Mayan Theater.

According to the website, the box office wouldn't be open until six. I glanced at my phone. One p.m. I was starving. And from where I was standing, at the edge of MacArthur Park, I could see the line already starting to form outside Langer's, where cured meat has been king since 1947.

After a short wait, I slid into a booth and ordered the #19: hand-cut pastrami, coleslaw, Russian dressing, and Swiss cheese on double-baked rye. The great thing about the #19 is you don't have to eat again for several days. Kind of like an anaconda after ingesting a capybara. While I was waiting for my food, Lieutenant

Hepworth called again. I wasn't ready to talk to him. Not until I had more information. A few minutes later, I got a text from Teddy, who asked if he could see me later in the evening. I panicked and said no, then thought it over, and sent him another text saying "maybe," which was ridiculous, so I had to follow it up with some emojis and an "okay, why not?" which was probably overkill, but I'm a Libra, which means I'm a people-pleaser.

Teddy didn't answer.

I ate my sandwich, then read a Buzzfeed listicle entitled "36 Things to Do while You Wait for Your Crush to Text You Back," which included signing up for a two-week free trial of Ancestry. com, and crying. Libras, I should mention, can also be self-indulgent and solipsistic.

Still no Teddy.

On the way back to my car, I was waylaid by a Luke Cutt fan from Des Moines, who blithely informed me that she'd lost her virginity to "Dreama, Little Dreama." After taking a couple of pictures with her, I drove to my favorite newsstand and paged through *Paris Vogue*, *Paper*, *Bon Appétit*, *Star*, and *US Weekly*, the last of which featured a side-by-side comparison of my mother and Taylor Swift clad in the same plaid crop top and mini (unsurprisingly, 93 percent of the respondents thought Taylor wore it best). That killed an hour. Three more to go until the Mayan opened for the evening. I could read more magazines. Check my phone again for texts from Teddy. Work on my Jewish foodie tour.

Or I could pay an impromptu visit to Maya Duran.

Maybe the doctor would be around, and she and I could have a chat without Miles breathing down our necks. Maybe I'd even bump into Lizeth the housekeeper again. Strange to have seen her there yesterday. She must've heard about Maya, and known that she and Carmen Luz were one and the same. I wondered what else Lizeth knew.

My grandmother taught me to always bring flowers. Maya liked roses, but $49.99 the dozen seemed excessive, so I chose a single long-stemmed rose with complimentary baby's breath for $7.99. The girl was in a coma, after all.

On the way up to the sixteenth floor I pondered what I might say if she happened to choose the moment of my arrival to wake up. Nothing appropriate came to mind. Not that it mattered. As soon as the elevator door opened I knew something was wrong.

It was a private floor, true. But last time I visited there were a couple of nurses milling about, a janitor pushing a mop, and Miles, standing there looking like death warmed over. Today, the place was empty. I mean empty like the morning after the zombie apocalypse.

My footsteps echoed as I made my way down the hallway to room 111. I knocked once, then pushed open the door.

There she was, all alone in her gilded bed.

Sleeping Beauty.

Who didn't exactly lead a charmed life.

Take the whole cursed-at-birth fiasco. As if that weren't bad enough, she gets booted from the enchanted castle and has to make do with a tiny cottage in the forest. *And* has to exchange her princess name, Aurora, for plain old Briar Rose. Not that that ruse does her any good. She pricks her finger anyway, and falls asleep for a thousand years. It was all sounding depressingly familiar.

"Maya?" I pulled up a chair and sat down. "It's Dreama. We met the other day. How are you?"

Awkward. I tried again.

"Carmen?" Pause. "Can you hear me, Carmen?"

Nothing.

"Listen." I took her hand. "You can call yourself whatever you'd like. It doesn't matter to me. I know who you are. And I know what happened to you. I'm truly sorry."

Against the pallor of her skin her large tattoo looked almost garish. A pink lotus flower, floating above the blue water. In Buddhism, the lotus symbolizes purity. Though rooted in mud, it remains unstained. It is immaculate, uncorrupted, order as opposed to chaos, silence as opposed to noise.

Noise.

That was what was wrong.

No birdsong.

No sirens.

No horns.

No voices.

No beeping heart monitor.

I spun around in my chair and looked at the machine. The red lights were off. The green indicator number was black. And her hand. I dropped it in horror. The IV was gone. It had been taken out, a tangle of tubes and clamps hanging off the edge of the bed.

I tore out of the room.

"Help!" I cried. "Is anybody here? We need help!"

I ran down the hall, flinging open doors as I went, calling out for someone, anyone. But there was no one. No one at the nurses' station. No one in the waiting area. No one in any of the rooms. And I was useless. I didn't know CPR. I didn't know the Heimlich maneuver. My head was filled with half-remembered song lyrics and celebrity trivia gleaned from daily scrutiny of the tabloids.

The stairwell. There had to be someone on the floor below. I turned around, ran back the way I came, but just as I was about to head down the stairs the elevator doors opened to reveal Miles McCoy, looking cooler, calmer, and more collected than I'd ever seen him.

"Dreama." He tucked his phone into his back pocket. "I'm glad you're here. I—"

"Stop! Listen to me! Maya isn't hooked up to any of her machines! We have to—"

"You're crazy." He started down the hall. "Where's the nurse?"

I raced to keep up with him. "I have no idea. This place is a ghost town."

"That's impossible." Sweat pouring off his brow, Miles threw open the door to room 111.

"What the *fuck*?" He ripped off his sunglasses and stared.

Pee Chee was sitting at the vanity, touching up her makeup.

"What are *you* doing here?" I asked her. "You don't do hospitals."

Miles stood in the doorway. "Will someone *please* tell me what is going on?"

Pee Chee put down her lipstick. "Nothing's going on." She turned to face us, flashing her long, slender legs. "The nurse had car trouble. This is her replacement."

She gestured toward a smallish woman in blue scrubs, who nodded, then hung a bag of clear liquid on the IV stand.

"I'm sorry," I said, "but you're full of it."

I walked over to the bed, picked up Maya's hand. The needle and tubing had been reinserted, a fresh piece of tape holding them in place. As for the E.C.G., it looked to be in perfect working order, the red line zigzagging in harmony with Maya's evidently still-beating heart.

I shook my head. "Somebody pulled out her IV and turned off the machine. And left her here all alone."

Miles turned to the nurse.

"No disrespect," she said, "but the line probably fell out. It happens. As for the electrocardiogram, the patient no longer requires it." She held up the chart. "Doctor's orders. I'm just double-checking right now. For my own piece of mind."

"Well, then." Pee Chee rose from her chair, tugged down her short dress. "I guess that's that." She walked over to the door and opened it. "I'm sure you have someplace else to be, Dreama."

"Actually," I said, "my schedule is wide open today."

Pee Chee leaned against the door. "Then you can get me a coffee. I take mine black. Miles is done with his detox tea, I see." She handed me the empty plastic bottle. "Would you refill this with a nice double chai soy latte? It's his afternoon treat."

"Excuse me," I said, "but I don't work for you."

"Right. You work for Miles." She touched the tip of her nose. "Oops. I forgot. Not anymore. Tour's off."

"Sorry to disappoint you," I said, "but I'm still on the payroll."

Pee Chee turned to Miles, her mouth an angry slash. "You never cease to amaze me."

"Right back at you." He looked at her. "On another note, you check in with Destiny today?"

"Bitch is back on board," Pee Chee said.

Miles scratched a note on his little yellow pad. "Thank you, Jesus."

Those two made quite a pair. But at this point I didn't trust either of them. In fact, I wouldn't put it past one or both of them to have gotten rid of the original nurse. To have yanked out that IV. And to have come slinking back to make sure the job was done.

"I'm leaving now," I said. "I just want to say goodbye to Maya."

I walked over to the bed and squeezed her hand one last time. And then I noticed something. At first I thought it was just a shadow. But then I looked again.

It wasn't a shadow. It was a black key, embedded into the seed-pod at the center of Maya's lotus flower tattoo. And I knew what it meant.

Tattoo artists often leave signatures. Initials, lucky numbers, pairs of dice, arrows, small black keys, even. But here's the thing.

Cat never leaves a signature.

Which meant that this was not Cat's tattoo.

Which meant that Miles's fiancée, Maya Duran—the sleeping beauty who kept coming back from the dead—was *not*, in fact, Carmen Luz.

As I left the room, I didn't hear anyone say goodbye.

All I heard was the ticking of the clock.

Chapter 15

WHENEVER I'M AT a loss I remind myself to stop, take a breath, and call my best friend.

"Ridiculous," Cat said by way of greeting.

"How'd you know it was me?" I asked.

"I'm talking about this place. It looks like hell, and I can't find the broom."

It was the last Friday of the month, and Cat House was going to be a zoo in a couple of hours. Normally, Cat didn't do the tidying, but Tigertail and Rory were M.I.A., presumably bringing baby Sprite into the world.

"Whatever," said Cat. "You sound upset. What is it?"

"I thought they were the same girl," I started. "I mean, they look basically *identical*. But they're two separate people. And all they have in common is Miles McCoy and a stupid lotus flower tattoo."

"Dreama—"

"Sorry, a *beautiful* lotus flower tattoo You're very talented."

"That's not—"

"Can you please stop interrupting?" I was just getting warmed up. "What's even *more* disturbing is the $40,000 Miles paid me—or didn't, if you want to take his word for it, not that I'm inclined to take his word for anything. Now it's missing, which is a real problem. Not so much for me—even though I'm broke, and pretty much living on Top Ramen Variety Packs—but for my uncle Ray. Uncle Ray, Cat! The only man who's ever stood by me!"

"Dreama."

"Yes."

"Can you please start from the beginning?" she asked.

I took a deep breath and recited the entire sorry tale. And at the end of it I was right back where I'd started.

I didn't know why Miles was carrying a picture of Carmen Luz.

I didn't know who might want to harm Maya Duran, or why.

I didn't know who would have turned off her IV, or why.

And most important of all, I didn't know what all of this had to do with me, my uncle, and the now-missing $40,000.

"Don't freak out," Cat said. "It ain't over 'til the fat lady sinks."

"I think that's 'sings.'"

"Wrong," Cat said. "It comes from pool. The fat lady's the eight ball."

"And your point is?"

She sighed. "The key. I know whose tattoo signature that is. It might be a place to start. Hold on. I've got another call."

It was Rory and a still-pregnant Tigertail. Apparently, they'd had a false alarm. Poor Rory, however, had been so flustered by the prospect of impending fatherhood that he'd misplaced his car keys so he and Tigertail had been forced to shell out fifty bucks for the cab to Cedars. Now they needed a ride home. And yours truly just happened to be sitting in the parking lot.

I put on my red Ray-Bans. "Lucky for them my mother taught me to say yes when I should say no."

"You're a doll," Cat said. "I've gotta go."

"Not so fast," I said. "About that tattoo. You said you knew who gave it to Maya."

"I do," Cat said slyly. "But not as intimately as you do." She paused for effect.

"What on earth are you talking about?"

"Dreama," Cat said. "*Please*. Do I need to remind you of the man you had sex with five times in a twenty-four-hour period after Luke Cutt left you? Who happens to be a *tattoo artist*? Whose name is Clayton *Key*?"

Oh, god.

Some things you will yourself to forget.

Cat said, "How funny is this? I ran into him recently, and he looked *totally* hot. And he was alone. *And* he made a specific point of asking how you were. I think you should go see him. Like, tonight."

I checked the rearview mirror. "I can't. I'll be chauffeuring your employees all over town."

"Afterward, then. He works late."

"I'm going to be busy."

"With Teddy? He's a booty call."

"And *Clayton Key* is my soulmate?" I backed out of my spot. "I can't talk anymore. There are two people waiting for me outside the emergency room, one of whom is extremely hormonal."

"Yeah," Cat cracked, "and don't forget about Tigertail."

I pulled into the circular driveway just as a nurse came through the double doors pushing Rory, who was seated in a wheelchair. Tigertail trailed behind, juggling her overnight bag, a pregnancy pillow, and a car seat.

"What happened?" I asked.

Rory shrugged, then emptied a box of raisins into his mouth.

"Low blood sugar," said Tigertail. "If he doesn't have a snack every two hours, he faints."

"I meant with you."

"False labor," she said. "It could be days, or even a week. I'm visualizing my cervix dilating and effacing."

"Watch out for the mucus plug," Rory said. "That thing can pop without any warning."

"Okey-dokey." I put Tigertail's things in the trunk. "Into the car. Just toss my stuff out of the way. I'll have you home in an hour, tops."

"An hour, tops?" Rory snorted. "It only takes half an hour to get to Echo Park from here. Unless you drive like a card-carrying member of the AARP."

I was cruising down Robertson now, hitting only green lights. Maybe my bad luck was over. "I hope you don't mind. We have to make one little pit stop. I think you two will enjoy it, actually."

"Less thinking, more drinking," said Rory.

"I could use some fun," offered Tigertail.

How convenient.

Fun is my middle name.

Chapter 16

"You didn't say it was Lucha Vavoom night!" Tigertail cried.

I helped her out of the back seat while Rory groomed his Snidely Whiplash mustache.

"Surprise, then!" I popped the trunk, and handed Tigertail her pregnancy pillow. "Let's go."

A couple of times a year, the Mayan does a special show, Lucha Vavoom, devoted to Mexican masked wrestling, striptease, and comedy. As it turned out, Rory and Tigertail were the perfect cover. The doorman took one look at us—Tigertail in a black lace romper they definitely didn't stock at Pea in the Pod, and Rory with the aforementioned mustache and sky-high spiked hair—and sent us backstage along with the rest of the performers.

"Godspeed, by the way," said the doorman. "Stage manager's in a bad mood."

Backstage, everybody else seemed to be having a riotous good time. Two Aztec dancers in full headdresses were shoveling down pre-show donuts, a sexy brunette was gluing gold tassels to her nipples, little people were rolling fringed hula hoops. A man in an iridescent chicken costume asked me to help zip him up. Then he wanted to know if I was single.

"Don't go there," Rory smirked. "She's merciless as fuck."

"I think we should focus." I turned to him. "We're looking for a gun."

"A *gun*? Why didn't you tell me?" Rory pulled out his cell phone. "I know this guy—"

"No guy. Please." I took Rory by the shoulders. "We are looking for a *specific* gun. It was left behind a few days ago by a friend."

"A 'friend'? Nice try, Dreama. We all know the kind of resentment you're harboring against your former lover, Luke Cutt. It's best to be honest. And perhaps find another way to channel your negative emotions."

I appealed to Tigertail. "I'm thinking that the gun *belonging to my friend* is probably somewhere downstage. It was the last place she had it."

"The stage." Tigertail looked wistful. "Sometimes I really miss the old days."

"Not me," Rory said. "I always felt exploited by management."

Time to get this show on the road. I pulled aside the brocade curtains and took a few tentative steps forward. The lights were blinding. I couldn't see anything.

Somebody in the audience shouted, "Take it off, baby!"

Good lord. The festivities didn't even start for an hour. "Sorry to disappoint," I said, "but I'm doing a sound check."

"Check *this*!" cried somebody else. Then he blew me a raspberry.

I spun around, nodding. "What did I tell you? The acoustics suck."

Suddenly, a long wooden cane extended from behind the curtains and whacked me in the hip.

"Sorry," said Rory. "But you're done here."

"Whoa." I tucked my top back into my jeans. "I thought that only happened in cartoons."

He shook his head. "You're hopeless."

"And I suppose you've got a better idea?"

His nostrils flared excitedly. "As a matter of fact, I do."

Tigertail said, "Honey? Please don't overdo."

Ignoring his wife, Rory emerged stage left, gave us a little one-two as he ducked in and out of the boxing ring they'd set up for the wrestlers, marched down to the apron, then jumped into the orchestra pit, landing with a deafening thud.

"Fuck!" he cried. "My ankle!"

"He's put on a wee bit of weight," Tigertail whispered.

"It's nothing to be ashamed of," Rory bleated. "It's called couvade syndrome. Sometimes there are also mood swings."

"The beautiful thing is Rory's been nesting," Tigertail said. "You should see the linen closet."

I had to hand it to him. The orchestra pit. Of course. The gun had gotten kicked off the stage and tumbled down there. Musicians are so oblivious that they easily could have missed a deadly weapon lying right there at their feet.

"What do you see, Rory?" I called out.

"A mirrored disco ball!" he cried.

"Not up in the rafters," I said. "Down there!"

"Cymbals!" A loud, sharp crash followed.

I turned to Tigertail. "Can you give me a hand?"

Tigertail lowered me down into the pit. I got down on all fours and crawled around the filthy wooden floor, steering clear of the water bottles, music stands, ancient cigarette butts, and somebody's discarded sudoku book. Nothing even remotely resembling a gun.

I rose to my feet, and dusted off my knees. "Let's go find the stage manager."

Back in the hallway we ducked our heads into various dressing rooms, upsetting a trio of mariachis, a woman riding a gold sequined broomstick, and somebody smearing cover-up all over his—don't ask.

Finally I saw a chubby, red-headed man wearing no discernible costume. He was holding a clipboard, another clue. I marched straight up to him.

"Are you the stage manager?" I was hoping he had a phone number for the janitor who'd worked that night.

He looked me up and down. "Auditions are held the first Thursday of the month. And I don't know how you got in here, but you need to go."

Rory pushed Tigertail in front of him. "Feast your eyes, mister."

He shook his head. "Got nothing to do with me. I've been celibate since 1997."

Rory shouted, "This woman's about to expel her mucus plug, and we don't have time to pussyfoot around! We need to see the video feed from last Sunday. Immediately."

The *video feed*? Oh, my god. I scanned the room. There were cameras everywhere. I tugged my beanie down low on my forehead, and stared at the floor. All I needed was to be caught on video poking around another crime scene. Not that I knew Carmen's house in Glendale was a crime scene when I was snapping pictures of it.

"*We need to go,*" I hissed.

The stage manager turned to Rory. "Good idea. Unless you've got a subpoena."

"Which we absolutely do not." I pulled my beanie so far down I could no longer see. "Rory. *Now.*" I swiveled around, bumping into a lighting cart.

"We are not leaving without getting what we came for," Rory said. "A 'friend' of my friend here left something behind on Sunday. Something very important." He was nothing if not determined. Back in Coney Island he'd trained himself to swing a ten-pound bowling ball from his earlobe.

The man whipped his phone out of his pocket. "Though it's none of your business, I'm going to put you out of your misery. The video you're looking for was recycled yesterday. I keep telling them, we need to upgrade to digital." Then he started dialing.

"You calling the janitor?" I asked hopefully.

He stared at me. "Is his number 911?"

Out on the street, we regrouped.

"It was a valiant effort," I said.

"We blew it." Rory looked crestfallen.

"It's going to be okay." I linked my arm in Tigertail's. "Why don't we stop at In-N-Out on the way home?"

That cheered everyone up. As we were pulling away from the curb, however, Tigertail realized she'd forgotten her pregnancy pillow down in the pit.

"I'll just be a second." She struggled to her feet.

"*Rory,*" I said.

"What do you want from me?" He downed another package of raisins. "The doctor said she needs exercise."

After a round of Double-Doubles, we went back to Rory and Tigertail's. They insisted I come in and see their collection of Super Mario Bros. memorabilia. Rory showed it off proudly, then grabbed a bag of Tostitos from the cupboard and said he was hitting the sack. Tigertail walked me to the front door. It had started raining again.

"You guys are troopers," I said. "Thank you."

"Before you go." Tigertail turned her head, making sure Rory was out of earshot. Then she reached into her purse, pulled out a brown paper bag, and handed it to me. I glanced up at her, puzzled, then looked at what was inside.

It was a gun.

Maya's gun.

My mouth fell open. "How did you *do* that?"

"When I went back for my pillow, I had a moment of inspiration." She blushed prettily. "The lost and found! We have one at Cat House, so I figured it was worth a try. You wouldn't believe what was in there. A couple of switchblades. A Trojan Pleasure Pack, unopened, thank goodness. And a gun!"

"How does a *gun* wind up in the lost and found?"

She said, "It looks like a prop. I told the guy it was mine, from my Divine in *Pink Flamingos* act."

"And he just handed it over?" I said.

"Naturally." Tigertail gave me a wink. "Don't you remember? Back in Coney Island I was a snake charmer. Drive safely now, Dreama. No talking, and for heaven's sake, no texting!"

Tigertail was going to be some mother.

As for me, well, I needed a drink. A vacation. And an umbrella. What I had was a trench coat, a beanie, and a gun. I put them on, said my goodbyes, and headed out into the cold, wet night.

Chapter 17

WHEN I SAW those lights flashing in my rearview mirror, my first thought was, this is turning into a bad comedy routine. My second thought was Vlad the Impaler had fixed my busted taillight, and I hadn't been talking on the phone, or speeding, or tailgating. Which made me kind of anxious. Not that I had anything to hide.

Except, perhaps, for the brown paper bag on my front seat.

The 101 was quiet, but given the pounding rain, it still took a couple of minutes to get over to the shoulder. I tried to stay calm. There was always a chance that I wasn't the one he was after, and that when I got out of the way, he'd just pass me by.

Surprise.

I was the one.

"Roll down the window!" came blaring over the loudspeaker.

I had to hurry. I kept my left hand on the wheel, where he could see it, and used my right to surreptitiously swat the brown paper bag onto the floor. If I'd had time, I would have kicked it under my trench coat, but no such luck, there he was, coming up on my left, a man in uniform, a man with a problem.

"Evening, sir!" I said. "How are things?"

He was all heavy brows and dead eyes, like the sadistic cop Matt Dillon plays in *Crash*. "License and registration."

I handed them over.

He studied them, then asked, "Where are you coming from?"

"Echo Park. A friend's house. Medical emergency."

"And before that?"

"The Mayan. Lucha Vavoom. You should go sometime. It's totally fun."

He wasn't about fun. "Where are you headed?"

"Back home. To Venice."

"Do you know why I stopped you?"

"No, sir."

"Do you realize it's a crime to evade the police and that I could haul you off to jail right now?"

He didn't wait for me to answer.

"Were you not aware of me signaling to you a mile back?"

"I had to get over to the side," I said. "I was trying to be careful. I'm not the greatest driver."

Good one, Dreama.

"Have you been drinking this evening?" he asked.

"No, sir."

"Is that a brown paper bag I see? On the floor, near your coat?"

"Brown paper bag?" I looked down. "Huh."

"If I opened it up, I wouldn't find an open container, would I?"

No, Officer, you would find a gun that was recently used in a probable attempted homicide, and was pilfered from the crime scene just this evening by my canny pregnant accomplice.

He pulled a flashlight out of his belt and shined it into my eyes.

"Ow!" I turned away. "Was that really necessary?"

Guess he liked asking the questions.

"Step out of the vehicle," he said.

It was very disorienting. All those cars whizzing past, engines throbbing, tires screeching, lights flashing and blinking. Also, I was getting soaked.

"Put your hands on the hood."

As I placed my hands on the hood, several things occurred to me at once.

Good thing I hadn't bothered with a car wash.

My beanie was angora, which shrinks when wet.

If he patted me down, I was going to sue.

If my mother hadn't spent the $3,000 Miles gave her for the Guns N' Roses photo, she could bail me out.

Then the light went off.

This cop hadn't made me open the brown paper bag. Or cuffed me. Or charged me. Because he had nothing to charge me with. This was a setup. Somebody was sending me a message.

Lieutenant Hepworth. I'd been avoiding his calls. And he'd said he'd be keeping tabs on me.

Then another light went off.

Uncle Ray had a lot of friends on the force. Maybe *he* was the one keeping tabs on me.

"I'm going to let you go," the cop said. "I don't want to see you again. Tonight, or ever. I hope I'm making myself clear. Drive safe now."

I was still kind of edgy when I passed downtown and transitioned onto the 10. Traffic was heavier now, and I wanted to be home. Home, where I was being watched by the L.A.P.D. Home, where someone had broken into my bedroom. Home, where someone had stolen $40,000 from under the mattress. Okay, maybe home wasn't sounding all that enticing right now. In any case I was stuck in the wrong lane behind a stream of cars that were exiting on La Brea. I merged into the middle lane, then the fast lane. And that was when I realized I was being followed again.

It wasn't a cop car this time.

It was a white van.

Did you know there are entire websites devoted to white vans? I didn't either until a bald man sitting next to me at the D.M.V. a few years back told me. Apparently, a disproportionate number of kidnappers, rapists, and road ragers favor white vans. My gardener, Jovani, has a white van. It says, "Green Thum [sic] by Jovani" on the side in big black letters. Not that I suspected Jovani of anything other than your run-of-the-mill misanthropy.

I was still holding out hope that despite being glued to my rear bumper this particular white van had nothing to do with me. But there was only one way to find out for sure. I zigzagged back across the two lanes I'd just traversed.

Shit.

He was still behind me.

I couldn't make the face out in my rearview mirror. The rain was coming down too hard, my wipers were squeaking and dragging, and the defogger was barely functional. All I knew was I had to get away. We were coming up to the exit on Robertson. I took one last look in my mirror, then floored it and went squealing down and around the ramp, right into that seamy under-the-freeway zone that was home to a defunct pet boarding establishment and a gentleman's club for people who simply couldn't wait. Which, of course, described me at the moment.

For a split second I entertained the idea of leaping out of the car and making a break for the club, where I could mingle undetected with the businessmen clients enjoying totally nude lap dances. But I was hardly going to abandon a vintage Mercedes I'd just spent $700 on, and the valet was nowhere in sight, so I just kept on driving west, hitting only green lights, which was a good thing, except for the fact that the white van was hitting those same green lights, which was a bad thing.

I swung my wheel sharply to the left, and then, praying I wouldn't spin out, took a hard left onto Washington. As I passed the old Culver Studios I leaned on the horn, hoping to attract attention. But nobody seemed to notice that I was driving close to eighty miles an hour on city streets with a death van on my tail. That was when I realized the streets were pretty much empty. People in L.A. stay home when it rains. This person could rear-end me and then shove me in the back of his vehicle and no one would ever know. I'd be just another statistic on the white van website.

I detoured onto Venice. The white van followed suit. Jesus. Culver City had come and gone. Mar Vista, too. Now I was racing through Palms. As I passed the former site of a Brazilian restaurant whose owner was strangled by her reality T.V. producer husband when they were on vacation in Cancun I had the fleeting thought that I should call for help. But my purse was in the back seat. As I twisted around to get it, I took my eyes off the road—for the merest fraction of a second—only to find myself up on the sidewalk and heading straight for a bus shelter advertising the latest Adam Sandler movie. I swerved just in the nick of time, my back wheels spinning on the rain-slicked asphalt, and wound up back in the street. Too bad I was facing the wrong way.

At least my course of action was clear.

I had to cross two lanes while dodging the two honking cars

heading straight at me, then hurtle across the median strip, steering clear of the flowering shrubs, and then merge into the traffic heading east without killing anyone.

It was kind of seamless, to be honest.

Didn't know I had it in me.

Unfortunately, the driver of the white van was equally skilled.

We were coming up to a red light at Centinela. There was no way I could barrel through a major intersection without getting hit. The rain was falling harder now, and the inside of the car was fogging up to the point that I could barely see. It was do or die. But I had an idea. I knew this spot. There was a guitar store on the northeast corner that Luke and I had visited when he was searching around for a vintage Gibson Les Paul Standard so he could pretend to be Jimmy Page.

I remembered that day well. There was no parking in front, and the residential streets in the area were all permit parking only, so Luke had me pull into the alley behind the store and wait while he went in to talk to the manager. After sitting there for over twenty minutes, I'd realized there was a nail salon right next door, and since I was waiting anyway, I might as well get a manicure. *And*—how convenient was this?—they had free underground parking.

Like I said, do or die.

The light turned green. I pressed pedal to the metal and went right, the white van pressing hard behind me, then swung an immediate right, and then another, diving down, down, down into the bowels of Happy Nail. I held my breath as I stared into the rearview mirror.

The white van barreled past me and disappeared into the pouring rain.

I don't know how I made it home that night. I can't remember which streets I took, or what songs I listened to on the radio, or a single thing I thought about. I suppose I was numb. And exhausted. When I saw Teddy's car parked outside his house I felt something surge through me. Relief? Joy? Vindication? I wasn't sure at the time.

I flew out of my car, ran up his walk, and pounded on the door.

"Teddy!" I cried. "It's Dreama! Let me in!"

"Dreama?" he said. "What's going on? You're drenched!"

He opened the door wide and took me in his arms.

"I'm so glad you're home," I murmured into his shoulder.

That's right.

I let him think it was him that I wanted when what I wanted most of all was not to be alone.

I told myself it was okay, given everything I'd been through that night.

But deep down, I knew better.

Chapter 18

"Dreama," Teddy whispered. "Wake up."

"No, no," I murmured. "I can't go to school. I didn't study for the test." I rolled over and buried my face in the pillow.

Teddy sat on the edge of the bed, and stroked my hair. "You're dreaming," he said. "There is no test."

I sat up, rubbed my eyes, took a minute to remember where I was and what day it was.

Teddy's house.

Saturday.

And just to clarify, there is always a test. The trick is to be prepared so you don't keep making the same stupid mistakes.

"Breakfast is ready," Teddy said. "Take this."

Teddy's robe was navy blue with thin white stripes. It was also the softest garment that had ever touched my skin. I pulled it on, went into the bathroom to splash some water on my face, then padded into the kitchen.

It was a beautiful day. The morning sun was streaming in through the open window. The *Times* was on the table, the pages riffling in the breeze. There was a jug filled with fresh daisies. And then there was the feast. A steaming French press, a bowl overflowing with raspberries, and a stack of pancakes, maple syrup spilling luxuriantly down the sides. If I hadn't been so hungry, I would've felt at least a twinge of guilt. Instead, I popped a handful of berries in my mouth and poured myself a cup of coffee.

Just then I heard the opening bars of Adele's "Someone Like You." Engelbart started running in circles.

"Hey, you." I bent down to scratch him behind the ears. "It's only my phone." I turned to Teddy. "Do you know—?" I didn't exactly remember where I'd dropped my basket the night before. Things had gotten pretty heated pretty quickly.

"I'll get it for you," he volunteered.

I took a bite of pancake. Oh, god. You could taste the tang of buttermilk.

"They hung up," Teddy called out from his bedroom. "Hey, I was thinking of taking Engelbart for a quick trip to the dog park after we eat. Wanna come?"

This is why you have to nip it in the bud. Homemade pancakes, the dog park, and the next thing you know, you've moved in, you've bought towels together, and one day you grab his phone to make dinner reservations only to find out he's sleeping with a supermodel *and* his publicist.

Then I heard a thud.

And Teddy's voice. *"What the—"*

"You okay?" I called out.

Teddy came walking into the room.

With a gun in his hand.

"Look what I found," he said. "A .38 special."

"That's not mine," I said automatically.

"What are you, fifteen, and your mom just caught you smoking weed?"

"You mean *hers*? I wouldn't have dared."

"Don't change the subject."

"C'mon, Teddy." I stood up, walked over to where he was standing, put my arms around his neck. He shook me off, the gun still in his hand.

"Fine." I backed off. "You want an explanation? I'm involved in a situation. I guess it's kind of messy."

"*Messy*? Pancakes with syrup are messy. My *living room* is messy. I want to know why you were shaking when you showed up last night. And why you were crying in your sleep. And why you asked me if I'd seen anybody trying to get into your house. In case you haven't noticed, I care about what happens to you. I would hate to see you thinking you had to carry a gun for protection. I mean, I know your uncle's a cop, but come on. Unless you know what you're doing, statistics show that you're the one most likely to get hurt."

It was the most I'd ever heard Teddy say at once. I was floored. Maybe he had more going on upstairs than I'd given him credit for.

"First of all," I said, "will you please put the gun down?"

He stood his ground. "I've already checked. It isn't loaded."

Wish I'd thought to do that. "Will you put it down anyway? It's making me nervous."

"Glad you're coming around to my point of view," he said, placing it on the table.

"Listen, do you really think I'm the sort of person who carries a lethal weapon in her basket?" I shot him a look. "Don't answer that. Okay, here's the deal. The gun was used in the commission of a crime."

"*What?*"

I gave him an edited version of the story.

He responded with: "You need to hand the gun over to the police immediately. You've already broken the chain of evidence."

"Under normal circumstances, that's exactly what I would've done."

"What's the problem?"

"I'm not particularly eager to engage with law enforcement right now. Can't we just leave it at that?"

He was silent.

"Which is exactly why a person needs friends," I said. "Friends who have computer skills. Like you."

He didn't look happy. "What do you want from me, Dreama?"

"I guess I was kind of wondering if you could maybe hack into a database or something and figure out whose fingerprints are on that gun. You think they sell CSI kits on Amazon? I have 1-Click."

He wasn't amused.

"We're going to find mine," I went on. "And yours. And a few other sets." Tigertail's, for one. And Maya's, of course. "But I'm looking for the prints of the person or persons who might have slipped a bullet into the chamber the night of Maya's debut. Which would make the aforementioned crime a murder, as opposed to a suicide. Actually, an attempted murder, since she's not dead. Yet." I dropped two more pancakes onto my plate.

"You're kidding, right? I mean, this is a joke."

I sighed. "Look, I can't go to the police. They're the enemy right now. They're out to get my uncle. What's more, they think I'm involved in whatever they're trying to pin on him."

I wasn't going to get into the $40,000. I'd already told him more than I should have.

"Listen, if you don't want to help me," I said, "that's fine. I totally understand. It's probably the smart move. But I'm not letting this go. I can't."

"Look," Teddy said. "Even if I could do some digital voodoo and get a couple of decent prints off the gun, and then break into the NGI—"

"English, please."

"Next Generation Identification. It's the central information repository of the FBI—sorry, *Federal Bureau of Investigation*."

"No need to get snarky."

"As I was *saying*," he continued, "even if I could get in there, this plan works only if this person or persons' prints are already in the system. Without something to match, there's nothing I can do."

"I'm one step ahead of you!" I wiped my mouth, sprang up from my chair and ran out to my car in my bare feet. Teddy stood in the doorway with his coffee, waiting, then followed me back into the kitchen. I set two items down on the table, and smiled triumphantly.

Pee Chee's red lipstick.

And Miles's plastic bottle of detox tea.

I'd nabbed them yesterday at the hospital.

"Impressive," Teddy said, getting into the spirit. "But it might actually be more useful to know who supplied Maya with the gun."

"Why?"

"Because there's no way she would've been rehearsing for weeks on end with a real gun. Performers use prop guns."

I gave him a blank look.

"Think about it," he said. "If someone wanted to kill her, they couldn't possibly have swapped a real gun for a prop that night and expected her not to *feel* the difference. They look the same, but they don't weigh the same. Not by a long shot."

"So what are you saying? Somebody gave her a real gun, but *told* her it was a prop?"

"Exactly."

It took me a minute. And then I understood. "Then, that night, all that person had to do was load the thing with a bullet."

He nodded. "And mission accomplished."

I said, "Too bad I can't just ask her where she got the gun."

Teddy picked up the gun, peered at the handle, then wrote something down on a napkin.

I grabbed the napkin out of his hand. "Eight three three one four four four." Then I looked up at him. "The serial number. You're brilliant."

He flipped open his laptop. "Give me twenty-four hours and I'm going to tell you who bought this gun and everywhere it's been since."

"And what would you like in return?" I asked, untying the robe I was wearing.

He smiled.

A couple of hours later, I left for Cellar Door. Things were not going well over there. Apparently my mother's savory seitan pie lover had left her last night for a raven-haired singer-songwriter, and Mom had driven out to Ojai at 5 a.m. for an emergency session with her life coach, leaving Gram all alone in the kitchen, where she'd burned herself pulling garbanzo flour banana breads out of the oven. When I came in, she was rubbing a stick of Satan's cudgel (i.e., butter) on her hand.

"I know," Gram said. "At least it's unsalted."

I gave her a hug. "Why don't you go home? I can handle things here until Mom comes back."

"Let's not rush your mother," Gram said. "You know how that can go."

After we bandaged up her hand, Gram went out front to check up on things while I mixed up a vat of alkalizing fiesta salad, which is one of our best-selling items, second only to our adzuki bean sliders, which are actually quite tasty. Just not compared to a Double-Double. I was getting started on the cilantro-cumin cakes when I heard a crash. I ran out. Gram had dropped a tray of freshly refilled agave dispensers, and the entire floor was awash in sticky nectar. One of the busboys was already mopping it up.

"Gram, please," I said. "You're going to hurt yourself."

"Stop fussing," Gram said. "Anyway, I'm glad you're done in the kitchen. I have to talk to the new waitress, and I'd like you to back me up."

"What did she do?" I asked.

"She asked some customers if she could start them off with drinks, then suggested rosemary lemonade."

"The nerve of her," I said.

"It's not funny. Then she asked if they wanted appetizers and mentioned that her favorite was the ancient grain pizza."

"I never thought that belonged on the menu. Kamut has a weird texture."

"You're missing the point." Gram's voice started to rise. "This is not the Cheesecake Factory! Or the Olive Garden! We do not upsell wine coolers and nachos and Mississippi mud pie and whatever else we personally might like to consume in our weakest moments when many of our diners are gluten-averse! Or allergic to nightshades! Or on juice fasts and starving to death!" Then she burst into tears.

"Gram." I maneuvered her into an empty booth. "Talk to me."

"It's nothing. I'm upset about a video I saw this morning."

"What kind of video?"

"A circus lion freed from his cage who feels the earth beneath his paws for the first time." She looked up at me, her beautiful blue eyes glistening. "I'm going to send you the link."

"I can imagine that was really moving, but I'm thinking there's something else going on. You can tell me."

In so many ways Gram was ahead of her time. She was a free spirit who lived life on her own terms and didn't care what others thought of her. But in other ways she was strictly old school. She lived, she breathed, she was made for love. It was Ray. Obviously.

"It's Ray," Gram whispered.

"What happened now?"

"I don't know," she said. "I dropped by last night to bring him something to eat and there was no answer at his door. And no answer on his cell phone. I was worried so I snuck around the back to check on things."

"And?"

"I peered into the bedroom window," she said, tearing up again, "and there he was, with his phone in his hand, so he clearly knew I was calling. And he wasn't alone. He was with some woman."

"What do you mean, some woman?"

"I don't know! *Some woman!*"

"Were they—?"

"Oh, I'd say they were well on their way." Gram stifled a sob. "The thing is, we were talking about getting married! I was planning to pledge myself for life!"

For the fifth time, that would be. "There's got to be an explanation. He's under so much stress with work, and—"

"There's something else I've got to tell you," she said. "About Ray."

"Hold that thought." I looked down at my phone. It was Teddy. I stepped out into the parking lot.

"I've got a name," Teddy said. "Omar G. Patterson."

Didn't ring a bell.

"He purchased the gun six years ago," he said. "It hasn't changed hands since. At least officially. And as far as the FBI knows, it's never been used in the commission of a crime."

"Do you have contact info for him?" I asked.

There was a long pause.

"Never mind." I checked Facebook and Instagram. Nothing. Twitter and Pinterest. Nope. There was always 411.com, but the basic search costs $19.95, and I didn't have a credit card handy.

"Dreama. This is a really, *really* bad idea."

"Yes!" I'd hit pay dirt with LinkedIn. "Omar owns a business. Called Omar's."

"You're Googling Omar's, aren't you?" Teddy asked.

"Absolutely not." It was located on 54th and Central Avenue, in South Los Angeles.

"Now you're mapping it."

"No way." Given current traffic conditions, I could be there in twenty-four minutes.

"Why don't you cut the crap? You're not fooling me. I get you, remember?"

Ouch. Every time a man says he "gets" me all *I* get is hurt.

"I've got another call," I said. "See you later."

It was only later, once I was in the car, that I realized I'd forgotten to say thank you.

The other thing I'd forgotten was to ask Gram what else she'd wanted to tell me about Uncle Ray.

Too bad.

Because that was when it all started to fall apart.

Chapter 19

I EXITED THE freeway at Alameda, and took Central Avenue the rest of the way. It was a colorful ride. Just after 4th Street, I passed the wholesale bong district. After Olympic, the best place to buy a counterfeit Disney princess piñata. Then there was the Streamline Moderne Coca-Cola bottling plant, built to look like an ocean liner, complete with portholes and a catwalk. By the time I crossed under the 10, I was in South L.A.

Back in the 1940s, this particular strip of Central was solidly African-American, full of jazz clubs and hotels that catered to the likes of Duke Ellington and Billie Holiday, who weren't welcome elsewhere in the city. I'd done some research on the area for the noir tour. In Walter Mosley's hardboiled classic *Devil in a Blue Dress*, Easy Rawlins gets into hot water there, looking for a white woman named Daphne Monet who liked to live on the edge. The same could be said of Velma Valento, the femme fatale in Chandler's *Farewell, My Lovely*, whose opening scene took place at Florian's, the dive on Central and 54th where Velma used to sing. These days, Central and 54th was home to Gomez

Appliances, La Bendicion Meat Market, and a *peluqueria* with a sign reading, "Fade/Taper/Fo Hawk/Mo Hawk." Something for everybody.

I pulled up in front of Omar G. Patterson's place of business. The sign read, "Granero del Gallo de Oro." According to Google Translate, that meant "golden chicken granary." My mind immediately went to cockfighting. Above the doorway were formal portraits of what seemed to be local pit bull V.I.P.s, as well as a photo-realist rendition of a twenty-pound bag of Iams ProActive Health lamb meal. Now I was thinking the full gamut of bloodsports.

Inside, however, things were somewhat more sanguine. There were Hannibal Lecter–esque muzzles, but also harmless items like flea powder and Skip to My Loo pet toilet training liquid. Yeah, it was yellow.

"*Puedo ayudarle?*" asked a young girl with thin, painted-on eyebrows.

"I'm looking for Omar G. Patterson," I said.

She called out to a guy behind the counter, who was arranging the choke chains. "*Ella esta pidiendo el gordo.*"

"*El gordo*" means "the fat one." I think.

"*En la puerta de salida,*" the guy said.

I typed the phrase into my phone. It was either a sexual reference, or Omar was just past the exit. I was going with the latter.

Out back there was a disintegrating brick garage with a small wooden sign nailed in front. "Omar's Car Service, Est'd 1931." A family business. Nice. Inside were a couple of limousines that looked like they'd seen better days. "Hello?" I called out.

A grizzled-looking man slid out from under one of the limos. "Afternoon, young lady. How can I help you?"

"I was wondering if Omar was around."

A younger man slid out from under the other limo. He looked like Michelangelo's *David*, with prison ink. He gave me the eye. "Sure you're not looking for me?"

"Shut up, Wilson." The older man turned to me. "Omar, Sr. or Omar, Jr.?"

I had no idea. "Omar G. Patterson," I said.

"G for gorgeous," he said. "That'd be Junior. He isn't here."

"*Gorgeous?* Omar G. looks like a hairy marble," said Wilson.

The older man said, "Wilson. Help this young lady out. Where is Omar?"

"Where do you think? At your house, in bed with your wife."

I liked their shtick, but I didn't have all day. "Excuse me—?"

The older man held up a finger, then turned to Wilson. "You know who's on tonight? 'Cause these cars aren't gonna be ready."

Wilson picked up a bottle of oil and shook it. "Empty. Damn. I don't know who's working. Check the schedule, Grandpa."

"I'm not gonna do that. *You're* gonna do that."

"Darling?" Wilson gave me a smile. It was something special, that smile. "Can you check that notebook sitting on top of that file cabinet there? My hands are dirty."

I walked over, opened the calendar, found today's date. "The only name here is Lucius Ramsay."

Lucius Ramsay.

That name sounded familiar.

Somebody had been talking to me about Lucius Ramsay.

Recently.

The older man nodded. "That's where Omar G. is. Kissing Lucius's butt."

Wilson said, "I'm thinking Lucius better be kissing Omar G.'s butt, if you know what I'm saying. Lucius is kind of cash poor these days."

Suddenly, I was getting the distinct feeling that Lucius was the one I wanted to see.

"I should've known." I shook my head. "I've been *wondering* where Lucius has been hiding lately."

Wilson jumped in. "Damn! He owes *you* money, too?"

Interesting. "Not *me* exactly. I wouldn't be this upset if it were about *me*." I smiled beatifically, then patted my stomach.

The older man took the bait. "You poor girl. Lucius is *incorrigible*."

I swatted away an imaginary tear. "I don't know what else to do. I thought maybe Omar could garnish his wages or something."

Wilson said, "I know where he's staying." My knight in shining armor. "At his sister's, two blocks from here. You need the address?"

"That would be wonderful. I'm sure she'd love to see the sonogram of her nephew." I smiled proudly. "Lucius Jr."

Wilson stroked his naked chest. "After you're done there, maybe you and I can go for a ride."

"Cars don't run, fool," said the older man.

"Well, shit," Wilson said. Then he doubled over laughing.

There was a massive sycamore tree across the street from Lucius's sister's place. I parked beneath it and rolled down the window. Then I slunk down in my seat and assessed the situation.

It was a nice block, lined with small, well-tended post-war homes. Apparently, Lucius's sister hadn't gotten the memo. Her lawn was patchy, her paint was peeling, her screen door was hanging off the hinges. I could relate. Home maintenance is expensive and time-consuming. And Lucius was clearly no help. I popped open the glove compartment and pulled out my opera glasses. Hopefully, I'd be able to spot Lucius through the front window, getting his butt kissed by a man who looked like a hairy marble, or vice versa. Suddenly, the front door opened, and a petite woman with a sexy blond weave came out. The sister, I presumed. I peered at her through my glasses. Her nails were amazing. Hot pink, and shaped like daggers. Now she was getting into her Prius, putting on her seatbelt, and backing out of the driveway. I watched as she drove to the corner, then screeched to a halt, backed up, swung a U-turn, drove back to her house, and pulled into the driveway.

She'd forgotten to lock up.

Well, that was that.

You don't lock up when somebody's still at home. But I had to make sure. I waited for her to get back into her car, pull back out of the driveway, drive down the block, and disappear around the corner. Then I waited another couple of minutes to make sure she was really gone.

No more stalling.

It was time to exit the vehicle and take a little walk—past the pink house with the shiny trike hanging off the front steps, past the blue house with the trash cans out front, past the gray house with the four guys in wifebeaters and baggy shorts sitting on the porch who were certain to have no interest whatsoever in a strange young woman with a Jane Birkin basket trespassing on their neighbor's property.

So maybe the plan wasn't fully formulated.

I slumped lower in my seat, and turned on the radio. Music always helps me think. I flipped stations until I found Destiny D-Low's chart-topping nineties throwback of this fall, "Oil Slick," which Miles had produced to great acclaim. He'd told her to forget about singing on key and just belt it out, and sure enough, the cracks and squeaks in the vocals were exactly what made the track so powerful.

Destiny D-Low.

She was the one who'd mentioned Lucius Ramsay.

She, Lucius Ramsay, and Big Fatty were thick as thieves.

Big Fatty had raped Carmen.

And Lucius Ramsay worked for the guy whose gun had almost killed Maya.

Oh, shit.

Looked like I'd cranked the music a little too high, because one of the guys in the wifebeaters had crossed the street and was heading straight for me. I tossed my opera glasses on the seat, and started up the car.

"Do. Not. Move," he said, his middle finger stabbing at the air.

No way out of this one. The rest of his friends were right behind him. And looked like they meant business.

"Hey." I leaned out of the window. "What's up?"

The first guy stared into my eyes, then reached into his back pocket for something, which turned out to be a Sharpie.

"Dreama, little Dreama, am I right?" He handed me the marker, then pointed to an open spot beneath his Tupac tattoo. "You think you could sign right there?"

After thanking me, he said, "Nice car like this shouldn't have that dent on the front bumper."

"Dent? *What* dent?" I exited the car and walked around to what was unequivocally a dented front bumper. Unbelievable. There was no *dent* in my car before Vlad the Impaler got his hands on it. No, I'll bet it happened at Cedars. This is why I hate valet parking.

"Me and my boys, we can take care of it for a hundred bucks.

You need anything else, we can do that, too. Tires, rims." He popped a small piece of plastic onto the end of his cell phone. "We use Square. But since we have to pay 2.75 percent per swipe to the gangsters at Visa we'd prefer cash, if you've got it."

The price was fair, but I really needed to economize. After I signed the other guys' arms, and everybody swapped numbers, we chatted for a few minutes. It was good timing, too. Because while we were sharing favorite Instagrams and debating the pros and cons of e-commerce, they missed the man in the black hoodie emerging from Lucius's sister's backyard.

It wasn't Lucius Ramsay.

Nor was it the hairy marble, Omar G. Patterson.

It was my uncle Ray.

Chapter 20

RAY HAD PARKED his Dodge Charger a block and a half away. I knew this because I trailed him in my car. Lucky for me there was a garbage man making his rounds so I could sort of idle in his shadow without calling too much attention to myself. It's a groupie thing.

Once Ray got into his car, he sat there for a few moments just staring into space. I tried not to read anything into it—paralysis, despair, or demoralization, for example. The truth is I had no idea why my uncle would be lurking outside Lucius Ramsay's sister's house. There was probably an innocent explanation. But this wasn't the time to figure it out. This was the time to gather information.

When Ray pulled away from the curb, I was ready. I shot forward, ducking around the garbage truck while trying to keep at least two cars' distance between us as Ray raced down Central at breakneck speed. Speeding is one of those cop prerogatives, along with parking backward in the red to get your Starbucks. Anyway, I was doing a pretty good job, if I do say so myself, until Ray cut over to Alameda without signaling and I lost him thanks to a slow-

moving family of tourists in matching bucket hats who were crossing the street single file. It was totally the baby's fault.

Just then my phone rang. The number was blocked. And I
wasn't in the mood for surprises.

"Hello?"

"Hey, Dreama."

Uncle Ray. Jesus.

"How about a late lunch at Philippe's?"

I shot a glance at the vintage neon sign just up ahead. "Philippe
the Original. French Dipped Sandwiches."

"Come find me after you park," he said. "I'm already in line."

I pulled into the lot.

"There are spaces to your left," Ray said. "But be careful. You
don't want to put another dent into that car."

The man had eyes in the back of his head.

"You do realize," he said, "that pedestrians always have the
right of way. Especially tourists in bucket hats."

That was it. "Don't you think you're enjoying this a little too
much?"

"I'm just getting started," he replied.

I whipped open the door to the restaurant so fast I almost
whacked myself in the face. Uncle Ray waved me over to where he
was standing.

"We can't keep meeting like this," he said.

"I wonder if I know what you mean," I said, channeling Barbara Stanwyck in *Double Indemnity*.

Ray didn't miss a beat. "I wonder if you wonder."

"Did you know that Billy Wilder and Raymond Chandler almost
killed each other working on that script?" I asked. "Chandler
thought Wilder was smug."

"And Wilder thought Chandler was arrogant," Ray answered. "Because when it came to movies, Chandler was an amateur." He looked at me pointedly. "And amateurs are the first ones to get hurt."

"Afternoon, Ray," said our favorite server. "What about it, Dreama? He behaving himself today?"

I gave Ray a sidelong glance. "Hard to say."

Ray tucked his phone into his back pocket, then ordered two beef dips, two pickled eggs, and one nacho cheese Doritos. After the server loaded our items onto the tray, we found a quiet booth in the back. I slid into my seat, and nonchalantly slathered my sandwich with hot mustard. Ray watched, trying not to laugh, as I washed down my first bite with an entire cup of water.

"You okay?" He reached across the table and started thumping on my back.

"I'm fine." I squirmed away. "Look, why don't we lay our cards on the table?"

"Great idea." He ripped open his bag of chips. "Why are you following me?"

"I could ask you the same thing."

"I'm not following you," he said.

"On Instagram, you are," I said. "Don't bother denying it. You've also kind of been around me, my house, the places I go, you know, a bit more than usual."

"Well, that's pretty vague."

"You want me to get specific?"

Ray shook the last of the Doritos into his mouth. "Sure."

I cut my egg into four quarters, then each quarter into halves. Out with it, Dreama. "Did you visit me the other day?"

"Yes," he said. "We had coffee. I brought a cherry pie from Dupar's. You ate three pieces. Ring any bells?"

"After that, I'm talking. Maybe when I wasn't home?"

Ray frowned. "How could I visit you if you weren't home?"

This conversation wasn't going exactly as I'd planned. I paused, then blurted out, "It's about the $40,000. Look, I just need to know if you took it. It's okay if you did. I just want to know."

"Stop right there. Please." Ray shook his head. "I don't believe this. That asshole has crossed the line."

"Which asshole?"

"Lieutenant Hepworth. I know you spoke with him."

"You see? You *have* been following me!"

"That's ridiculous. I haven't been following you. I just know how the man operates. He's a good talker, I'll give him that. I'm betting he played with your head, made you doubt me, but he's wrong. I need you to understand. I am *not* a dirty cop."

"Ray—"

He held up his hand. "He scared you, didn't he? Made threats. Maybe he even told you it would go easier for me if you gave him some information he could use. What a piece of shit, dicking around with my *family*." He leaned forward. "Do you hear that? I called you a piece of shit, *Doug*."

Oh, my god.

He thought I was wearing a wire.

"Ray," I said. "I am not recording this conversation. I would *never* do something like that to you. I do not for a second believe that you took a $40,000 bribe. Or kickback. Or whatever."

He put his head in his hands, then looked up at me, his eyes red. "Then why are you asking me about the money?"

I stared at him. It was obvious he had no idea what I was talking about. I didn't know who broke into my house and stole that money, but it wasn't my uncle Ray.

"I'm sorry," I said. "I'm so confused about everything these days. My career's in shambles, my love life's a complete mess—"

"Join the club," he said. "Scoot over, okay?" He got up from his seat, slid in next to me, and gave me a hug. He smelled like cigarettes. So much for breaking old habits. "I'm really sorry for what I said. It was out of line. I know you'd never do anything like that. It's the stress getting to me—everybody asking me questions, putting me on the defensive. It wasn't fair to assume you were part of it. You can ask me anything you want, anytime you want. As far as you're concerned I'm an open book."

I smiled. "That goes both ways."

"I am so glad to hear you say that. Because I'd really like to know what you were doing in South Central today."

Damn, he was good. "I want to know what *you* were doing in South Central today."

"I'm a cop, Dreama. I go places. I check on things. It's my job."

"You've been suspended."

"I'm going to repeat my question," he said. "What were you doing in South Central today?"

"I was looking for someone," I said.

"I gathered. And who exactly were you looking for?"

"A guy named Lucius Ramsay."

He slammed his fist on the table. "Goddamn it!"

"*What?*"

"This is *exactly* what I'm talking about. What the hell did Hepworth ask you to do?"

"I told you! Nothing!"

"Are you *crazy*? Do you have any idea who *Lucius Ramsay* is?"

"He's some kind of rapper," I said. "I needed to talk to him.

He's a friend of a friend of mine, Destiny D-Low." That was 100 percent accurate, if not the whole story.

"Might I suggest that your friend Destiny get herself a new friend? Because Lucius Ramsay is a criminal and extremely dangerous. Do you understand me? I don't want you *anywhere* near him."

Just then Ray's phone rang. He looked at the number and something dark passed across his face. When he picked up, a woman started yelling at him.

She didn't sound like Gram.

He hung up after a minute, then rose to his feet. "I have to go. So please listen to me. I love you, but I'm worried about some of your choices. You need to stop and *think*, Dreama. *Think* before you act."

Easier said than done.

I finished my food, and ate the rest of the sandwich Ray had left behind, then I looked at my phone.

One text from Teddy. He was checking up on me.

Another missed call from Lieutenant Hepworth.

And a text from Cat, all in caps: *WHERE ARE U? MEET ME AT 11345 SUNSET BLVD. IF YOU KNOW WHAT'S GOOD FOR YOU!*

Experience suggested that I did not, but I was absolutely open to new approaches. The 10 was backed up, but I got there within the hour. It wasn't until I pulled up right in front, however, that I realized where I was.

And that Cat's days were numbered.

Chapter 21

"TELL ME THIS is a coincidence," I said to Cat. "That you are standing in front of this particular establishment."

Low Key Social Club.

L.A.'s number one tattoo shop.

Owned and operated by one Clayton Key.

And in case you were wondering, rebound sex is always a mistake.

"I prefer to think of it as serendipity," Cat said. "How often do you find an open parking space on the Sunset Strip on a Saturday evening?"

"Show-off," I said. "I had to pay fifteen bucks, and it's not even dark yet."

Cat looked up. "The sun is going down. In any case, I like to get to parties early. Before everything goes to hell."

I pulled a Colgate Wisp out of my basket and ran it over my teeth. "You could've warned me."

She studied my white eyelet camisole and black and white striped hip-huggers. "You look great."

Though not as festive as she did, in a rainbow-striped satin pencil skirt, a baby tee that read, "KATE MOSS AND SOME PIZZA SLICES," and Birkenstocks that I think used to be mine.

"Oh, no," I said. "Across the street. Don't look."

Outside the Roxy box office there was a group of conservatively dressed twenty-somethings pointing their phones at us.

"Could be a church group," I said.

"Ooh," Cat said. "They're jaywalking."

One of the girls came right up to me. "Excuse me, but—"

"She is, and she doesn't mind," said Cat.

We posed for pictures. By then I needed a coffee. But Cat was anxious to put her plan into action before her meter ran out.

"What exactly is your plan?" I asked.

Cat said, "We go inside, you lock eyes with Clayton, realize what you threw away, and move in together. I need you settled."

"When did you become such a Clayton fan?"

"He's a good guy, in spite of the artful stubble. And like I said, he's pining for you. Here." Cat handed me a black eye pencil. "You look washed-out. Do an Amy Winehouse eye."

I shook my head, then rifled around in my purse until I found some sparkly highlighter, which I rubbed onto my cheekbones. "I've already been down this road. It's not going to work."

"Didn't you once tell me that Clayton was the one that got away?"

"We were together for half a second," I said.

She took my hand, and pushed open the door. "My point exactly." Inside, the lights were off.

"Where is everybody?" I asked. "Do you smell smoke?"

Cat sniffed the air, then nodded. "Mark my words. Someone threw a joint into the trash last night and started a small fire." She walked over to the front desk and pushed the service bell.

A voice came from the back. "We're not open yet!"

"Let's go," I whispered.

Cat poked me in the ribs. *Say something.*

"Fire marshal," I cried. Oh, my god.

A chair scraped against the wooden floor. Then footsteps. Half a second later Clayton Key appeared—shirtless, I might add—backlit against the office doorway. He still looked good enough to eat.

"Hi," I said. "Cat and I were in the neighborhood, so—"

"What took you so long?" He broke into a grin.

I'd totally forgotten he had dimples.

Cat said, "Uh, Clayton? You might want to—"

He looked down at his bare chest, then grabbed a Low Key T-shirt off the desk and tugged it on. "Sorry about that. Air conditioner's messed up. So, Dreama. Man. You look *amazing*. How have you been?"

"Good," I said.

Cat interrupted, "Is that smoke I'm smelling?"

Clayton nodded. "Somebody tossed a joint into the wastebasket last night and started a small fire."

Cat turned to me. "How totally weird."

Clayton put his hand on my shoulder. "So you changed your mind."

"Changed my mind?" I asked, heart pounding.

He nodded. "About that tattoo."

"Oh, that." In spite of myself I was disappointed. "No, I haven't changed my mind."

"Too bad," he said. "I was kind of looking forward to leaving my mark on you."

"You left your mark," Cat said. "Trust me on that one."

I glared at her, then turned to Clayton. "Do you have a minute to talk?"

He led me over to a couch in the back of the shop. We sat down next to one another. "You have my full attention."

I felt myself blush. Stupid. You are not a schoolgirl. You are a mature woman. Mature women know what they want. Proceed. "I wanted to ask about your tattoo signature. A key, right? Pretty cute."

"Yeah," he said cautiously. "That used to be my signature. But I had some legal issues recently, and I don't sign my work anymore."

"What happened?"

He sighed. "I did this awesome Thor tattoo. Covered this guy's entire back. Took an entire month. On the last day, after I finished up the cross-hatching, I put a key on the handle of Thor's hammer. The guy okayed it, but I guess he was wasted at the time and didn't remember, so he took me to court."

"And?"

"I got lucky. The judge dismissed the case. The guy was a loser. Whatever. It's part of the job. Right, Cat?"

"Yup," she said. "People change their minds all the time."

"It's usually women," Clayton said. "No offense."

"Actually, I wanted to ask you about a woman," I said. "You gave her a tattoo. Anything you could tell me would help. Her name is Maya Duran."

"Doesn't sound familiar."

I said, "Very beautiful, with pale, short dark hair, tall. A dancer. Young. Early twenties?"

"What kind of tattoo was it?"

"A pink lotus flower, on her arm. Large-ish."

"I do a lot of large-ish pink lotus flowers."

I closed my eyes and visualized the tattoo on Maya's arm. "This one was special. It was black with a wash of pink, kind of like a veil, and these abstract black whorls of water. Like bull's-eyes. No other colors. And your signature was embedded into the seedpod at the center of the flower."

Clayton nodded. "I remember that one."

He got up from the couch and went over to a large black book tucked behind the front desk. I followed, watching over his shoulder as he thumbed through the pages looking for the right sheet of paper.

"Here it is," Clayton said. "She came in last May. A little less than a year ago. She brought a picture. She wanted me to copy it. This is how it came out."

There was a Polaroid clipped to the sheet of paper. Clayton handed it to me and Cat.

Cat immediately recognized the tattoo. It was a carbon copy of the one she'd given several years ago to Carmen Luz.

I immediately recognized the girl. It was Maya Duran, proudly showing off her brand new tattoo. Only in this photograph she wasn't a pale, edgy beauty with a dark glossy bob.

She was a California dream girl, with masses of long, blond hair.

"She was really nervous about the whole thing," Clayton said. "It was her first time."

"Anything else you remember?" I asked.

Clayton frowned. "She was with this older woman who seemed to be running the show. She was pretty much covered in ink, so maybe she thought she was some kind of expert. Anyway, she gave me a really hard time, standing over me, barking orders, intimidating the girl."

"I'm surprised she let you sign your work."

Clayton looked at me. "She didn't."

Cat raised an eyebrow.

"The older woman left for a while," Clayton explained. "So I asked the girl if it would be okay. I mean, it was her body, right?"

Cat turned to me. "The man's a feminist."

Ignoring her, I asked Clayton if there was anything else.

He took a breath. "I don't want to be rude, but the older woman had these huge—" He cupped his hands over his chest. "And this wild hair."

I should have seen this one coming a mile away.

"Was it the color of Flamin' Hot Cheetos?" I asked.

Clayton laughed. "Sounds like you know her."

Cat looked at me.

"I do," I said. "Her name is Pee Chee Lowenstein."

Clayton looked down at the piece of paper. "Nope. Definitely not Pee Chee Lowenstein."

Impossible.

"What is it then?" Cat asked.

"Phyllis," he read.

"*Phyllis?*" asked Cat.

"Yeah," Clayton said. "Phyllis Dietrichson."

Of course.

Cat asked, "*Who* the hell is Phyllis Dietrichson?"

I punched the name into my phone and up came the iconic film noir image: Barbara Stanwyck in dark sunglasses, dark lipstick, and a garish blond wig. A garish blond wig chosen by director Billy Wilder to complement her character's garish nameplate anklet.

I turned my phone so Cat could see the picture.

"Phyllis Dietrichson is the name of the femme fatale in *Double Indemnity*," I explained.

And *Double Indemnity* is the story of a murder that—at least on first inspection—looks like a suicide.

Chapter 22

CLAYTON'S ASSISTANT SHOWED up with a couple of six-packs of Corona and some paper towels, and Cat and I stuck around and helped them clean the place up. By that time there was already a crowd milling around outside. After Cat took off, the assistant starting signing people in, and Clayton walked me back to my car. We didn't say much, but he took my hand and I didn't pull it away. I can't say it felt right, but it didn't feel wrong.

On the ride home, I had a lot to think about.

Start with the obvious.

Pee Chee Lowenstein (sorry, Pee Chee's alter ego, Phyllis Dietrichson) and Maya Duran (a blonde at the time) had showed up last May at Clayton's shop wanting a tattoo for Maya. Not just any tattoo, though. An exact replica of the pink lotus flower Cat had given Carmen Luz.

That would be Carmen Luz, whose photograph I'd taken from Miles's wallet, and who'd been raped and left for dead by Big Fatty.

That would be Big Fatty—rapper, ex-felon, and close personal friend of Destiny D-Low.

That would be Destiny D-Low, whose career had been resurrected by a man she loathed, Miles McCoy.

That would be Miles McCoy, who had or had not given me $40,000, and had or had not stolen it back, compromising the reputation of Uncle Ray in the process.

That would be Uncle Ray, whom I'd just caught sneaking around the house of the sister of Big Fatty's and Destiny's old drinking buddy Lucius Ramsay.

That would be Lucius Ramsay, employee of Omar G. Patterson, whose gun had recently been used to spectacularly ill effect by Maya Duran.

Did I leave anything out?

Only that if his name wasn't cleared soon, Ray was not only going to lose a promotion he'd worked two decades to get, he was going to wind up in prison.

And that if *that* happened my grandmother was going to have her heart broken yet again.

Oh, and that Maya was about to start walking and talking again, and there might well be somebody out there who didn't want that to happen.

Now I *really* needed a coffee.

I pulled into the closest Coffee Bean and ordered an Iced Blended with an extra shot. There was the usual discussion when I gave the server my name. The kid didn't think much of Luke's recent solo album, but apparently his mom was so into Luke's sultry Bvlgari Man fragrance ad that she'd bought her son a bottle for Christmas even though he didn't wear cologne.

On the way out of the mini-mall, I thought I saw a white van pull out behind me. But when I checked my rearview mirror, I saw that the van was actually sort of ecru, and that the driver was like a hundred years old. Maybe it was a bad idea to suck down so much caffeine at night. I took a breath. Visualized a mountain stream and daisies. And told myself that every white van in Los Angeles was not out to get me. Which turned out to be 99 percent accurate.

As I pulled into the driveway I saw Teddy waiting outside my door with Engelbart, who was wearing a red bowtie.

"He went to the groomer," Teddy explained. "Petco got fancy on me."

I bent down to scratch Engelbart behind the ears. He closed his eyes in ecstasy, puffing hot, moist dog breath into my face. It wasn't all that pleasant, but I was stalling. I didn't know what to say to Teddy. I felt like I'd just cheated on him. Even though Clayton had only kissed me once in the parking lot. Okay, twice.

"Are you going to tell me what happened with Omar G. Patterson?" he asked. "I've been worried."

I stood up, got my key out of my purse, opened the door. "Would you like to come in? I need a shower, and then we should talk."

"Okay," he said carefully.

"Grab yourself a drink, or whatever," I said. "I'll be quick."

I stayed in there as long as I possibly could.

After half an hour, Teddy poked his head into the bedroom. "You still breathing?"

I was in my robe, wet hair streaming down my back. "Sorry. It was a long day."

He grabbed my hand, pulled me into the kitchen. "Look." He tossed some lemon wedges into the disposal and turned it on. "I fixed the garbage disposal."

"You didn't have to do that." I'd had no idea it was broken.

"I also brought in the trash cans."

My gardener wasn't going to like that. We have our rhythms, Jovani and I. He drags my garbage cans out on Thursdays, and brings them back in on Mondays. In between, I let the trash pile up inside my house. It works for us.

"I changed the lightbulb in the dining room, too," Teddy said.

Well, that sealed it. The guy was too nice. Too thoughtful. Too concerned about my safety and well-being. So I did the logical thing. I started a fight and broke up with him. Who wouldn't have done the same? Who wouldn't prefer a player like Clayton Key, who'd probably never changed a girl's lightbulb in his life? And who kissed girls in parking lots and then didn't so much as mention wanting to see them again? Hot one minute, cold another. Yeah, a person would never be bored with Clayton.

After Teddy left, I went straight for the freezer. No ice cream. I was starving, and all there was in the fridge were softish radishes and an English muffin showing the first signs of mold, so I called the Indian place around the corner and ordered a mango lassi and three orders of samosas. They forgot the chutney, so I ate the samosas with ketchup.

After that hearty repast, I sat down on the couch and Googled Pee Chee Lowenstein.

What a nasty piece of work she was.

Her real name was Phoebe, but her second-grade teacher had nicknamed her Pee Chee, after the school folders, because even then she'd been obsessive about organization. I'm talking hitting the children who wouldn't line up single file. I'm talking arranging the crayons in alphabetical order. Those fun facts I got from a profile that ran in the *New York Times* when Pee Chee was named Editor-in-Chief of *Spin*, after going straight from college to a career as an A&R executive at Roc-A-Fella Records. When she was running *Spin*, the magazine became known for promoting hip-hop and rap, as well as covering non-mainstream cultural phenomena, like monster trucks and Japanese anime. Pee Chee herself became known for her hair, her boobs, and her relentlessness. Also, for bullying her employees, several of whom filed a class-action lawsuit, which effectively caused her to resign.

Pee Chee had no kids. No significant others. No charities. Hobbies included needlepoint and scrapbooking—just kidding about the last part. No hobbies. Only work. And Miles McCoy.

No one was surprised when Miles seduced her away from some post-*Spin* freelance producing and made her 25-A-Day's second-in-command. Miles was riding high at the time, and his charisma was legendary. By all accounts, they made a great team. Miles, the artist, and Pee Chee, the head to his heart, the one who greased the wheels, and tied up the loose ends. She even officiated at two of his four weddings. When asked by a *Vanity Fair* reporter what her own relationship to Pee Chee was like, Miles's third (and fourth) wife, socialite Petal Collings, said, "What do you think? Pee Chee is Mrs. Danvers and I'm the second Mrs. de Winter."

That got my attention.

A socialite known for her blond ringlets and a guest appearance on *Gossip Girl* referencing Daphne du Maurier's *Rebecca*? I wondered if Petal Collings wasn't smarter than she seemed. And if she had anything more to say on the subject of Pee Chee and Miles. I polished off the last of the samosas while I looked her up online.

Turns out Petal was no shrinking violet. She had 14,100 Twitter followers. On Facebook, 7,003 friends, plus four canines—Horst, Horst Jr., Horst III, and little Quattro. From Facebook I also learned that she was descended on her father's side from

Thomas Jefferson, and that her defunct handbag line had been remaindered at Nordstrom Rack. She was more active on Instagram. Summer house pictures, views out of Manhattan penthouse pictures, views out of private jet pictures, and—because some PR person must've told her she wasn't relatable—bowls of chili with onions pictures. By the time I finished a scintillating profile of Petal in last December's *Los Angeles* magazine I realized why the woman might want to be more relatable. She was launching a line of Nantucket-themed china, glassware, and tabletop accessories, which would be available exclusively at Barneys in Beverly Hills. And according to their website, the launch party was tomorrow.

I wandered into the kitchen and threw open my cupboard doors. There wasn't much in there: a cracked mug from Fairfax High, the alma mater of my mother and two of the Jackson Five; three random wine glasses from a trip to Napa with Luke Cutt; and four white plates, which were all that remained of the original set of eight I'd picked up at Target before my last dinner party, eighteen months ago.

Shameful.

Anyone could see that what I needed was a nice set of whaling ship dessert plates and some jaunty sailboat-printed highball glasses.

And I knew exactly where to get them.

Chapter 23

"I WISH WE'D gone to one of our usual places," my mother grumbled. "Or just eaten at Cellar Door. Gram could've whipped us up some nice tempeh hash."

"Barneys is centrally located," I said. "And known for its people-watching. Look." I pointed to a spindly person of indeterminate age whose curly hair matched that of her French poodle. A service animal, no doubt.

"Don't stare," my mother scolded.

"Don't start," my grandmother cautioned.

So there we were, three generations of strong women, squeezed into a booth for two, enjoying Sunday brunch. My grandmother was having borscht, hold the sour cream. Beets support detoxification and fight inflammation. My mother chose sauerkraut. According to Dr. Oz, fermented foods keep you young. And I was stuffing my face with several of my favorite ancestral treats: blintzes, bagels, cream soda.

"Beverly Hills brings back bad high school memories," said

my mother as she dumped an ungodly amount of sugar into her coffee. Her commitment to renunciation was shaky at best.

Gram nodded. "I remember when they kicked you out of that boutique for shoplifting those jeans."

My mother said, "I was thinking of the time they kicked me out of that club on Rodeo Drive. I'd been going there since ninth grade, no problem."

"It was a private disco," Gram said. "What was it called?"

"Oh, my god," my mother said. "You're losing your memory *already*?"

"The Daisy," I piped up. "I was just reading about it. They filmed a scene from *American Gigolo* there."

My mother said, "That's right. The scene where Richard gets together for a drink with his pimp."

That would be *Uncle* Richard Gere, who had a thing for my mother in between the (alleged) gerbil and Cindy Crawford.

"Leon was the pimp's name." My grandmother turned to her daughter. "And don't you worry. I remember everything."

"Excuse me, ladies," I said. "Do you want to know why I was reading about the Daisy? Speaking of gigolos?"

"You can stop right there," my mother said. "I'm not having you say a word against Daniel."

"Who is Daniel?" I asked.

"The savory seitan pie maker," my grandmother supplied.

I turned to my mother. "Why would you think I was talking about him?"

"You said, 'speaking of gigolos,' and I know exactly what you meant. And I do not appreciate it."

"I wasn't talking about your lover, Mother."

"Ex-lover. Not that you care about my feelings."

"More coffee, ladies?" asked the waiter.

My mother placed her hand over her cup. "Habituation to caffeine leads to increased risk of mortality related to cardiovascular disease." She fixed me with one of her stares. "And I want to live forever so I can torment you."

Like a red flag to a bull. But not this time. "When I said, 'speaking of gigolos,' it had nothing to do with you, Mother. It was about me."

"Teddy's a gigolo?"

"Teddy is not a gigolo. And Teddy is no longer in my life."

My mother almost choked on her sauerkraut. "He dumped you?"

"As a matter of fact, I dumped him."

She shook her head. "Not smart. He's hot and nice. Who dumps hot and nice?"

Gram started to cry.

"Now look what you did," my mother said. "She's upset about Ray."

"I am not upset about Ray." Gram blew her nose with her napkin.

"Ray is cheating on her," my mother said.

"That is so not true," I said.

"Stop it, both of you," Gram said. "Not another word on that subject today." She asked for the check. "You were about to tell us why you are pursuing a gigolo. Or gigolos."

My mother said, "It's a bit hypocritical, isn't it? You made such a fuss about me going on Tinder."

"I am not pursuing gigolos," I said. The couple at the next table turned to look at me. I lowered my voice. "*Gigolos* are pursuing me."

Gram looked shocked. "I didn't realize it had come to that. If you need money, we can give you more hours at Cellar Door."

My mother handed the waitress her credit card. "Remember

what happened to Leon the pimp." She ran her finger across her throat.

I'm not going to recount the rest. Let's just say it took me twenty additional minutes to make it clear that I'd just been hired to organize an *American Gigolo* tour for Cowboys4Angels, which is a company that provides straight male escorts to women looking for the "boyfriend experience." The C.E.O. believes in perks—trips to Disneyland, spa days, etc.—to keep the gentlemen motivated. My mother and grandmother were beyond thrilled to hear that my career was not over, and that I was moving on from the Miles McCoy debacle. And I *was* moving on. Just not quite yet.

After we'd properly digested, the three of us headed to the third floor.

Home accessories.

There was a sizable crowd of people hovering around a blonde perched on a high stool.

There are blondes, and then there are *blondes*.

Petal Collings was the second kind, all pale skin, red lips, and cascading curls, dressed in a body-hugging white dress that would have been virginal if it weren't actually pornographic. This was a woman who never waited in line. Never paid. Who made people stop and smell the roses and crave blueberries fresh off the bush and feel suddenly happy to be alive. Big whoop. I had cunning. Like a fox.

"Please back up!" barked an older woman wearing khaki walking shorts and a Nantucket red visor. "Miss Collings is claustrophobic and feeling faint!"

"Oh, please," pooh-poohed my mother.

Indeed. Petal was drinking champagne and looked to be safely ensconced behind a barricade of acrylic and faux-leather trays and

Lucite ice-buckets with logo-embossed brass handles, though it was true that people were grasping at these objects as if they were holy relics and Petal herself had the power to heal the lame.

"I repeat, put away your phones," the older women shouted through her megaphone. "Miss Collings will only pose for pictures with a purchase." She frowned at a passel of youngish Asian women who were frantically waving around selfie sticks. Apparently, Petal was huge in Japan.

I got into line behind a woman who was live-tweeting standing in line to buy coasters. My own set of coasters in hand, I cursed silently to myself about the injustice of having to shell out actual dollars merely to approach this woman who may or may not have information she was willing to share about Pee Chee Lowenstein and/or Miles McCoy. My mother, meanwhile, had set her sights on the last set of starfish napkins, and was battling it out with an equally determined Orthodox Jewish matron juggling several toddlers and what looked to be one of the discontinued Petal Collings purses from Nordstrom Rack.

"Wouldn't you prefer this, Desirée?" Gram pointed to a pink and green catchall tray.

"You know I hate paisley," said my mother, who had attracted the attention of several of the Japanese teenagers, who were now pointing their selfie sticks at her while chanting, "I WANT MY, I WANT MY, I WANT MY MTV."

Thrilled to have been recognized, my mother surrendered the starfish napkins to the Orthodox woman and, backing up to fix her lip gloss, careened into the vertiginously stacked ice buckets, which went crashing to the floor. My grandmother, rushing in to fix things, as is her wont, tripped over the older woman in the Nantucket red visor's megaphone, which certainly shouldn't have been left lying in the middle of the floor, and went flying directly into Petal, who, in trying to catch her balance so as not to topple off of her swivel stool, inadvertently yanked out her own hair extensions.

Oh, yes.

They kicked us out.

After escorting my mother and grandmother back out to their cars, and going all the way back up to the restaurant to get my ticket validated so I didn't have to pay even more handsomely for this fiasco, I wandered into the lingerie department. It was by accident, really. Not because all my bras and panties were ratty and there might be a time in the near future that I'd like to own at least one matched set that could make a lothario like Clayton Key go weak at the knees.

They were having a sale. After fighting off several determined women, I grabbed some tiny, silky things and waited for a vacant dressing room.

The first ensemble I tried on—red with leopard accents—was something my mother would wear.

The second made me look like a pre-pubescent boy.

The third—well, I was studying myself from all angles in the full-length mirror at the end of the corridor when I heard someone say, "You look hot enough to make a bishop kick a hole in a stained-glass window."

I whipped my head around.

Petal Collings, in a full-on bondage ensemble.

Not only could this person reference Daphne du Maurier, she could quote from Chandler's *Farewell, My Lovely*. But why was I surprised? The woman *had* married Miles McCoy. Twice.

I scooted back to my dressing room and attempted to wrap

the pink curtain around my body while maintaining eye contact with Petal. God forbid I should glance down again. That's right. Crotchless.

"I'd kill for your legs. " Petal waved around her ostrich feather tickler for emphasis.

"Thanks," I said.

"What do you think of this?" She pirouetted out of her own dressing room. "I've got an event."

No way was I asking.

"Stunning. The tassels are so bouncy."

"Dr. Kamerinsky." She nodded conspiratorially. "His boobs defy gravity."

We were bonding.

"So you like this teddy?" I dropped the curtain. "I'm not 100 percent sure."

She smiled. "*I'd* do you."

That wasn't the kind of bonding I had in mind. "I'm kind of involved with someone."

"No worries," she said. "I'm straight. And engaged! I'm a big believer in marriage."

Good thing. The Nantucket-themed china, glassware, and tabletop accessories—like her handbags—were nothing to hang a future on.

She passed me her phone. "Type in your number, and I'll invite you to the wedding. I don't mean to be weird, but you're Dreama Black, aren't you?"

If you've been famous for fifteen seconds and you meet someone else who's been famous for fifteen seconds, boom, instant friendship. Sometimes they have their assistants text you, or they find you on social media and invite you to drinks. Or to their weddings.

I punched in my number, and handed her phone back. "And you're Petal Collings. I was upstairs earlier. I was going to buy the coasters, but—"

She leaned in. "They're crap. Made in China. Wait for the fall line. My fiancé found me this guy in Italy."

"Excuse me, ladies," said a wizened little woman holding a bathrobe. "Can you maybe wrap it up?"

Petal beckoned me into her dressing room. We sat down next to one another on the tiny wooden bench. We were both more or less naked. It was kind of awkward, actually.

"Hey," she finally said. "You know that Victoria's Secret supermodel with your ex? I can't believe he cheated on you with *her*." She clucked disapprovingly.

"Luke Cutt isn't exactly the faithful type."

Petal nodded. "I get it. My ex-husband Miles made a fool of me, too."

At last.

"No way," I marveled. "How is that even possible? You're so beautiful. And so smart."

"I know," she said. "But Miles never really appreciated me. I think he was swayed by this horrible woman working for him who was, unfortunately, way smarter than I'll ever be. She took care of his needs. And I mean *all of them*."

This was a twist. But why was I not surprised? Miles and Pee Chee were joined at the hip. And not just metaphorically, apparently.

"That is so crossing the line," I said. "Sleeping with your employer? Your *married* employer? What kind of woman does that to another woman?" I leaned forward, poised for something juicy. And then Petal's phone started ringing.

"Never a moment's peace." She rummaged through her purse,

pulling out a rhinestone-encrusted iPhone and two linty red Life-savers. She popped one into her mouth, and offered me the other, which I accepted. Price of doing business.

"Shit." Petal studied the screen for a minute, then mumbled, "Evil old crone."

"The woman who worked for your husband?" I asked hopefully.

Petal stepped out of her leather teddy and pulled on her white dress. "No, my mother. Did you meet her upstairs? In the Nantucket red visor? She's a nightmare, but the woman my ex worked with was even worse. Tattoos on her chest, hair like a fright wig. No way Miles would've touched *her*. No, the person he was screwing during the entirety of our second marriage was a hot, young thing looking for a free ride. Totally the opposite of me."

A hot young thing looking for a free ride.

I could think of two people who might fit the bill.

Petal kicked off the marabou-trimmed sandals and slipped back into her white Christian Louboutins. "I'd love to keep talking, but unfortunately, Mommy Dearest says I need to go back up to the third floor and make nice to my fans. By the way, you should try on this bikini." She handed me two tiny scraps of emerald green fabric. "It matches your nails."

She couldn't go yet. I needed more information.

"I'm worried about you," I let slip.

She laughed. "I think I can handle some Japanese teenagers."

I shook my head. "That's not what I'm talking about. Remind me again, when did you and Miles get divorced?"

She looked confused. "Which time?"

"The second time. I mean, you want to be sure enough time has passed. You know, before you get married again. Just to be sure it's going to stick."

"You silly goose." She smiled. "The divorce was final a year ago this March, thanks for asking."

The hot young thing Petal was talking about wasn't Maya Duran. Miles hadn't even met her until after his divorce from Petal had been finalized.

That left Carmen Luz.

"I celebrated on the white sand in St. Barts with an underaged fuck-buddy of my own," Petal said. "It was *heaven*. And all I had to buy him was one, lousy Versace suit. Miles, on the other hand—" She shook her head.

"What?" I was hanging on her every word now.

"He likes to do things big, you know? He didn't rent his little slut some apartment somewhere. He bought her a *house*. For a girl like her, it must've felt like a dream come true."

Those were Lizeth the housekeeper's exact words.

But how could I be sure?

And then it came to me.

That day, standing by the trash cans, I'd shown Lizeth the wrong picture.

I shouldn't have shown her *Carmen's* picture.

I should have showed her *Miles's*.

Chapter 24

THE DRIVE TO Glendale took under an hour, counting a pit stop at Porto's for a *café con leche*, half of which spilled in the car, and a guava pastry I'd intended to save for later.

Like my mother says, delayed gratification is for suckers.

I was still wiping the crumbs from my mouth when the woman in Madame Anna's house who was not Madame Anna opened the door. The dog went straight for my ankles this time.

"Be nice!" the woman chided.

The dog let go of my jeans, hung his head in shame, and trotted away.

"Ace of Swords," the woman said. "I knew you would come back."

"You must be psychic," I said.

"Funny girl," she said. "You are here on good day." She waved an enormous diamond in my face. "I meet rich man online, and yesterday he come over, make dinner, and propose."

"Beautiful ring," I said.

"Is not real diamond, do not worry. Real diamond is in safe. This is fake one to wear to Bootylates class and if somebody steal it, no problem. Sometimes, people are jealous—" She puffed out some air, then led me inside.

The Real Housewives of Beverly Hills was on T.V. Everyone was singing, "Happy Birthday," and a skeletal woman in a bustier was blowing out a prodigious number of candles.

"I know you're busy," I said, "so I'm going to get right to the point."

She hit the mute button. "I am not busy. Are *you* busy? I think too busy. I worry for your negative energy. For sixty dollars, I help you fix it."

"I think we already went over that," I said. "I'm not here for me. I just wanted—"

She grabbed her water bottle and took a long slug of something yellow that definitely wasn't Gatorade. "You want, you want." She burped delicately. "What about me?"

No way I was paying this woman again. "Is Lizeth here today?"

She scowled at me. "Who?"

"Your housekeeper. She was here last time I came by. A week ago Saturday?"

"Oh. Lisa. I call her Lisa. Is easier to pronounce."

"Okay, Lisa. Is she around?"

The woman cupped her ear. "What do you hear?"

The dog was snoring loud enough to wake the dead.

"Nothing," the woman declared. "Do you hear vacuum? *No.* Do you hear dishwasher? *No.* That mean Lisa is not here."

"Do you have any idea where I can find her?"

"I will check crystal ball." She strolled over to a plastic globe from the dollar store and plugged it in. Then she waited for the green mist to start spewing. Then she looked at me.

After I handed over sixty bucks, she typed Lizeth's address into my phone.

Lizeth lived in neighboring Eagle Rock, a rapidly gentrifying hillside enclave known for a large eagle-shaped outcropping you can see from the freeway, and for being the stomping grounds of one of L.A.'s best-known serial killers, the Hillside Strangler, who was actually two people.

Lizeth's apartment building was newish and surrounded by a ten-foot iron security fence, which was too bad for me. I searched the directory for "Pimentel." Apartment 339. I pushed the buzzer a couple of times, but there was no response. So I pushed all the buzzers. Yeah, well, it works on T.V.

Sure enough, somebody let me in. The lobby was sparsely furnished, with a leatherette couch chained to the tiled floor, a large clock that read one o'clock, which was three and a half hours ago, and a healthy-looking Boston fern. I pinched a leaf. Plastic.

A teenaged boy wearing an Eagle Rock High wrestling shirt was sitting on the couch texting. He glanced up.

"No school today?" I asked.

He gave me a pitying look. "It's Sunday."

We took the elevator up to the third floor. He went left and I went right. Lizeth's apartment was at the end of the corridor.

Now I was getting nervous. Uncle Ray had nailed it. I was an amateur, and amateurs blow it when the pressure is on. I pulled myself together. I could do this. I *had* to do this. Because Lizeth was the only one who could tell me whether or not it was Miles who'd bought Carmen that house. And whether or not it was Miles who'd given her that black eye. And if that was before or after Big Fatty had raped Carmen. And if Lizeth could tell me all that, maybe she could also tell me why, in spite of everything, Miles still carried Carmen's picture in his wallet. Because if he still loved Carmen, well, I'm not entirely sure what that meant for Maya. It certainly didn't augur well.

I knocked for a solid minute.

Lizeth wasn't home.

I had one last trick up my sleeve.

The kid took his time opening the door.

"Hi again," I said. "I was wondering if you knew where your neighbor Lizeth might be today."

"Huh," he said.

"She and I have some business to discuss," I said.

"Huh," he reiterated.

"Who's at the door?" came a voice from inside. Thank you. An adult.

"Is that your mom?" I asked.

"Whatever." He stared at his phone.

A harried-looking woman appeared at the door. "My son hasn't left this apartment all weekend." She pointed down. "Check his ankle monitor."

"I'm not interested in your son. I'm trying to find your neighbor. Lizeth Pimentel?"

The woman told the kid to clean up the kitchen. She waited until he was gone, then said, "You another cop?"

Another cop? "Do I look like one?"

"Not really. Actually," she said, studying my face, "you look like that girl from the song. That's *you*, isn't it? Dreama! Oh, my god!"

It never fails.

"I follow your mom on Twitter. Is she broke, or what? I know it's none of my business, but I totally think she should go on *Celebrity Apprentice*." The woman fluffed her hair, then grabbed me by the arm. "Why don't you come in? I'll make us some coffee."

After shoving aside some pillows, she sat me down on the couch, then raced into the kitchen.

"How do you take yours?" she called out. "Move it," she hissed at the kid, who came scuttling out of the kitchen with a Hot Pocket in one hand and a bong in the other.

"Black," I said.

The woman had a lot to say about a lot of different things. It took some doing to get her to focus on Lizeth, but eventually she did, though I have to admit to being confused by what she had to say.

Earlier in the week, a man had come by to see Lizeth. They'd had an intense conversation, apparently, because she and this man went into her apartment and neither of them came out for several hours. Not that the woman was keeping tabs. She was just observant. When she'd asked Lizeth about it, Lizeth said that he was a cop, and that he was questioning her about something.

Maybe I was off base, but there was one cop I could think of who was turning up in a lot of unexpected places lately. I asked the woman if she could describe the man.

"I didn't exactly—"

"Yes, you did," I said. "So why don't you just tell me?"

"Fine." She scratched her nose. "Tall, good-looking, sixtyish—"

"And African-American? Dead ringer for Denzel Washington?"

She blinked. "How did you know that?"

I drained my cup. "Just a lucky guess."

"Actually, I'm a bit worried," she said. "Lizeth isn't legal. I mean, she's been here since she was a little kid, but she doesn't have a green card. Maybe he had her deported."

Suddenly, I got a very bad feeling. "Why would you think that?"

She started to clear the coffee table. "Because we usually bump into one another, you know, in the elevator, or the laundry room, or by the mailboxes. And it's been I don't know how many days since I've seen her."

I stood up. "Would you excuse me for a minute?"

I went into the hallway and called the woman who was not Madame Anna.

"When was the last time you saw Lizeth?" I asked her.

"Who?"

"Lisa!" I said. "Your housekeeper. Please. It's important."

"She always come on Saturdays. But she did not come yesterday. She did not call, she did not explain. Is very bad. My man find dog hair in his salad."

I walked back into the apartment. "I think there may be a problem."

Lizeth was probably fine. It didn't necessarily mean anything that she hadn't been seen around her building in days. And what if she hadn't shown up to work yesterday? Sometimes people need a break. There was no reason to assume it had anything to do with Uncle Ray. He was hardly the only African-American on the force. And lots of people look like Denzel Washington. In any case, I had only Lizeth's word that the man on her doorstep was a cop. And why should I trust Lizeth? She was another one who kept popping up in unexpected places. Like the hospital where her friend Carmen's ex-boyfriend's current fiancée was under sedation and totally helpless. Maybe Lizeth was the one who'd come back and pulled out that IV.

Okay, that seemed unlikely.

I turned to the woman. "Do you have a spare key to Lizeth's apartment?"

"No," she said. "Why?"

"Who would have one?"

She thought for a minute. "The manager, I guess."

Her cell phone was on the coffee table. I picked it up and handed it to her. "I think you should get him down here right now."

She said, "He can't just go into someone's apartment when they're not there."

"Sure he can." I took her by the arm and marched her down the hall to Lizeth's apartment. "I smell gas. Do you smell gas?"

When she saw the look on my face, she called the manager and explained that we smelled gas coming from Lizeth's apartment.

He was there in a matter of seconds, jeans halfway down his butt, keys jangling on his belt loop.

"I don't know what you ladies are talking about." He hoisted up his pants. "I don't smell anything."

"Better safe than sorry," I said. "You don't want a lawsuit or anything."

He knocked on the door several times, and when there was no answer, let himself in. We stood there listening to him trip over something, open a window, slam a door.

"I probably should have called the police," I said. "It's not a good idea to trample a crime scene."

"Come on," the woman said. "Don't you think you're being a little paranoid? I mean—"

She didn't get to finish her thought, though, because at that moment the manager came running out of the apartment, dropped to his knees, and threw up right there in the hallway.

Just because you're paranoid doesn't mean there isn't a dead body on the other side of the door.

Chapter 25

"WELCOME BACK," LIEUTENANT Hepworth said. "Just a couple of questions."

I crossed my arms and leaned across the big wooden desk. "I already told your colleagues. I'm not talking to you until my attorney arrives."

It wasn't for nothing that the family motto was, "lawyer up."

"He must be caught in traffic." Lieutenant Hepworth checked his computer monitor. "Yup. Accident on the 10 near at Grand. The left two lanes are closed and it's backed up for half a mile." He shook his head. "Always wear seatbelts. But I'm sure I don't have to remind a law-abiding citizen such as yourself."

Lieutenant Hepworth stuck a pencil into the electric sharpener and hummed through the high-pitched buzzing. When he was done, he picked up another pencil and did it again.

"I'd like to use the restroom," I said.

"I think it would be best if you waited," he said. "Coffee?"

"This is ridiculous," I said. "I've been cooped up here for hours. I gave my statement to the detectives. You, I'm not talking to."

Lieutenant Hepworth tapped his pencil on the desk. "I suggest you calm down. You have nothing to be concerned about. Unless, of course, you happened to have murdered Lizeth Pimentel. Not that anyone is jumping to that conclusion. I mean, just because you spent much of today making inquiries about the victim's whereabouts to multiple people, starting with—" He flipped through his papers. "Miss Rodica Balan of Glendale—"

"The woman pretending to be a *psychic*?" I broke in. "She's a *con artist*."

"Haven't the Roma been discriminated against enough?" he asked. "And then you accosted young Tyler Loomis—"

"The *stoner*? Another model citizen, with his ankle bracelet."

Lieutenant Hepworth said, "Perhaps you are unaware that juveniles placed under house arrest have much lower rates of recidivism than those who are incarcerated. So there's every reason to be hopeful."

I leaned back in my chair. "Guess I'm a realist."

"And finally we have—" He flipped through his notepad again. "Ah, yes. Mr. Conor Gilligan. The residential manager out there in Eagle Rock. Hard-working fellow, just minding his own business. Then you come along, threatening him with legal action unless he opens the door to Lizeth Pimentel's apartment. Someone could argue that you sent him in there knowing full well he'd contaminate the crime scene."

"Don't you think you're reaching?" I asked. "I met Lizeth Pimentel exactly once." Twice, if you counted bumping into her at the hospital, though I saw no need to mention that. "Why would I wish her any harm?"

Lieutenant Hepworth turned up his palms. "I don't pretend to fully understand the criminal mind."

"This is all very interesting," I said, "but I'd appreciate it if we could just sit here in silence until my attorney arrives."

Lieutenant Hepworth looked up at the clock. Well, his good eye looked up at the clock, and the other looked in a vaguely westerly direction. "I hope it isn't much longer."

Nope. He couldn't stop.

"You do realize these big-shot attorneys hit you up for transportation time," he said. "What does he charge? $400 per hour? $500? But then you probably aren't hurting for money, what with the extra cash your uncle has been socking away lately."

It kept coming back to Uncle Ray.

"Maybe now you understand why I'm so interested in someone else's murder investigation." Lieutenant Hepworth smiled. "That's right. We're a team here at the L.A.P.D. We help each other out when we can, pool our information. Here's a choice tidbit: your uncle was seen at Miss Pimentel's a couple of days ago. But maybe you already know that. What you might not know is he ran an illegal search on her phone records immediately thereafter. Food for thought, am I right?"

If Lieutenant Hepworth was right, I didn't want to know who was wrong.

"You don't have to answer," he said. "I get that you don't like me. You don't return any of my calls. But don't feel guilty. Even if you had called me back I still would have shared my intel with the higher-ups. Some of them, for god knows what reason, still support your uncle for Deputy Chief."

"Just stop!" I burst out. "I told you before. You're making a terrible mistake."

"There's always a first time." He looked up at the clock, then pushed back his chair. "I'll tell you what I'm going to do. My wife's holding dinner for me. Lamb chops, which are my favorite. To save all of us a little time, I'm going to kick you out of here. So feel free to call off your overpriced attorney. But if you don't mind some unsolicited advice, be nice. I have a feeling you're going to need him later."

From police headquarters, I drove straight to Gram's.

Gram lived in the time-warp that is Laurel Canyon, immortalized by Joni Mitchell and Crosby, Stills, Nash, and Young as a cannabis-scented Neverland just above the Sunset Strip where pretty girls in bell-bottoms wandered from backyard to backyard and the soulful thrum of guitar chords reverberated 24/7 through the sage-covered hills. Gram's house was perched at the edge of a steep drop-off, behind a grove of eucalyptus. It wasn't unusual to see deer wander past the bedroom window, a raccoon peering through the screen door, even a possum who'd let himself in through the cat door. At night, especially when there was a full moon, you could hear coyotes howling, owls screeching, feral dogs barking. I'd always thought it was magical.

Gram's doorbell hadn't worked since the seventies.

"Knock-knock," I called out as I let myself in.

The lights were on, but no one stirred. The only sound was the wind whistling through the bamboo chimes, which had been a present from Glenn Frey, who was not one of my uncles. As opposed to Don Henley, that is.

Then I heard someone coughing.

The lights were on in the bedroom.

"Gram?" I tiptoed over to the bed. "Are you sleeping?"

She turned around, sat up. Her eyes were wide open. And red.

"Sweetie." Her cats—Three, Dog, and Night—hopped off the bed and hid behind the beaded curtains. "What are you doing here?"

Gram's silky hair was a mess, and she was wearing a baggy sweat suit. I'd never seen her like this. She wore top hats, antique lace, and toreador pants to clean the litter box. "I wanted to check on you. Are you sick?"

"I'm fine." She ran her fingers under her eyes, forced a smile. "You just saw me this morning."

I sat down next to her on the bed. "A lot can happen in a day."

She nodded. "Let's go into the kitchen and make some nice kombucha tea."

"Yum," I said. "Kombucha tea makes everything better."

"That's my girl." She stepped into her dressing area and came out a minute later in an antique kimono, her hair tucked into one of her shawl-cum-headwraps. She seemed more like herself already.

I sat at the kitchen table while she pulled out a gallon-sized mason jar covered with a white cloth.

"I used to use paper towels," Gram said, "but these do a better job of keeping the fruit flies and gnats out."

Oh, happy day.

"It's been a full week, so it should be ready." Gram opened the jar, and pulled out a festering spongy mass with brown stringy bits hanging off of it. She studied it for a minute, then shoved it in my face. "I don't smell cheese. Do you smell cheese?"

I assumed it was a rhetorical question.

"I like seeing those bubbles collecting around the scoby," Gram said. "It's a sign of healthy fermentation."

She poured us each a glass and downed hers immediately. "Did you get anything at Barneys after we left?"

"A green bikini," I said. "I'm broke, so I put it on my credit card."

"Good girl. Anything else?"

"A teddy," I said.

"A *teddy*," Gram repeated. "Interesting."

I told you she was good.

"So spill it," Gram said. "Why *did* you dump hot and nice?"

I broke in, "Because I'm an idiot? There's also this other guy. Clayton. A tattoo artist. He's way more my type."

"A scoundrel?"

"Gram."

She shook her head. "I only say that because I've been there, done that. More times than you can possibly imagine."

Not sure about that. When I was in ninth grade, my teacher assigned a paper on influential people of the sixties. I chose Gram's nemesis, Pamela Des Barres, which totally pissed her off. After that, she'd insisted on sharing her entire romantic history with me. It took weeks. No detail was spared.

Gram got up and walked over to the freezer. While her back was turned, I poured half my tea into the cat bowl. I would've poured all of it, but I was afraid of poisoning innocent animals.

"I thought I finally had it right." Gram set two frozen bananas on the table. "You know, it's always been me and Ray. I just didn't see it. I wasted so much time. I guess was blinded by the sparkle: spotlights, flash bulbs, disco balls, a tight pair of black leather pants."

"Stop right there," I said. "With the pants."

"Sorry." Gram sucked lasciviously on one of the bananas.

I stared at her. "You can't help yourself, can you?"

She gave me a look. "*Excuse me*, but what was the tattoo artist's name again? Clayton?"

I nodded.

"Yes, well, apparently, the apple doesn't fall far from the tree."

She had a point. I picked up my banana and stuck it into my mouth. "I didn't come here to talk about me."

"Okay, then," she said. "What do you want to talk about?"

"The woman you saw Ray with the other night."

She stood. "Are you going to finish your tea?"

"Gram, please. It's important."

"I don't want it to go to waste."

I put down the banana and sucked down what was left of the evil brew, then rummaged around in my basket until I found my phone. While Gram nervously tidied the kitchen, I went to the *L.A. Times* website and clicked on local news. I scrolled past an article about a rash of stingray attacks in Huntington Beach, another about three human skulls found at a nursing home in Palmdale. Then I found what I was looking for.

Lizeth Pimentel.

They'd dug up her senior picture from high school. God, she was so much younger than I'd thought. My age, in fact. She'd had her whole life in front of her. It was heartbreaking.

"Is this the woman?" I turned my phone around and showed Gram.

She took the phone out of my hands, studied the picture for a minute, then looked up, confused. "I don't understand. This woman was just murdered."

"I need to know if she was the person you saw with Ray."

She handed the phone back to me. "It was dark," she said. "I have no idea."

"Gram, it's going to be okay."

"You're scaring me," she said. "Ray is a good man."

I put down the phone and took her hands. "I know that. I'm just trying to get to the bottom of this. I want to help him."

Gram dropped my hands. "All right! *Yes! Yes*, this is the woman I saw at Ray's house! Who is she? What is going on?"

I looked her in the eye. "What did you see that night?"

She took a deep breath. "It was hot. The windows were open. They were in his room, talking. The conversation was intense. They were standing very close to one another."

"Did you hear what they were saying?"

She paused. "Some of it."

"Why didn't you tell me?"

"I tried to," she said.

It was true. She'd tried that day at the café. But I was distracted by Teddy's call. It was all about the gun then, and I couldn't even remember why. As usual, I'd obsessed about the wrong things.

Gram said the conversation wasn't what she'd expected. It wasn't personal. It was about work. Specifically, the preliminary hearing Ray was testifying in on Tuesday. The situation was pretty cut and dried. Ray was off-duty. He'd gone to a dive bar with some friends. There was a guy there who was drunk and waving around a weapon. Ray called it in, and a couple of beat cops came and hauled the guy away. That was it as far as Gram knew.

"So what's the big deal?" I asked.

"I have no idea. And Ray hasn't told me. I don't know why he shuts me out. I want to be part of his life."

"Think back. What *exactly* did Lizeth say about the prelim?"

"She told Ray that it was the guy's third strike, and that there would be trouble for Ray if he testified. More trouble than he'd ever seen."

"Oh, my god," I said. "Was she *threatening* him?"

She shook her head. "I didn't get that feeling at all. It was more like she was stating a fact." Gram looked down at her hands. "She didn't want to see him hurt."

"She said that?" I asked.

"She didn't have to." Gram looked up, her beautiful face as worn and tired as I'd ever seen it. "I saw it in her eyes." Then Gram turned away from me and headed back to the bedroom. It was late and she needed to sleep. I hugged her goodbye, and told her everything would look brighter in the morning.

I said it.

I hoped it.

But unfortunately, I didn't believe it.

Chapter 26

THE ALARM WENT off at 6 a.m. I slammed down the button before the beeping accelerated from the mildly annoying to the heinous.

"Jesus," mumbled Clayton. "I haven't been up this early since—ever, actually." He rolled onto his side.

I rubbed the sleep out of my eyes, and glanced over at Clayton's bare, hairless, perfectly sculpted back. Yeah, I'd known I was going to wake up feeling mighty *conflicted* so I'd organized my penance in advance.

Five miles, with ankle weights.

I'd even curated a Monday-themed playlist, which turned out to be more downbeat than anticipated, between "Monday, Monday" by the incestuous Mamas and the Papas, "Rainy Days and Mondays," featuring the vocals of poor, anorexic Karen Carpenter, and the Boomtown Rats's ripped-from-the-headlines "I Don't Like Mondays," which is what sixteen-year-old Brenda Ann Spencer of San Diego reportedly said when asked why she'd opened fire on a school playground. But who can say what made me feel worse: the depressing music, the grayish day, or the fact that Teddy's car wasn't parked in the usual spot in front of his house.

At six in the morning.

You do the math.

My run took me from Venice Beach to the Santa Monica pier, with a short detour to the 7th Street stairs. By the time I came home, Clayton was gone. He didn't leave a note. I spent twenty minutes cleaning up the mess he'd left in the kitchen, then showered, dressed, and headed back out the door.

The sun was now shining, the birds merrily chirping, the homeless guy in the alley contentedly sipping his morning coffee. Another day in paradise. Not even Miles McCoy could screw that up.

Last night I'd received a text summoning me to the offices of 25-A-Day. Miles had an urgent matter to discuss. That was convenient because I, too, had an urgent matter to discuss. Actually, several. I only hoped Pee Chee had taken the day off. I wanted Miles alone, and preferably unprepared. Which is why I'd decided to show up an hour early.

Miles's Chandler obsession ran deep. Not only was the name of his record label an homage to Philip Marlowe, his offices were located in the same building—the former Security Trust and Savings Bank at the corner of Hollywood and Cahuenga—on which Chandler had modeled the fictional detective's office. I took the rickety elevator up to the sixth floor. But instead of being greeted by the sight of Marlowe with a Camel, I got Mookie with an Android. He was playing *Grand Theft Auto: San Andreas*. I recognized Ice-T's voice.

"Sorry to interrupt," I said. "But Miles asked me to come by."

Mookie looked up, dazed. "Miles?"

"Your boss."

"Oh. He isn't in."

"I'm early." I pointed down the hall. "Which door again?"

"Nice try." Mookie rose to his feet.

"I like your suit." It looked like he'd bought it yesterday and had yet to master all the moving parts.

"Uh-huh." He walked toward me, and when he was about four feet away, kept right on walking.

"I see you had a Spanish omelette for breakfast," I said.

Mookie stepped back. "Do I have something—?"

I tapped my front tooth. "Little bit of green pepper."

He extracted a toothpick from his pocket and removed the offending speck.

"We good now?" I asked.

"You should come back another day," he said. "Boss canceled all his meetings."

"Why?"

Mookie flicked the toothpick into the trash. "He went to the hospital to collect Maya."

I stared at him. "That isn't possible."

"Not sure where you get your information." He glanced at his wristwatch. "They're probably home by now."

I was dumbfounded. "But it's only *Monday*. The doctor said Wednesday or Thursday. I was standing right there. I heard her myself."

"Lady must've changed her mind."

It didn't add up. "So you're telling me Maya woke up and just walked out of there?"

"Guess so." Mookie went back to his seat, and pulled out his

Android. Suddenly, the room was filled with the rat-a-tat-tat of gunfire and the squealing of tires. "Sorry, but I gotta get back to work."

This wasn't happening. "I need to speak to Pee Chee."

Mookie said, "Not sure where she is. Look, I don't know why you're so upset. This is good news."

Bullshit.

Maya was up. Maya was talking. And at some point in the very near future I was betting she was going to be making it known to all and sundry that she hadn't tried to kill herself, and was looking forward to wearing all her new clothes from Neiman Marcus. And then what?

I'd wasted enough time with Mookie.

I had to make sure Maya was okay.

It took fifteen minutes to get to the Eastern Columbia.

"Good day, Miss Black." The concierge called upstairs, then gestured toward Miles's private elevator. When the doors opened Pee Chee was standing there, a butcher knife in her hand.

"Was it something I said?" I asked.

"I wouldn't know." She crossed her arms in front of her chest. "I tend not to listen when you're moving your lips."

"My mother says distraction is a big problem in the perimenopausal years."

"From what I read online," Pee Chee said, "your mother has a lot of problems."

"One of them being trolls who stalk her on the internet," I shot back.

There was a large cardboard box at her feet. Pee Chee knelt down and slit it open with her butcher knife. Inside were dozens of full-sized yellow legal pads. Pee Chee let loose with a string of epithets, then looked up at me.

"This had better be good." She tucked a few stray hairs back into her gold lamé turban. "Because I *really* don't have time."

"Miles wanted to see me."

"He's busy now."

"I hear Maya left the hospital."

"You heard correctly."

"She up for a visitor?" I asked.

"I'm sorry, but are you a friend of hers?"

At that moment, I was guessing I was the best friend Maya had. "Actually, I have something for her." Not true, but I'd address that problem on an as-needed basis.

"Nobody wants anything from you."

"I can slip it under the door."

"*Unbelievable.*" Pee Chee shook her head. "Maya can't be disturbed. She's tucked into her gondola bed, fast asleep."

"You moved her entire room back here already?"

"Lock, stock, and barrel. It's a service economy, Dreama. You pay people, they do shit for you. Speaking of that, don't move."

Pee Chee left me standing there for a couple minutes. I knew the name of Maya's doctor. I could call and find out if she'd actually released the patient early. But before I'd had a chance, Pee Chee had returned, juggling several stacks of hundred-dollar bills.

"Think you can fit all of this into your little basket?" she asked.

I backed away. "What is this?" I knew exactly what it was. A bribe. She wanted to be done with me.

Pee Chee said, "It's the $40,000 we owe you."

There was that number again. "I can't accept it."

Pee Chee dumped the cash onto a low console. "What is the matter with you? The wedding is back on, and so is the wedding present! Get the fuck out of here and get back to work!"

I tapped my foot. "What does Miles have to say about this?"

She whipped out some packing tape and started sealing up the cardboard box. "What do you think? He's like a pig in shit! His fiancée lived through a suicide attempt, she's back home good as new, his life is rainbows and snow cones and unicorns! Fucking hashtag blessed is what he thinks! So take the money, and get ready for your close-up!"

Pee Chee kicked the cardboard box and me out, and retreated into the apartment, slamming the double doors behind her.

Yeah, I took the money.

But she wasn't getting rid of me that fast.

Chapter 27

Twenty minutes later, I was sunning myself by the Eastern Columbia's rooftop pool, a glass of Cristal in my hand.

The path there had been only mildly circuitous.

After Pee Chee bounced me to the curb, I walked back to my car and drove to the closest pay lot, which seemed prudent given that there was now $40,000 in my trunk. Then I put up the top, scooted down in my seat, stripped out of my clothes, and slipped on the tiny green bikini Petal Collings had made me buy the day before. My white peasant blouse kind of worked as a cover-up, but unfortunately, the only shoes I had were my knee-high moccasin boots. Pocahontas meets Bunny Lebowski. Could've been worse.

"Welcome back, Miss Black," the concierge said. "Forget something?"

"Nope!" I said brightly. "Just heading back up for a swim with Pee Chee!"

"I'll let her know you're on your way." He picked up the phone.

"Oh, no," I cried. "I want to surprise her."

The concierge shook his head. "Against the rules."

Just then a group of blinged-out Russian gangster types strolled into the lobby. I don't know if they were already drunk at 11 a.m., but they were making a lot of noise—laughing, high-fiving, bellowing into their phones. One of them shook the concierge's hand, then slipped a hundred-dollar bill into it. Then they headed to the elevator at the rear marked, "Pool/Spa."

"Hey, guys!" I called out. "Perfect timing!"

They turned around en masse.

I flashed my bikini top. "Who's ready for Marco Polo?"

They were into it.

The one with the hundred-dollar bill got me settled onto a striped chaise lounge, then helped me out of my cover-up. What a gentleman. After making a couple of phone calls, he produced a bottle of Cristal, poured some for each of us, and offered to buy me a plane. Well, that's what it sounded like. Maybe he just wanted to take me on one. I couldn't understand most of what he was saying, but I figured if I kept on smiling and nodding and evincing vague delight at the sight of him and his friends in Speedos I could stay up there long enough to figure out how exactly I was going to sneak into Maya's bedroom window to make sure she was still breathing.

"Dreamy!" That was what my new boyfriend was calling me. "I have question for you."

I hit stop and looked up from my phone. I'd found a video on YouTube posted by the real estate broker who'd handled the listing when Miles had bought the penthouse several years ago. Apparently, it was 3,800 square feet and took up the entire northwest side of the building. On the first level was the living room, dining area, and kitchen, stocked with stainless steel appliances. On the third level, there was a wraparound balcony and full production suite. I was interested in the second level, which had the marble bathrooms with the sunken tubs, and the bedrooms with the walk-in closets. If only I could figure out which side Maya's was on.

"Dreamy, would you like the mozzarella sticks or the fried calamari?" my boyfriend asked. "We get it sent from the restaurant downstairs. Lev!"

Lev was in the hot tub, sipping a frozen margarita. *"Da?"*

"Call for the fried calamari for Dreamy. I will have the nachos."

"Sauce on the side?" Lev asked me.

A girl could totally get used to this.

While Lev was calling in our order, and another one of the henchmen was adjusting the umbrella so I wouldn't get too much sun on my alabaster skin, I Googled floorplans of the penthouse. The day we'd met, Miles had dragged me into his bedroom to show me his collection of *Black Masks*. Through his window I'd seen the neon roof sign of the Orpheum Theater, which, according to the blueprint on my screen, meant his room faced east. Maya's bedroom, Miles had said, was directly across the hall, which meant it faced west. Right?

Right.

In theory.

But sometimes theory is all you have.

I downed the rest of my champagne, then stood up. I told my new boyfriend that I needed to stretch my legs. I appreciated his saying they were perfect as they were, but I had work to do.

The turquoise clock tower was even more spectacular up close. At its foot a lushly landscaped private terrace extended out from the penthouse's first floor. And all I had to do was get through the locked gate, tiptoe through the bougainvillea, and scale the wall to get to the second level, where I was going to find Maya and save her from a perilous fate.

Just as I was approaching the gate, the opening guitar chords of "Someone Like You" sounded. Shit. I'd forgotten to put it on silent. I fumbled with my phone, and said, "Hello?"

It was Miles.

I took a header into the nearest petunia bush.

"Sorry I missed our meeting this morning," he said.

"No problem," I whispered.

"Do you have a cold?" he asked.

"It's just a bad connection." I spat out some leaves.

"Well, there's something I need to talk to you about. I'm here now, if you can make it."

"Here *where*?" Not here *here*. Please.

"At the office."

One down, but he was hardly my only problem. "What about Pee Chee?"

"What about her?"

"Is she at your penthouse, or there with you?"

"Hello—Dreama? I can't hear you. Just come by when you can."

He hung up on me.

I was pushing my way out of the bush, trying not to think about the carnage that would ensue if Pee Chee were to catch me in the act, when I heard a clatter behind me. I turned around. It was a guy carrying a weed whacker and a rake. The gardener. He walked toward the gate and pulled out a key.

I cut him off at the pass. "So glad you're here!"

He looked at me, then drew himself up like a puffer pigeon. "Really?"

"I came out to work on my tan and forgot my sunscreen inside. Would you mind letting me back in?"

"I'm sorry, but you are—"

"Miles's baby sister. Visiting from our hometown of Detroit. Go . . . Steelers!"

"The Steelers are from Pittsburgh," he said.

"You think I *like* Detroit? Anyway, I've been calling Miles for an hour, but he's at work. What else is new?" I shook my head. "*Finally*, he calls me back." I turned my phone around and showed him my recent calls. "He's kind of a douche, if you want to know the truth. He told me to go downstairs and get a key from the concierge, but I don't exactly feel comfortable parading around half-naked." I looked down at my bikini and smiled demurely. "I'm not like these L.A. girls."

The poor guy let me onto the terrace.

"Word to the wise," I said. "Miles is not happy about that fig tree over there." I pointed around the corner. "You might want to start there."

I gave him a little wave as I reached for the French doors to the living room. But as soon as he turned right, I turned left. West. Where the ocean is. Where the sun sets. Where Maya lay sleeping. It all made perfect sense.

Once I was standing there, one flight below her bedroom window, I was less certain. First of all, how was I supposed to get up there? If only a window-washer had left behind some scaffolding. Hmm. There was a drainpipe. One option was to shimmy right on up that thing.

I was reckless, but not that reckless.

And then I noticed the fire ladder. Standard issue back in 1930 when the building was erected. Designed for safety. I slipped my phone into my moccasin boot, and climbed up onto the first rung, flattening myself against the ladder as much as I could, trying not to tremble, promising myself I wouldn't look down. By the time I was halfway up, I was basically on the ledge. All I had to do was step off the ladder. I reached for the top of the window frame, hooked my fingers around it, and pushed off. Yes!

So there I was, standing on a window ledge, at the top of a thirteen-story building, in a Bunny Lebowski bikini. If I could have reached my phone without losing my balance and plunging to my death I would've documented this milestone, like the people who make it to the top of Mount Everest. Of course, climbers say the getting up isn't the hard part. It's the getting down.

There was more room to maneuver up there than I would have expected, though I was kind of distracted by the birds flapping their wings in my face. At least they weren't landing on my head, which is what happened in that episode of *I Love Lucy* Gram and I had watched at least half a dozen times. Anyway, if by some miracle the window was unlocked, I could just crouch down, shove it up, and step on inside.

It was.

And I did.

Only to hear someone out in the hall turning the doorknob.

I darted into the walk-in closet, pulling the door closed behind me.

The closet was truly something. Huge, with built-in shelving and drawers and matching black velvet hangers. I sank down onto the plush ottoman and wondered what it would be like to be the sort of woman who nibbles on chocolates in a closet like this while trying to figure out which pair of Christian Louboutins would look best with her outfit. The thing is, there were no outfits in the closet. No shoes. No purses. No *negligées*. Where was the mountain of stuff from Neiman Marcus?

"I can't believe this! Where the *fuck* did I leave them?"

I'd recognize that voice anywhere.

Pee Chee Lowenstein.

I waited for Maya to wake up and tell Pee Chee she'd had quite enough of her filthy mouth. But there was only silence. I slipped deeper into the closet and cowered behind a mirrored pillar just as the closet door swung open and banged against the wall. Pee Chee was so close I could smell her perfume, a hideous amalgam of incense, stale Halloween candy, leather, and fresh blood. Well, maybe that was an exaggeration. Anyway, I wanted to retch, but I didn't so much as flinch as she turned on the light, stepped inside, and yanked open the drawers. After what felt like a very long time but was probably only thirty seconds, she gave up. The light went off and she stomped out of the closet. Then the door to Maya's room closed.

I stood there for another minute, listening for sounds. Nothing. I opened the door to the closet as quietly as I could, and peered through the gap. The lights were off, so I couldn't see very clearly. But I could see clearly enough.

No slipper chair.

No vanity.

No brass lanterns.

The only thing in the room was Maya's gondola bed, shoved in the corner, its sheets and blankets stripped, its beautiful gilded headboard cracked in two.

And it was empty.

Chapter 28

THE FRIED CALAMARI looked delicious, but I'd lost my appetite. My boyfriend didn't seem to mind. While I was gone, he'd plowed through the nachos and a slice of blackout cake, and was now trying to decide if he should order some beef and cheese empañadas. I handed over my plate. After he finished it, he said he liked a woman who ate like a bird, which was yet another reason he and I were not going to make it.

On my way down to the car, I called Cedars, and was informed that Maya Duran had been discharged at eight this morning. I asked to be transferred to the nurses' station on the sixteenth floor, where they refused to tell me to whom she'd been released, and whether or not it had been against medical advice. When I inquired as to the doctor's whereabouts, the nurse asked me what my relationship to the patient was. I wasn't sure, so I hung up.

Here's another thing I wasn't sure about: if Maya wasn't at the hospital, and she wasn't home in her gondola bed, where was she?

That was going to be the first question I asked Miles when I finally sat down with him in his office. And after I asked him about

Maya, I was going to ask him about Carmen. And after I got an answer about Carmen, I was going to ask him what he knew about Pee Chee taking Maya to get an exact copy of Carmen's lotus flower tattoo. And who exactly came up with the pitch-perfect pseudonym "Phyllis Dietrichson." And what he knew about Lizeth Pimentel. And that was just for starters.

Twenty minutes later I'd wriggled out of the bikini and back into my clothes, then pulled into a pay lot across the street from Miles's office building. Another ten dollars down. Going up in the elevator I'd felt somewhat apprehensive, but by the time the doors creaked open I had on my game face.

"Boss is waiting for you." Mookie had evidently wearied of *Grand Theft Auto: San Andreas* and was now shooting rubber bands one after another into the trash can. "Down the hall."

The door was open. Miles was sitting in a chair, his back to me, looking outside. At what? Telephone poles, trees, birds, neon signs. Nothing special. Business as usual. But not for long.

"Miles?"

He rose, straightened his big white T-shirt, hiked up his baggy pants, and for a split second, I had the feeling he was going to hurl himself through the window. But then he turned around.

"Thanks for coming, Dreama." He walked toward the door, brushing against me. "Mind if I close this?"

"Don't you like the cross breeze?" I asked. "It's kind of hot in here."

He kicked the door shut. "I'll turn on the A.C."

It wasn't exactly like I had a choice. Not if I wanted to get to the bottom of things. But Miles pre-empted me.

"Enough bullshit." He sat back down in his chair. "I know what you did."

"What *I* did?"

He opened the drawer, pulled out a USB flash drive, stuck it into his laptop, then spun it around so I could see what was on the screen.

And there I was, less than two weeks ago, sitting on the white chaise in Miles McCoy's living room, a wallet in my hand. I didn't have to watch the rest. I knew what happened. I'd stolen Miles's photograph of Carmen Luz. End of story. Actually, that had been just the beginning.

"Mookie goes through the surveillance footage every Sunday night," Miles said. "Last Sunday was the night of the shooting, so we were all kind of preoccupied. He got caught up yesterday. And look what he found."

"I can explain," I said.

Miles shook his head. "I don't want to hear it. I just want you to return what you took from me."

"I didn't mean to take it," I said.

He put up his hand. "Look, I don't know what kind of game you're playing, if it's blackmail, or you just get off fucking with people's heads—"

"*Blackmail?* What are you talking about?"

"You're going to deny it? Please. Don't make me call Mookie in here."

Jesus. "Can't we just talk about it?"

"Secrets never stay buried," he said. "I am such a fool." He put his head in his hands.

"Will you listen to me, Miles—"

He looked up. "No, why don't *you* fucking listen? Sorry to ruin your little scheme, but the truth is *I don't give a shit* anymore!" He laughed out loud. "That's right! I didn't realize it until this very second. *I do not give a shit!* So go ahead. Tell the whole fucking world what I did. The only person that matters to me is Maya. And she already knows. *Obviously.*"

"What exactly are you saying?" Was he admitting he'd tried to murder her?

"Nothing," Miles said. "I just want my picture back. What about that don't you understand?"

"I'm sorry," I said. "It's not here."

"Stop fucking *lying.*"

"I'm not! Look, I was curious about Maya. I thought it was a picture of her. I didn't know it was a picture of Carmen."

"Don't you *dare* say her name!" he cried.

"Sorry," I said, stunned. "I meant no harm. Really."

"Maya found out what I did to Carmen." Miles nodded robotically. "Just like you did. That's why it all fell apart. We were so fucking happy. We were going to have this fucking amazing life."

I shifted my weight, turned around, looked longingly at the closed door. But I couldn't go. I wanted to hear what Miles had to say.

"I put on a good show for you that day at the hospital, didn't I?" He pulled his prayer beads out of his pocket and started pacing. "Goddamn *fraud*, that's what I am. Pretending to look for someone to blame for what happened to Maya when all I had to do was look in the goddamn mirror! *I'm* the one who's to blame! *I'm* a fucking monster! *I'm* a fucking *defiler*! *There!*" He threw his beads against the wall, and the string broke, little balls of green sandalwood rolling into the corners of the room. "You happy now?"

I wasn't happy. I was confused. And from the looks of it, so was Miles. I thought he might be having a heart attack. His face was flushed, his pupils dilated. I dug in my basket and handed him a water bottle. "Drink this."

He downed the entire thing.

"You okay?" I asked.

He stared at me. "Why do you give a shit?"

"I have no idea."

"You don't know? About what I did?"

I shook my head.

"It's an ugly story," he said.

I said, "It won't be the first I've heard."

"It's the reason I don't touch alcohol anymore. It's the reason I became a Buddhist. It's the reason I still carry Carmen's picture in my wallet. To remind me every single day of the worst thing I've ever done."

Carmen's black eye.

That was Miles.

But evidently, that wasn't the end of it.

"I raped Carmen," he declared.

"You did *what?*"

"I raped Carmen," he repeated.

"No, you didn't," I said in a rush. "Freddy Sims—Big Fatty—*he* was the one who raped Carmen. *He* was the one who went to jail."

"Lots of innocent people go to jail." Miles shrugged. "I got shit-faced, I blacked out, and I beat and raped the woman I loved."

We always hurt the one we love.

But I'd thought that was *Maya.*

"You obviously don't get it," Miles said. "I used to black out. *A lot.* I did terrible things and had no fucking idea I did them. I wasn't conscious! I didn't remember! But you know what they say. You don't remember the things you drink to forget."

"Miles, I want to understand. But you need to slow down."

He sighed. "It was one stupid night. One stupid night where everything went to shit. Pee Chee needed me. It was 4 a.m. I wasn't in the office, and I wasn't home with Petal, so Pee Chee figured I was with Carmen. She drove over to our place in Glendale." He shook his head. "It was chaos. She found me on the kitchen floor. She slapped me awake, then dragged me into the bedroom. Carmen was lying there, barely alive, glass everywhere, on her, in her." He was crying now. "I tried to call 911, but Pee Chee said it was okay, Carmen was going to be okay, the doctor was already on his way. But now, she said, *now* was the moment for me to sober up and finally make some good decisions. Those were her words exactly."

Because Pee Chee was the head to Miles's heart, the one who greased the wheels and tied up the loose ends.

"Carmen was a girl who wanted to live big," Miles said. "She was *incandescent*. She burned brighter than the sun or the moon or the fucking stars! But sometimes she took it too far. She drank too much. She'd been out partying, she was out of it, she had no idea who'd raped and beaten her. And how was she going to feel when she found out that the man she loved and fucking *trusted with her life* was the one who'd crushed her, body and soul? Carmen's brother had overdosed the year before. Carmen had gone through a pretty serious depression. Pee Chee said it was too much of a risk. And we were lucky. Pee Chee knew one of the guys who'd been out with Carmen earlier that night, and for the right price, she said, he'd be willing to take the fall. Pee Chee would fix it so he'd be guaranteed a short sentence. It was a win-win, right? Fuck it, I was so out of it that night, I agreed."

Miles was a rapist.

Miles was a liar.

Miles had bought his own freedom with another man's suffering.

"It's karma, Dreama." He walked over and rested his foot on one of the beads for a second, then kicked it across the room. "You can't fucking escape it. Maya found out what I did, and she couldn't bear it. That's why she shot herself, and that's why she did it in front of me. So I'd understand. So I'd feel her pain."

"You can't know that," I said.

"Yes, I can," he said. "I told you there was no suicide note, but that was a lie." He reached into his pocket and pulled out a scrap of paper, and handed it to me. "I found it on my bed when I came home that night."

I looked at the piece of paper. It said, in big black letters, "**I KNOW EVERYTHING. I CAN'T DO IT ANYMORE.**"

"The only thing I don't know," Miles said, "is who told her." Then he looked at me, his eyes glazed over.

I shook my head. "I didn't know until now."

He looked utterly broken. "I wish I could believe you."

Just then there was a knock on the door.

"Boss? You got that appointment." Mookie handed Miles a cup. "Your double soy chai latte."

"Thanks." Miles rose from his seat. "You need to go, Dreama."

There was so much more I had to ask him. I needed to find out about the $40,000. About Lizeth. About that tattoo. But there wasn't time. So I asked him the one question that really, truly mattered. I asked him what happened to Maya.

Miles walked over and opened the door. "Get out, Dreama."

"*Where is she?*" I repeated.

He shook his head, then whispered, "I don't know."

I walked out into the sunlight and collapsed onto the curb. I was hot, I was cold, my entire body was shaking. It wasn't so much what Miles had just told me. It was my own ambivalence about it. The thing is, I understood his pain. And, bizarrely, what I felt for him—more than loathing, more than contempt—was pity.

When I was a child, my mother used to black out. Gin was her poison. Martinis, Negronis, Tom Collinses, it didn't matter, as long as a bottle of Tanqueray was involved. To this day, I can't stand the pungent, flowery smell of it. Gin made her do and say things she was ashamed of. Gin made her doubt her sanity. At least once, gin made her want to die. I was four years old. She'd gone on a bender. It took two whole days until she could straighten herself up enough to make it home. The only problem was she'd left me there, all by myself, with nothing to eat. Uncle Ray was the one who'd found me. He and Gram hadn't heard from my mother, and figured that meant nothing good. He drove straight over, heard me inside crying, and broke down the door. After Ray calmed me down, he took me straight to Du-par's, where we polished off most of a cherry pie. When my mother sobered up, she begged me to forgive her. Of course I forgave her. I was her daughter. I loved her. But even then, I understood that she was damaged, and that I could never fully trust her.

I couldn't trust Miles either.

But I knew what I had to do, and where I had to go.

Then I saw my car.

And realized that I wasn't going anywhere.

Chapter 29

MY CAR HAD four flat tires.

I'm talking no air whatsoever.

I'm talking flat as pancakes.

Yes, it's tough on the road, what with all the potholes and debris. And sure, it's possible to have a slow leak and not know it until you hear your rim grinding against asphalt, or you return from a tense meeting during which your client reveals he's a rapist only to discover that your lovingly maintained vintage automobile has collapsed to the ground. But I knew this was not about a slow leak. I crouched down and took a closer look.

No puncture holes, no embedded nails, no screws.

Just some big, ugly slashes.

Someone had done this intentionally.

To me.

Before the panic took over, I slowed my breathing and practiced gratitude. It's trickier than it sounds. Still, it was kind of working until a new thought started to worm its way into my consciousness.

No.

There was *no way* it could have happened again.

I raced around to the back of the car, popped the trunk, rifled through the contents, then spewed every four-letter word I could think of.

But it had.

$40,000 gone. Vanished into thin air. *For the second time.*

"Everything okay, miss?" The parking attendant had snuck up behind me.

"No, it's not okay!" I snarled. "Something was stolen out of my trunk."

"That's terrible," he said. "I hope it wasn't anything valuable."

I started laughing hysterically.

"Miss, are you all right? Is there someone I should call?"

There was no one to call. I was all alone in this. I couldn't call Uncle Ray. I couldn't call Gram. My mother was useless. I'd cut Teddy loose. Clayton was a cad. I could've called Cat, but to be perfectly honest, I was too embarrassed.

"Yes," I said, pulling myself together. "I think you should get your boss over here. I paid ten dollars to park in this lot and you are supposed to keep an eye on these cars. Look at this!" I pointed to my tires.

"If you check your ticket, you'll see the garage isn't liable." The attendant was backpedalling furiously now. "The legal term is assumption of risk."

"Assumption of *risk*? What about pride in your *work*?" I demanded. "What about that?"

"You're supposed to read the fine print," he said with a shrug. "Look, I'd be happy to call the cops."

"God, no," I said. "No cops."

"I get it." He looked me up and down. "We all have things to hide."

Who *was* this person? "Speak for yourself."

"No need to be rude. I was just about to invite you into the booth to look at the surveillance footage."

Never thought I'd say it, but thank god for surveillance footage.

The booth was a tight fit for the three of us: me, the attendant, and the attendant's labradoodle, who needed to be taken out to pee first. Finally the conditions were optimal, and the attendant rewound the tape. Not that it was particularly helpful. Turned out there was only one camera. It was trained on the booth, where the cash box was located, as opposed to lot, where the cars were, meaning we didn't catch anybody in the act unless you counted the dog, who by all appearances was responsible for the theft of his master's Egg McMuffin.

"You could make an insurance claim," the attendant said. "Though your rates will skyrocket."

"Hold on," I said. "Can you go back three minutes?"

And there it was.

An unmarked white van.

Entering the lot at 2:05 p.m., and exiting the lot at 2:08 p.m.

"Stop!" I cried. "Right there! Now go forward."

The white van was passing the booth on the way into the lot. Unfortunately, I couldn't see inside because the windows were tinted.

I turned to the attendant. "Can we talk about that white van? You gave a blue ticket to the person driving it."

He nodded in acknowledgement.

"So was it a man or a woman? Old or young? Bearded or clean-shaven? Any distinguishing marks?"

"I get a lot of people in and out of here."

"Come on."

He furrowed his brow. "The only person I remember was a woman. She seemed like a wack job. Something about her eyes, you know?"

A woman.

Not again.

"What did she look like?"

"She reminded me of my aunt. But now that I think of it, that woman was driving a blue Jaguar."

Oh, my god. "Why don't we approach this from another angle? Can you zoom in on the license plate?"

"What do you think this is?" he asked. "A rerun of *Law and Order*? You can't just *zoom in* anymore. Not with digital surveillance systems. The resolution is better than your old school VCRs, but the compression makes the digits unreadable. It's all about saving bandwidth."

"So that's it?" I was feeling extremely sorry for myself now.

The attendant smiled. "Nope."

He grabbed the keyboard, pressed a couple of buttons, then swung the screen around for me to see.

And there it was, clear as day.

K11 OBY.

"I thought you said it wasn't possible," I said.

"To *zoom in*," he said. "You didn't ask about using a deblocking filter."

After jotting the number down, I went back to my car and sent a couple of texts. Thirty minutes later, the guys I'd met outside Lucius's sister's house pulled into the parking lot in a tricked-out Ford Raptor, with four new tires stacked neatly in the back. By the time they'd finished installing them—and popping out my dent, free of charge—one of their moms, who serendipitously worked at the D.M.V., had texted back the name and address of the person who'd stolen my money, ripped through my tires, and chased me through the rain-slicked streets of greater Los Angeles.

Somebody had some 'splaining to do.

Chapter 30

HIS NAME WAS Charlie "Chick" Churchill, he lived at 9633 Beachwood Drive, and I was pretty certain that he worked for Miles McCoy.

It seemed like the obvious conclusion. I mean, Miles *had* caught me stealing from him. And thought I was capable of blackmail. And believed that I'd told Maya about his having raped Carmen. Why *wouldn't* he have hired someone to follow me? But I needed proof.

Beachwood Canyon is a small community located in the Hollywood Hills just below the famous Hollywood sign. First developed in the 1920s along the wooded ridge abutting Griffith Park, Beachwood has its own market, its own coffee shop, and its own riding stables, which I once visited with my uncle Axl, whose brief domicile in the neighborhood—and my mother's life—came to a spectacular end the night he pushed a $38,000 piano through the side of his one-and-a-third-acre fixer-upper.

Charlie Churchill's house was hard to miss. It was the ersatz Victorian from the seventies with the unmarked white van parked in front of it.

Let me reiterate. It was broad daylight. There was an elderly woman walking a dog, a FedEx truck down the block, a Time Warner Cable guy parked behind him, and a pool man carrying a net into the house next door. I didn't feel particularly threatened. So I walked straight up to the van and peered into the back.

"Excuse me?" called the old lady with the dog.

I spun around. "Hi there! So nice to see you again!"

She looked confused. "Have we met?"

"You don't remember? With Charlie? You were walking—what's the little guy's name again?"

She said, "Alison."

"Look at those chubby paws," I said. "Aren't puppies the best?"

The woman said, "Alison is a senior. And morbidly obese." She shook her head. "That's what the vet says. *I* think it's a load of hooey." She crossed over to my side of the street, stopped short in front of me. "You're Charlie's girlfriend?"

I said, "It's still kind of new." Then I bent down to pet Alison. Close up, she was a lot bigger. In fact, her face was so fat you couldn't see her eyes.

"Well, isn't that nice? I keep telling him it's not good to keep to yourself."

So White Van Charlie was a loner. Big surprise. "Yeah, he's gone through a lot."

"Life is hard." The woman looked at Alison, who was valiantly attempting to do her business. "Isn't that right, my angel?"

I cleared my throat. "So where is he? He's not answering his phone."

The woman said, "You just missed him. He went out for a walk maybe twenty minutes ago. If you hurry, you can probably catch him."

"That's a great idea!" I exclaimed. "Charlie loves surprises. Which way did he go?"

She fished around in her pocket for a baggie, then bent down to pick up the fruit of Alison's labors. "The usual way. He does the steps, winds up by the reservoir. You know."

I nodded. "I know. The usual way. Steps, reservoir. Yup."

"When you see him," the woman said, "would you tell him FedEx left a small box with me?"

"Oh!" I clasped my hands together in glee. "The small box! *Finally!* Why don't I grab it right now?"

She didn't look entirely happy with that idea.

"Trust me." I gave her a wink. "It will make the surprise even more memorable."

We walked back across the street and she ducked into her house and got me the box. I waved goodbye, then stalled for a minute, pretending to dig around in my basket for my sunglasses, while she and the dog headed down to the coffee shop. As soon as she was out of sight, I tossed the box and my basket into my car, and took off to find Charlie.

After Googling "Beachwood Canyon steps," I found a detailed map and itinerary posted by @happyhiker. Apparently, there were six sets of stone steps in Beachwood, and it took an hour to cover the 2.6 mile loop, which meant half an hour to get to the reservoir. At least I wasn't wearing heels.

As instructed, I headed north on Beachwood. I found the first staircase just after the house at 2800. It was dark and littered with dead leaves. I landed at the top, already panting. Not a good sign. I consulted my phone, then took a right onto Westshire Drive, and looped downhill a ways until I got to the next set of stairs. These were steeper and shadier, framed on either side by huge clumps of lantana, which, according to my gardener, Jovani, is attractive to butterflies but invasive. He'd ripped all mine out.

I counted 149 steps up, the last 84 in a single unbroken run. Once I'd caught my breath, I turned left on Hollyridge, stopping to take a picture of the crenellated wall of a *faux* castle for my Instagram. The next staircase was at 3057. I followed it down for 178 steps, then walked straight up for a while, admiring the houses— which ranged from modernist boxes to Robinson Crusoe–esque treehouses—and wondering how the Time Warner Cable guy, who'd just pulled up in front of a bungalow with a Spanish galleon weathervane, could possibly be this efficient. Whenever he came to my house, he took forever.

The next set of stairs was constructed in 1928 and originally had a stream running down the middle. About halfway up, I heard some rustling in the leaves, then saw a lizard dart across my path and disappear into the brush. In dreams, lizards symbolize resurrection, which I took as a positive sign. I trudged onward, following Belden Drive around a couple of bends to the next staircase.

At the top of Durand Drive I stopped to catch my breath. The view was amazing, with the Hollywood sign behind me, the Griffith Park Observatory to my left, and downtown Hollywood spread out in front of me, a tinselly oasis teeming with key locales from my biography: the stacked platters of the Capitol Records Building, where I once played jacks with Uncle Bob Seger while Gram mended his leather jacket; the neon roof sign of the French château–style Fontenoy, where Nicholas Cage mixed me my first cocktail, a Tequila Sunrise; and the outsized W of the W Hotel, at whose rooftop bar Luke Cutt had humiliated me for the very last time. It was somehow very sobering.

Finally, I arrived at my destination, the hairpin corner at the intersection of Durand and the unpaved fire road. Just below my line of sight, framed by lush groves of oak, pine, eucalyptus, and sage, was the shimmering mirage of Lake Hollywood, a reservoir held back by a dam designed by William Mulholland himself, immortalized as Hollis Mulwray in Roman Polanski's noir throwback, *Chinatown*. This would have been a great location for my tour, not that I had to worry about that anymore, much less the whole "satisfaction guaranteed" thing, given that the client in question had hired a man in a white van to stalk me, among myriad other crimes, small and large. Anyway, I snapped a couple of pictures, then started down the dirt path.

And there he was, on the other side of a massive clump of agave.

Suffice it to say he wasn't exactly what I'd been expecting.

Chapter 31

IN HIS SHRUNKEN hoodie and skinny jeans, Charlie "Chick" Churchill was a classic L.A. type: young and slight, with a shaved head and gauges in his ears. He was a Moby fan, a juicer, a defender of animal rights. I could take him with one hand tied behind my back.

"Surprise!" I called out.

He spun around. Yeah, I'd nailed it. Right down to the black-framed glasses and "BITTORRENT IS NOT A CRIME" T-shirt.

"Oh, shit," he said.

"'Oh, shit' is right," I replied.

His face was bright red. "I can explain."

"I hope so. Because I'm not exactly happy at the way our relationship has been going."

"I like your sense of humor." He grabbed the camcorder at his feet. "Do you mind if I record our conversation? There's a release form you have to sign, but we can worry about that later."

"You've got to be kidding."

He unzipped his fanny back and pulled out a fluffy brush and HD powder. "You are looking a little shiny."

"That's because I've been trudging up and down steps for the last half hour." I bent down to rub my ankle. "And I now have a blister."

"Sorry about that."

"Are you also sorry about following me and trashing my car? And does Miles know you stole my money? Or were you doing a little unauthorized skimming?"

He put up his hands. "Slow down. I have no idea what you're talking about. I'm a lover, not a fighter."

"TMI, Chick."

"Don't call me that."

"I'm not sure you're in a position to ask for favors."

"Look, I didn't steal any money, and I didn't trash any cars. Stalking is all I'm admitting to. That, and filming you."

"*Filming* me? Give me that camera." I grabbed for it, but he clutched it to his scrawny chest.

"God, you're aggressive," he said admiringly.

"Don't change the subject. Why have you been filming me?"

"I think you should sit down." He pointed to a boulder with the words "Dare to Dream" spray-painted on it.

I ignored him. "Answer the question. Why have you been filming me?"

"Because you're part of the story."

"*What* story?"

"The Miles McCoy story."

My jaw dropped. "Are you telling me you're a paparazzi?"

"It's paparazzo, singular."

"Don't you get there are laws in this state you've been breaking?"

"In all fifty states," he said, "free speech and public interest trump any purported rights to privacy. In any case, I'm not a paparazzo. I'm a documentary filmmaker. Graduated from U.S.C. two years ago. And I've got the loans to prove it."

This required some rethinking. I sat down and wiped the sweat off my forehead. "Let me get this straight. You're making a documentary about Miles, and you've been following all the people who come into contact with him?"

"Like his proctologist? Or the guy who delivers his Chinese food? That would be stupid. I'm only following the important ones."

I took off one of my moccasin booties and shook it out. Several pebbles dropped to the ground. "I can assure you I'm not that important."

He shook his head. "That was part of the problem with Luke Cutt, wasn't it? Your lack of self-esteem?"

This was getting weirder and weirder. "You know about me and Luke?"

"Of course. I do my research. On the women Miles sleeps with, in particular."

"Hold on, buddy. You are *way* off base." Even *my mother* wouldn't sleep with the man.

"Hey, I'm not judging. I mean, just because he's engaged."

"Let me state it for the record. I am not sleeping with Miles McCoy."

"I think we can let the audience decide," he said.

I turned to him. "This is insane. Since you've done your research, you know that for the past two years I've been designing and leading custom tours of L.A. Miles *hired* me to design a film noir tour for his fiancée. That's it. Not that I have to defend myself, to you of all people. Your ethics are pretty non-existent."

Charlie gestured theatrically. "How far do I go? How dark do I go? These are important questions. In film school, they taught us not to upset the talent, but I'm not sure that's always appropriate. Not when you're going after the truth. And the truth is, Miles needs to be taken down. The man is toxic. Everything he touches turns to shit."

Now I was getting interested. Charlie had been filming Miles and all the so-called important people who'd come into contact with him. He'd seen something. He knew something. It was time to stop antagonizing him.

"Sorry I accused you of stealing from me," I said. "You're obviously not that type."

"Thank you," he said grudgingly.

"It's so good to be sitting down." I sighed. "Do you by any chance have any water?"

He reached into his satchel and handed me a bottle. "It's sparkling."

"Perfect." I took a long slug. "It's really beautiful up here. You ever see rabbits?"

"Yeah," he said. "Deer, too. And coyotes. One time, a hooting owl."

"A hooting owl! Wow!"

"Okay, now you're playing me," Charlie said. "Don't bother. I'm making this film, and no amount of cajoling is going to change my mind."

I said, "There's going to be no cajoling from me. I'm on Team Charlie. But I've got to come clean with you. I'm concerned about Miles's fiancée. Maya."

"I get it. I've been keeping a close eye on her lately. And I'm concerned, too."

"Why? Because of what happened at the Mayan? Or because she's missing?"

"Missing?"

"Miles took her out of the hospital, but she's not at home."

"*Shit!*" he said. "This is *exactly* what I worried about, after—"

"After what?" I asked. "Her so-called 'suicide' attempt?"

He looked away.

"What?"

"Listen, all I know is that once you sleep with Miles, you're screwed." He shook his head. "I tried and tried to warn her, but she was totally in denial. She was too in love with the guy."

"You tried to warn her? You've been talking to Maya?"

He grabbed his satchel. "I want to show you something. Back at my place. What do you say?"

I hesitated.

"C'mon," he said. "What do you have to lose?"

I should have realized it was a trick question.

Chapter 32

CHARLIE KNEW ALL the shortcuts, so we made it back in under fifteen minutes. I started up the path to his front door.

"No," he said. "This way." He led me down the cobbled driveway into the backyard, which had gone to the dogs. I'm not talking potted plants in various states of decay or leaves in the pool. I'm talking mountains and valleys and rolling hills of dog shit. I literally didn't know where to step.

"Sorry," he said. "I've been kind of busy lately."

At the far end of the backyard, hidden behind a wall of cacti, was a rusted-out Airstream trailer. Charlie wiped his feet on the mat and removed his sneakers. Then he turned to me.

"Just in case," he said.

I took off my moccasin booties, padded inside behind him.

Oh, god.

One look around, and my heart was pounding, my palms were wet, and my chest tight. I wanted out. But Charlie was already locking the door.

"I thought we should have some privacy," he said.

I gave him a thin smile.

"Make yourself comfortable." He pointed to a cot in the middle of the space. "Sorry, I didn't make the bed. I wasn't expecting visitors."

"You live here?"

"Yeah," he said. "My mom lets me park on her property. Like I told you, student debt is a bitch."

We were avoiding the obvious. His trailer looked like something out of a slasher film. Every surface was covered with photographs—not of all the so-called important people in Miles's life. Just one of them.

Maya Duran.

Maya getting into her car, Maya getting out of her car, Maya laughing, Maya crying, Maya eating. Aside from the night she'd shot herself, I'd only ever seen Maya in her gondola bed, unconscious and hooked up to machines. These photographs changed everything. Now I understood exactly what Miles had fallen for.

It wasn't her beauty.

It wasn't her youth.

It was her *radiance*.

You could see it in her eyes, in the way she moved her body. Even in a photograph, she was so *alive*. And Charlie had hunted her like an animal.

"Are you proud of this?" I blurted out.

He looked around the room. "Kind of. I mean, it's been hard getting information on her. Maya's wiped from the internet. I don't know how Miles did it, but he did it. So I've had to do a lot of first-hand research."

No shame, no regrets. "If this is what you wanted to show me, I'm leaving."

"Wait." Charlie walked over to the kitchen counter, pulled

something out of a large file folder, handed it to me. "*This* is what I wanted to show you."

It was a strip of pictures from a photo booth.

"Please," Charlie said. "Just look."

I saw a boy and a girl. Teenagers, it looked like. Goofing around, the way teenagers do. He was skinny, awkward, tow-headed. She was intense, with wild, green eyes. You could tell he adored her, but she wasn't having it. This girl was waiting for bigger, better things.

I looked up to find Charlie staring at me. "Do you understand now? That's *us*."

I was confused. "You and Maya?"

"*Maya?*" He shook his head. "I don't know Maya. I mean, not personally."

Then I got it.

The girl Charlie adored wasn't Maya Duran.

It was Carmen Luz.

Charlie spent the better part of an hour telling me the story.

Carmen was his best friend's little sister. He'd known her forever. When they were kids, she followed the two boys everywhere. Bike riding, skateboarding, hanging out at the pool. When they got older, Charlie wanted more, but Carmen wasn't interested in him that way. Charlie was fine with it. They stayed friends. After her brother overdosed, they mourned together, and Charlie thought he might have another chance. But then Carmen met Miles McCoy.

Carmen fell for Miles, hard. She was in love. She said she was happy. But there were problems. Miles was married, for one thing. Then there was the drugs and drinking. All of a sudden, Carmen was partying every night, surrounded by users, haters, bloodsuckers. Charlie warned her she was going to get hurt, but she didn't listen. And then, one night, she was raped. She could've handled that, Charlie said. She'd handled worse. What she *couldn't* handle was the fact that afterward, Miles wanted nothing more to do with her. Refused her calls. Wouldn't see her. Never, in fact, laid eyes on her again. Carmen was devastated. Ashamed. She blamed herself for everything. And then, one day, she'd simply vanished, heartbroken.

And now Maya had vanished, too.

Charlie took the photo strip out of my hands. "It's a lot to take in, I know."

I nodded.

"But now you need to go," he said. "I've got stuff to do. I can't let that man destroy another woman's life."

I stood up, took one last look at Charlie. He seemed like he was telling the truth, but something was stuck in my head, something Miles had told me the day we'd met. He'd said Maya had stalkers, and that was why she couldn't be found on the internet. Maybe Miles was talking about Charlie. How did I know Charlie was a documentary filmmaker? Maybe he was just a man with an unhealthy obsession with another man's fiancée.

Back in the car, I picked up the box his neighbor had given me and studied the return address. Ship4U Mailboxes in West L.A. Not particularly helpful. I held the box up to my ear and shook it. No clues there either. I hesitated for maybe half a second before using the sharp end of my car key to rip through the tape, open the top, and shake out the Styrofoam peanuts. Out slid a DVD in an unmarked black case.

I was going to take a wild guess.

White Van Charlie liked dirty movies.

But now was not the time to confirm or deny my suspicions.

Now was the time to drive home to Venice, take a hot bath, and go straight to bed. Eight uninterrupted hours. In the morning, when I was rested, I'd sort everything out.

It was a lovely fantasy.

Which lasted until the very moment I turned onto my street, and saw the "For Rent" sign on Teddy's front lawn.

I felt like I'd been punched in the gut.

Teddy was moving.

Teddy was *leaving*.

I was such a fool. I'd taken one of the best things that had ever happened to me and thrown it away. For *Clayton Key*, of all people. And why?

I knew exactly why.

Because Clayton was a cartoon character. A bad boy I could tame. A reflection of my own vanity. Anything but a *real person*. Which meant he could never hurt me. And two years after Luke Cutt, I was still afraid of getting hurt.

The phone was ringing as I stepped inside. I tossed Charlie's DVD onto the couch, and ran to pick it up. It was Gram. She was calling to remind me that tomorrow was the day Ray was due at the criminal courthouse downtown. Department 30, fifth floor. I told her I hadn't forgotten. She also wanted to remind me about what she'd overheard Lizeth saying to Ray. I remembered that, too.

"That woman warned your uncle he'd regret it," she said. "I want to support his decision to do the right thing," Gram said. "But I can't just show up with things the way they are. You understand, don't you?"

"Of course I do," I said.

She was trying not to cry. "That's why I need you to be there for him. Regardless of what's happening between us, I don't want him to feel alone."

I told Gram I'd been planning on it. And then I told her how much I loved her.

After we hung up, I sat on the couch for a while, thinking. They were unbelievable, those two. Ray had asked me to be there for Gram, and now she was asking me to be there for him. Circumstances were keeping them apart, but they were going to find their way back to each other. I was certain of that. They were fighters, and both of them knew they had something worth fighting for.

Shortly before midnight, there was a knock at the door. It was Clayton, who'd just gotten off work. I let him in, and sat him down on the couch. He wasn't in the mood for talking, but I had something to say. Afterward, he kissed me goodbye, and it was sweet, the way last kisses can be.

I set the coffeemaker for 7 a.m., and walked around the house, locking the doors and windows. Before I turned out the lights, I left a message on Teddy's home phone. It definitely went on too long, but it came from the heart.

Turns out I had something worth fighting for, too.

Chapter 33

TUESDAY MORNING, 8:30 a.m. The sky was gray, which is nobody's favorite color. I descended into the underground parking garage kitty-corner from the courthouse, spiraling downward until I finally found a spot, between a hearse and a Dumpster. It didn't bode well. Nor did setting off the metal detector in the lobby. But what did I expect?

The last time I'd visited the Clara Shortridge Foltz Criminal Justice Center it was for jury duty, which I'd needed to get out of because I had plans to fly to New York the following day with Luke. The night before we'd brainstormed various strategies: I could show up in the jury pool dressed as Princess Leia; remind the prosecutor he'd once slept with my mother; proactively change my name from Dreama Black to Jesus Christ. As it turned out, I was put on a dog bite case that lasted two weeks, and Luke went to New York without me, to perform in the Victoria's Secret fashion show. The rest is history. But I digress.

After removing my shoes, belt, and bracelets, I cleared the security line. From there I headed up to Department 30, which was a riot of activity: the bailiff was playing *Fruit Ninja* on his phone; the court reporter was plucking her eyebrows; the assistant D.A. was attempting to tear a file folder in half. There were maybe a dozen people in the audience. The jury box, however, was empty. And no Uncle Ray in sight. Knowing him, he was going to show up at the last minute, brandishing the key piece of evidence.

The room grew quiet as the judge took her seat at the bench.

"May I approach?" asked the A.D.A.

The judge nodded, then crooked her finger at the defense attorney. "Why doesn't opposing counsel join us up here? Might as well get this over with."

The defense attorney consulted with his client, who turned to consult with the older woman sitting behind him, who listened carefully, then started whooping in delight.

"Order!" snapped the judge. "Or the bailiff will escort you out!"

"Apologies, your honor," the older woman said. "But he's my only son."

Just then the door to the courtroom swung open and banged loudly against the wall. Everyone turned around as a petite African-American woman in a tiger-striped maxi-dress made her way to the front of the room.

"Sorry I'm late." She tossed her long, blond hair as she slid in next to the older woman. Then she brought a hot pink dagger finger to her lips, and whispered, "My bad."

Hot pink dagger fingers, and a sexy blond weave.

I had a sudden flash of déjà-vu.

And then things started moving quickly. The lawyers returned to their seats and the judge said, "Will the defendant please rise?"

Up shot a small African-American guy in a sharp green suit. He could barely contain his excitement. His feet were tapping, his shoulders were twitching. I looked over my shoulder. Still no Ray. Was he stuck in traffic?

"You are one lucky man." The judge flipped through some papers. "Not too smart for a two-time felon to be waving firearms around a crowded bar. Third strike would've gotten you twenty to life."

The younger woman grabbed the older woman's hand.

"But," the judge said, glaring at the A.D.A., "due to a series of police and prosecutorial *missteps*, let's call them, I have no choice but to dismiss this case."

The two women threw their arms around each other.

"I don't want to see you in my courtroom again," said the judge. "Next time I won't be in a such a good mood."

"You have my word, your honor," said the defendant.

"In which case," said the judge, slamming her gavel on the desk, "Lucius Ramsay, you are free to go."

Lucius Ramsay.

Lucius Ramsay.

No wonder Uncle Ray didn't want me anywhere near him.

Lucius Ramsay was the person Ray was supposed to testify against. He was also a friend of the man who'd raped Carmen Luz, and an employee of a man whose gun had almost killed Maya Duran. And now, because Ray wasn't here, Lucius Ramsay was going free.

The A.D.A. zipped up his briefcase, and stormed out, stony-faced.

"Have a nice life!" Lucius cried. Then he turned to his attorney and pumped the man's hand several times before embracing his mother and sister.

"Son of a bitch," the sister said with a grin.

"Watch your tongue, young lady," the mother said.

I bent down, pretending to look for something I'd dropped, as the three of them exited the courtroom. Then I stepped out into the hallway and hid my face behind a discarded take-out menu while they waited for the elevator, laughing and joking so loudly one of the security guards asked them to please tone it down. At that point, Lucius got so pissed-off I half expected him to pull out a gun, since that was his M.O., apparently, but before he had a chance to do anyone any bodily harm, the elevator doors opened and his mother grabbed him by the collar and yanked him inside. I waited for the doors to close, then flew down five flights, just in time to catch them stepping out of the elevator and traversing the bustling lobby to the rear exit, where they parted ways, the ladies heading toward the parking garage, Lucius going south on Broadway.

It's not like I planned on following him.

It just kind of worked out that way.

I stayed on the opposite side of the street, keeping pace as Lucius made his way through the thicket of working people, hipsters, tourists, and homeless individuals that constituted the midday downtown crowd.

"Excuse me," I said, ducking around a bearded man who'd stopped to study a mouthwatering display of seashell-shaped *conchas*, buttery *mantecaditos*, and crispy, cinnamon-dusted *buñuelos*.

"Coming through," I said, pushing past a family of four who were picking through piles of sweat socks displayed outside a discount store.

And then, without warning, Lucius was darting across the street and heading my way. Running wasn't an option, so I spun around, put my hands up on either side of my face, and peered into the Guadalupe Wedding Chapel, a marvelous locale where, it turns out, you can not only get married, you can get divorced, buy gold jewelry, straighten out your immigration issues, and file a tax return. I stood there, motionless, my shallow breath fogging up the window, until the very moment Lucius marched past me.

Time to get serious.

I flipped up my collar and put on my red Ray-Bans.

Camouflage is the soul of surveillance.

Now Lucius was at the corner of 3rd Street, waiting for the light. Opposite him was the Bradbury Building, its undistinguished brick exterior concealing a light-flooded, steampunk marvel, with birdcage elevators and neo-Victorian wrought iron, familiar from countless film noirs. What most people don't know is that the Bradbury Building is also the headquarters of L.A.P.D.'s Internal Affairs Division. I wondered if Lieutenant Hepworth was holed up in there right now, plotting against somebody else's family. Or maybe he was still too busy trying to destroy mine.

The light turned green.

Lucius looked both ways before crossing, then swung left into Grand Central Market. I checked my phone. 11:45 a.m. Guess we were having lunch.

Unfortunately, I wasn't able to savor the myriad smells wafting through the sprawling, hundred-year-old food hall—Mexican limes, fresh coffee, handmade tortillas—because Lucius was practically sprinting now. Past Las Morelianas, known for its Michoacán-style *carnitas*, made up of fourteen slowly roasted nose-to-tail pig parts. Past Ana Maria's, which specialized in *gorditas* the size of a baby's head. Past Sarita's, where you go for old school *pupusas*. Finally, he slowed down. Something had caught his eye at one of the produce stands. Plantains. Delicious, fried, sautéed, or baked. Lucius starting squeezing them, one by one.

"No touching the *frutas*," cautioned the proprietress.

"Fuck that," he said.

I planted myself in front of the persimmons while he mauled the avocados.

"These are hard as rocks," he complained. "*Comprendo?*"

The woman dug around until she found a ripe one, then weighed it. "Ninety-two cents."

Avocado in hand, Lucius continued down the middle aisle. I thought he might be leaving, but just before hitting the Hill Street exit, he checked his phone, then circled back to the China Cafe, which looked straight out of the 1940s, with a U-shaped red counter, spinning ceiling fans, and what was probably the original neon "CHOP SUEY, CHOW MEIN" sign. While Lucius parked himself on one of the green vinyl stools, I found a spot maybe twenty feet away, belly up to a coffee bar, which offered an unobstructed, 180-degree view of the erstwhile felon. Now he was flirting with the pretty waitress. She was blushing and playing with her hair, which is kind of unappetizing around food, but whatever. After she went to place his order, Lucius took off his tie and stuffed it into his pocket.

"Ahem." The barista planted himself directly in my line of sight. "What can I get you?"

I peered at him from behind my sunglasses. "Coffee, please."

He looked disappointed. He was wearing a lab coat and holding a beaker. It was that kind of place. And he wasn't budging.

"Fine." I glanced up at the menu. "Make it an iced macadamia nut cappuccino."

"Good choice."

"In a to-go cup." In case I had to move quickly.

Once the barista was out of the way, I saw the waitress ferrying a steaming bowl of wonton soup over to Lucius. He took out the avocado he'd bought, sliced it into his bowl, doused the whole thing in Cholula, and slurped it up. When he was done, he made the pretty waitress laugh and smile until she stopped laughing and smiling as another woman approached the counter and slid in next to Lucius, who didn't look particularly happy to see her.

The woman was covered up in a blue coat and matching scarf, so I couldn't make out her face, but I could tell she was yelling at Lucius. After a minute or two, he passed her something, which she put into her purse. Then they put their heads together and started whispering, at which point Lucius signaled for the check.

"Almost ready, miss." The barista poured some coffee beans onto a scale.

"Oh," I said. "Thanks, but—" I craned my neck. They were paying. The woman was slinging her purse over her shoulder. Lucius was checking his phone. I leapt to my feet, fished a ten-dollar bill out of my basket, handed it to the barista. "Keep the change." This investigation was really costing me.

"But your beverage—"

They were standing up now. The woman was taking Lucius's arm. And as she turned her head, the scarf slipped and I caught a glimpse of her hair.

Unbelievable.

"Forget it," I said to the barista. "I have to go."

"Your *beverage*," he insisted, "comes to eleven dollars. No tipping. It's a growing national movement."

Cursing gentrification, I rummaged around until I found another dollar, which I threw onto the counter. Then I plunged into the crowd. It was chaos—kids running underfoot, people juggling trays. But I kept sight of them up until the very moment an elderly man pushing a shopping cart bent down to tie his shoe, blocking the aisle. By the time I'd dodged his cart, detoured in and around a spice stand, then elbowed my way back out to Broadway, it was too late.

I stood there like a fool, clutching my overpriced iced macadamia nut cappuccino—which tasted like feet, by the way—as Lucius Ramsay and Pee Chee Lowenstein slipped into a yellow cab and sped away.

Chapter 34

Lucius Ramsay and Pee Chee Lowenstein.

Talk about strange bedfellows.

But then this had been the strangest two weeks of my entire life.

Back at home, I put some coffee on and paced the living room, ruing the day I'd snapped up those floor-to-ceiling bookshelves at Ikea because if I'd just had some wall space I could've obsessively arranged and rearranged my documents and print-outs until they magically revealed what was going on, and how I was supposed to fix it.

Hey, it worked for Carrie Mathison.

But maybe it was the CIA training.

Also, I didn't have documents or print-outs.

I did, however, have Post-it notes, a perfectly serviceable kitchen table, and—according to the woman who was not Madame Anna, nor, in fact, a psychic—a desire for truth and justice.

I poured myself a cup of coffee and uncapped my pen.

Post-it #1. That was easy. Post-it #1 was going to be Miles

McCoy. I stuck him onto the middle of the table. All trails began with Miles McCoy.

Post-it #2 was Carmen Luz. Miles's ex-girlfriend. Rape survivor. Current whereabouts unknown. I gave her pride of place on Miles's right.

Post-it #3 was Freddy Sims, a.k.a. Big Fatty. Not, in fact, a rapist. A rapper. Current whereabouts likewise unknown. I positioned him directly to Carmen's right.

Post-it #4 was Maya Duran, yet another person in Miles's orbit who'd disappeared off the face of the earth. She went on the man's other side.

Post-it #5 was Pee Chee Lowenstein. She went below Miles, right next to a smear of cherry jam I'd left behind a few days earlier, when I'd consumed three English muffins before 8 a.m. (a personal best).

Post-it #6 was Pee Chee's unlikely confidant, would-be three-time loser Lucius Ramsay, who was probably out celebrating the fact that Post-it #7 was a no-show today. Lucius I put to Pee Chee's right.

Post-it #7 was, of course, my uncle Ray, suspended from the force, accused of corruption, inexplicably involved with the ill-fated Post-it #8. He went on Lucius's other side.

Post-it #8 was the late Lizeth Pimentel, former neighbor and friend of Post-it #2. Lizeth went on Ray's other side.

Post-it #9 was Charlie "Chick" Churchill, another old friend of Post-it #2, obsessed with Post-it #4, bent on destroying Post-it #1, and guilty of stalking yours truly in his white van. I had no idea where to put Charlie. At first I gave him some prime real estate next to Carmen, but then I moved him directly above Miles. Since he had a God complex and all.

I would have been Post-it #10, but apparently I'd run out of Post-its. Which was kind of a shame, really, because no matter how many times I shifted those babies around, I was at dead center—me, Dreama Black, and the $40,000 that I'd lost not once, but twice.

Let's consider that $40,000.

It was the exact sum Miles had promised to pay me for the star-crossed noir tour, as well as the exact sum that was ruining Ray's life. The conclusion was inescapable. Somebody wanted it to look like Ray was dirty, and using me to launder his money. But here's where it starts to get interesting.

Perhaps you are familiar with the concept of cui bono, which is Latin for "who benefits?" Cui bono, as I learned years ago from an especially compelling episode of *Monk*, is the key forensic question in all police investigations. So who benefitted most immediately and most directly from Ray's fall from grace? That would be Lucius Ramsay, whom I'd now linked to Pee Chee Lowenstein, who, in turn, lived to serve Miles McCoy. Taking it one step further, why would Pee Chee and/or Miles want to hand Lucius Ramsay a get-out-of-jail-free card? And what lengths would they go to in order to do so?

Just as I was trying to wrap my head around that one, the doorbell rang.

Teddy.

Please let it be Teddy.

But it wasn't exactly my lucky day.

"What are you doing here, Mother?" I let her in, then high-tailed it back into the kitchen, yanked off a length of paper towels, and camouflaged my Post-it note flowchart. The woman asks too many questions. "You know I hate surprises."

"Don't be silly," she said. "You adored your thirteenth birthday."

I poked my head out. "Really? You mean when your boyfriend showed up at my school and serenaded me with his latest power ballad?"

"That song made the Billboard Top Ten," she said defensively.

"It was about your private parts." I grabbed a box of graham crackers. "Listen, I need lunch. And then I have to get back to what I was doing."

"Would you please come out here?" she asked. "We have to talk about something."

She had a look on her face I didn't recognize. "Gravitas" came closest to describing it. All of a sudden, I was terrified.

"Okay." I sat down next to her. "What is it?"

"You're a good and loyal person." She stopped, searched my face. "I'm really proud of you, Dreama. Do you know that?"

"Yeah," I said warily.

"So here's the thing." My mother stood up, interlaced her fingers. "You came over the other day and asked me about your uncle Ray."

I stopped her right there. "Ray didn't show up in court today, and the judge dismissed the case. This *hardened criminal* just walked out of there, free as a bird. I don't get it. Ray would never let something like that happen."

"Not under normal circumstances," she said.

"Which these are not," I supplied.

She nodded.

"Because under *normal* circumstances," I went on, "if somebody told Uncle Ray not to testify, you know, tried to intimidate him or whatever, he would never back off. Right?" I don't know why I was asking, but I was asking.

"Dreama. You know him. No." She tried to smile. "Ray would never back off."

"So what is it then? Is he sick?"

My mother took my hands. "He's gone."

My stomach lurched. "Gone? What do you mean, *gone*? As in *dead*?"

"There's no reason to believe that at the moment," she said grimly.

I got up, grabbed my phone out of my purse.

"What are you doing?"

"Calling Gram."

"Put the phone down. I'm not finished."

I put the phone down and looked at my mother. She had left the house without makeup or her water bottle fanny pack. It had to be bad.

"There's no easy way to say it so I'm just going to come out and say it," she said. "A warrant has just been issued for your uncle's arrest. Which makes him not just missing, but a fugitive."

I wanted to speak, but no words came out.

She closed her eyes for a second. "I know. I'm in shock."

My mother had been through a lot in her life—alcohol abuse, drug abuse, domestic abuse, depression. Despite everything, she'd always been weirdly indomitable. But this thing with Ray had thrown her. She was devastated. Not just for me and for Gram, but for herself. Ray had been like a father to her, too.

She opened her purse and pulled out a pack of cigarettes. "Do you mind?"

I shook my head. "You know you can't do that in here."

"Fine." She stomped into the kitchen and came back with the

graham crackers, which she started stuffing in her mouth two at a time. "What are these things? They're *delicious*."

"Hand them over," I said. "They're poison. Full of preservatives and GMOs." I shoveled several into my mouth.

"There's more, by the way." My mother wrestled the box back from me. "A pair of cops came banging on Gram's door at 6 a.m. this morning, then grilled her for three solid hours."

"Is she okay?"

My mother nodded. "She's at my house now. I gave her a Xanax and she went to sleep."

"Xanax? I thought you weren't supposed to keep that kind of thing around," I said.

"Let me live vicariously, okay?"

"Whatever." I couldn't deal with her stuff right now. If I could just stay focused I might be able to figure out where Ray had gone.

"Look," my mother said. "I don't want to bicker."

"Me neither."

"All I wanted was to be here for you, in case you needed me. I know how much you care about Ray."

Leaning in for a hug, I whispered into her shoulder, "I love you."

"What was that?" she asked. "I didn't quite hear you."

"Don't push it," I said.

"Hey." She pulled back to look at me. "Whatever happened with your neighbor, Teddy?"

I shook my head. "I can't believe I'm saying this, but something you said actually resonated with me."

"Something *I* said? Impossible."

"Okay, it was something Gram said. After she and I hung up, I called Teddy and left a message."

"Saying?"

"That I was sorry for behaving so stupidly, and asking for another chance. I don't know if you noticed when you came in, but there's a "For Rent" sign on his front lawn. I wanted to be sure he knew how I felt, I mean, considering he might be moving."

My mother said, "You were never exactly good with timing."

"I don't get it."

"The 'For Rent' sign is gone." She cocked her head. "And did you not see the U-Haul?"

"What U-Haul?"

I ran over to the front window and pulled back the curtains.

The U-Haul was latched onto the back of Teddy's car. And pulling away from the curb. Which meant nothing I'd said on that message had changed his mind.

It was too late.

My mother looked uncomfortable. "You're not going to *cry*, are you?"

"Cry?" I blinked a couple of times. "Me? I'm your daughter, aren't I?"

"I'm going home to check on Gram." She got up from the couch, grabbing Charlie's DVD out from under her. "Here you go. I've been sitting on this."

Another thing I'd been careless about.

"And if you don't mind me saying, you might think about working on tidiness. Remember what Jerry Hall used to say. To keep a man you've got to be a maid in the living room, a cook in the kitchen, and a—"

"Okay, okay," I said. "I know the rest."

My mother tossed her legendary mane. "Dreama, you are such a prude."

"Oh, really?" I asked. "What would you say if I told you that the minute you leave I'm going to sit down and enjoy some adult entertainment?"

"I'd say you really are my daughter." She shook her head. "But kind of an oversharer."

When it comes to my mother, I just can't win.

Chapter 35

I SLID THE DVD into the machine, then took a seat on the couch. Call me crazy, but I had a feeling that Charlie "Chick" Churchill's taste in porn wasn't going to go down easy. But it wasn't porn. At first, I didn't know *what* it was.

The sound was terrible, and the picture worse. All I could make out were streaks of color—gold, blue, and purple—as the camera whipped from left to right, and right to left. Then, the thump of heavy bass, and a shot of people milling around, illuminated by flashing strobes. Then I got it.

This was cell phone footage somebody had shot inside a dance club.

After a minute or two, the camera stopped on a woman making silly faces, then on her friends, screaming with laughter. They were standing at the bar, bathed in a noxious green light, the bottles behind them reflected endlessly in the mirror. More screams, more laughter, as the woman knocked over her drink, then dumped the contents of her purse on the table.

"Can't find my lighter," she mumbled.

"Show's starting," someone said.

The camera whirled around, following a beam of white light. And then an enormous man in basketball shorts, a baseball cap, and dark glasses stepped into the spotlight.

Freddy Sims, a.k.a. Big Fatty.

"Everybody doin' all right?" he bellowed into his mike.

The crowd roared.

"If it's okay by you, I'm going to try out a song we've been working on." He hitched up his shorts, started pacing around. "My producer ain't happy I stole it." He grinned. "But y'all know I'm an unrepentant gangsta."

They roared again.

He turned his head. "Now bring it on out here."

Three young women dressed in crop tops, booty shorts, and glittery platforms pranced onto the stage, shaking it for all they were worth. And then, as the music came up—an idiosyncratic mix of dancehall, old school hip-hop, and gospel ecstatics—Fatty brought down the house.

It took me a minute, but I recognized the song.

Fatty was singing "I'll Be Your Mirror," the ninth track on the Velvet Underground's debut album of 1967. Lou Reed wrote it for his muse, the German model Nico, who sang the lyrics in a thin, tremulous voice, as if she were nodding off after yet another hit of heroin.

Big Fatty, however, flipped the script.

While his dancers stamped their feet, whipped their hair, and thrust their asses, he spat out the words in syncopated beats, chewing up every one of the song's poetic sentiments, a ghetto soothsayer with killer timing.

The Velvet's manager Andy Warhol wanted to sell the album with a crack in it so the song's title would be repeated over and over again until somebody lifted the needle. But Lou Reed had bickered with Andy, and nothing came of the idea. Until Fatty transformed it into performance art.

Over and over Fatty chanted the words, "I'll be your mirror, I'll be your mirror, I'll be your mirror." But it wasn't just the repetition. It was also the dancers. They were mirror images of one another— identical costumes, identical movements, identical body types, though one was a brunette, another a blonde, and the third had black hair.

That's right.

Black hair, pale skin, red lips, huge, green eyes, and what looked like a large lotus flower tattoo on her arm.

I pressed stop. Then rewind. Then play.

It was Carmen Luz.

The blonde was Maya Duran.

And the brunette?

She'd changed so utterly that I almost didn't recognize her.

Lizeth Pimentel.

Poor, dead Lizeth Pimentel.

Suddenly, the image blurred as a woman intruded into the frame. She looked ready to pounce, like a wild animal.

Hello, Pee Chee, I thought to myself. *You keep showing up in all the most interesting places.*

"Give me the fucking phone!" she screamed. "You were supposed to turn it in at the door!"

There was a scuffle, then the screen went to black.

I turned off the DVD and sat there for a few moments, lost in thought.

I won't say the pieces were falling into place, but at least they were starting to look like parts of the same puzzle.

And suddenly, I knew just who could help me.

Chapter 36

ACCORDING TO HER Instagram, Destiny D-Low was holed up at home, baking treats to be auctioned off at a PETA fundraiser the following night. Despite the fact that her "famous" red velvet cupcakes looked like something out of *Saw VII*, I deluged her with likes, but after an hour of radio silence it became apparent I was on the woman's shit list. Clearly, a more aggressive tack was in order. After checking *Daily Mail*, I learned that Destiny had recently bought an Art Deco mansion in Hancock Park's venerable gated community, Fremont Place—which, as it so happens, has a mythical significance in the Black family lore.

May I digress?

When she was a precocious girl of fifteen, my mother was obsessed with Mick Jagger. After failing to meet him backstage, and then embarrassing herself trying to sneak past the guard station at the entrance to Fremont Place, where he was living at the time, my mother came up with an idea. She and Gram were going to pretend to be shopping for a Fremont Place mansion of their own, and once inside the gates, while Gram distracted the broker with a slew of bogus questions, Mom was going to make a break for it, burst in on Mick, have sex with him, and live happily ever after.

You know what they say about the chip and the old block. Gram was all in. Unfortunately, Mick was out of the country the day the dynamic duo connived their way inside, but it wasn't a total loss as my mother met one of Mick's roadies, who introduced her to a funny little guy he knew who wound up opening for the Stones at the Forum in 1981. Yeah, it was Prince. But that's another digression.

Anyway, it isn't often that my mother has a good idea, and I saw no reason this one couldn't be recycled. Which is how, at five o'clock that afternoon, Cat and I found ourselves outside a magnificent 1925 Spanish Colonial estate at the southern end of Fremont Place, waiting for a real estate broker named Lisa Chen.

"I can't believe she's late," I said.

"Seriously," Cat replied. "Do you know what the commission is on $7,350,000?"

"I'm not going to pay *asking price*," I said. "I'm going to lowball. Obviously."

"Do you think you're taking this a little too seriously?"

Just then a black Mercedes sedan pulled up behind us, and out popped a tiny woman with large glasses, a bowl haircut, and annual sales topping $150 million.

"Hello!" she cried. "Which one of you is Dreama?"

We stepped out of the car. "That would be me. Thanks for coming on such short notice."

"My pleasure! As you can see, the house is a roomy eleven thousand square feet, with six bedrooms, eight bathrooms, a wine cellar, and lots of counter space in the chef's kitchen. So bring your panini press! Your Vitamix! Your Crock Pot!"

Cat turned to me. "You do love stew."

"Sold!" Lisa sang out.

"What about the neighbors?" I asked. "We heard lots of celebrities live here."

"Oh, yes!" She pulled off her glasses, leaned in conspiratorially. "Most of the homes up and down this block have been photographed for *InStyle*."

I exchanged looks with Cat. "Yeah, I remember the feature on Destiny D-Low's house." Which looked like it had been decorated by Marie Antoinette after one too many Vodka Red Bulls.

Lisa put on her poker face. "You certainly don't see many topiary dollar signs these days."

Bingo.

I started to wheeze. "Why don't you two go on inside?" I doubled over, coughing. "My inhaler's in the car. I'll be along in a minute."

"We can wait," said Lisa.

"Not necessary," I replied. "Cat has amazing instincts. Come on, Cat. Don't be modest."

Cat said, "Dreama's kind of impulsive. I help ground her."

"*Oh,*" said Lisa, eyes twinkling. "Now I get it. You two make a beautiful couple, if you don't mind my saying. Perhaps you're not aware, but I represented Portia de Rossi before she was with Ellen De Generes, who, sadly, came to the relationship with her own longtime broker."

"Their loss." Cat took Lisa's arm. "Shall we?"

I watched as the two of them climbed the front steps. When the door slammed shut, I raced down the block, skidding to a stop in front of Destiny D-Low's spread. I remembered it from when we drove in. In addition to the topiary dollar signs on the front lawn there were also topiary swans and what looked like a topiary Louis Vuitton steamer trunk, but could just as easily been a scraggly hedge.

Destiny herself opened the door.

"Some gated community," she said.

"Can I come in?"

She wiped her hands on a lacy apron. "Suit yourself."

She'd done some remodeling since she was featured in *InStyle*. The living room was cool and minimalist, with beige couches and a water feature, but somebody had clearly forgotten to feng shui the pit bull, who growled at me, incisors bared, from inside a flimsy-looking kennel.

"That's Tootie," Destiny said. "She's all bark and no bite."

I doubted it.

"Thanks for the likes," Destiny said. "Snickerdoodle?"

"No, thank you," I said.

"You probably don't eat gluten."

"Actually, I *love* gluten."

She went into the kitchen and came back with a cinnamon-dusted piece of cardboard she was pretending for some reason was a cookie.

"Delicious," I lied.

Destiny pushed aside a striped Hermès blanket and flopped down onto the ultrasuede couch. "So why are you here? Miles said we were good, but that man lies like he breathes."

I sat down opposite her. "Miles didn't send me."

She picked up a hand mirror, idly tucked a stray curl back into her headwrap. "Then what do you want?"

I was tired of the subterfuge. "I'm here about Big Fatty. I need you to help me find him."

Destiny bolted upright. "How *dare* you? Who *the fuck* do you think you are, waltzing into somebody's house like you own the place, asking about folks you've got no business asking about? I thought we were finished with all that. I thought you understood my *position*. Fatty is my *friend*. You ever heard of a concept called loyalty?"

I sighed. "I'm not asking you to betray a friend."

"Oh, really?"

"I just want to talk to him."

She got up, grabbed a decorative pillow, pummelled it within an inch of its life. "You want to talk to a *rapist*? What, you have a *death wish*?" She beat another pillow into submission.

I stood up. "Look, I'm sorry about the other day. Fatty did his time, and I respect that. It's all in the past."

She spun around. "You think it's behind him? You think because he's out of jail he gets to have a life now? I don't think so. He's finished. Nobody's ever going to listen to Fatty's music again without thinking of what happened to that girl. There's some things you don't come back from, Dreama. Wake up."

I said, "Maybe there's a way for Fatty to redeem himself."

"Damn straight," she said. "It's called prayer."

"I'm not talking about that. You know Maya Duran? Miles's fiancée?"

Destiny walked over to the burner in the kitchen, leaned in and lit a cigarette. "Uh, *yeah*. I was sitting right next to you when she tried to kill herself."

I followed Destiny in. "I'm thinking she didn't try to kill herself. I'm thinking someone slipped a bullet into her gun. I'm thinking all signs point to Miles."

Miles had raped Carmen. Maya had found out. Miles couldn't risk the information getting out. It left a lot of things unexplained, but it was the best I had.

Destiny took a long drag. "You have any proof?"

I drummed my fingers on the counter. "Not exactly."

Her nostrils flared in anger. "Well, why don't you just plant some? That's what the cops do."

"Listen to me," I interrupted. "Maya's vanished. And she's not the first person in Miles's life who has. Do you know who Carmen Luz is?"

"The girl who got Fatty in trouble?"

Talk about flipping the script. "Yeah. Well, Carmen's gone, too. And here's the thing. Did you know she was Miles's girlfriend at the time of the rape?"

That stopped her dead in her tracks. She dropped her cigarette into a cup of water and turned to face me. "How is it possible that this is the first time I'm hearing that?"

"Miles was married to Petal Collings. His relationship with Carmen was a secret."

I stopped, and let her take in the myriad possibilities that that particular factoid opened up.

"That man has lots of secrets," she finally said.

"Apparently."

Her eyes were glittering now. "You want to hear one that'll blow your mind?" She didn't wait for me to answer. "Miles McCoy did a bad thing." She stuck her finger into an open box of powdered sugar, then pulled it out and licked it. "A *very* bad thing."

"What are you suggesting?"

She shrugged. "I'm not suggesting *shit*. You're the one who's suggesting things. You're suggesting that women who get near Miles get fucked over, then disappear. I'm *telling* you something. They don't just 'disappear.' One of them was murdered. Two days ago in Eagle Rock."

Now I was the one stopped dead in my tracks. "Are you talking about Lizeth Pimentel?"

"What if I am?"

I felt a chill go up my spine. "What makes you think Miles has anything to do with her murder?"

Destiny said, "I went back into the studio yesterday. Overdubs. Obviously, Miles doesn't trust me to be punctual. So first thing in the morning he sends Mookie to pick me. I forgot my phone, and I was bored stiff stuck in rush hour traffic, so I reached into the seat pocket looking for something to read, and there was one of Miles's little yellow legal pads."

"So?"

"So do you think it's strange that a dead woman's name and phone number were scrawled on the first page in fucking red ink?" She nodded. "Yeah, I thought so."

Just then a small, mouse-like girl crept into the room. "Excuse me, but it smells like the lemon squares might be burning."

"What am I paying you for?" Destiny snapped. "Pull 'em out!"

The girl put on an oven mitt, and pulled a sheet of charred lumps out of the oven. "They don't look that bad," she said brightly.

Destiny scowled at her. "Get out of my sight."

I waited until the girl left, then said, "Do you think I could maybe see that notepad?"

"Sorry." She dumped the burned lemon squares into the sink and turned on the water. "I put it back where I found it."

Shit. "Why would you do that? Don't you think the police should see it?"

"For all I know Miles left it there on purpose. As a test. You think I want to disappear, too? Look, all I want to do is finish my new album, win my Grammy, and go home to Barbados for a while. My mother misses me." She turned off the water, opened the fridge, pulled out a bowl of dough, slapped some onto the marble slab, and started whacking it with her rolling pin. "No offense, but can you get out of my house now?"

"Don't you see?" I asked. "What you just told me is all the more reason I need to talk to Fatty."

Whack, whack, whack. "You sound like a crazy person, do you realize that?"

"Fatty knew Lizeth Pimentel."

She was really putting her arms into it. I could see the muscles working. "How on earth would Fatty know Lizeth Pimentel?"

I said, "A while back, Fatty was working on a remix of an old Velvet Underground song. 'I'll Be Your Mirror.' Does that sound familiar?"

From the look on her face it definitely sounded familiar. But she wasn't ready to give anything away. She turned, reached into the cupboard for the flour. "Stupid dough is sticking to my rolling pin."

"Destiny."

"Yeah, I heard some outtakes once. Fatty was working with some inexperienced producer and they couldn't get the permissions. The deal fell through."

"Fatty performed the song one night in a dance club. I saw the footage. There were three girls backing him, and one of them was Lizeth Pimentel."

Destiny looked sick.

"The other two were Maya Duran and Carmen Luz. Are you hearing what I'm saying? The three of them are connected. None of this is a coincidence."

Destiny put down her rolling pin. "You think Fatty is going to help you pin all this shit on Miles, but that's not going to happen. Fatty never worked with Miles. Fatty never even knew Miles."

"Destiny," I said. "Come on. Think for a second. Who do you think that inexperienced producer working with Fatty was?"

She looked at me. Paused. Swallowed hard.

"Yeah," I said. "Now you get it. Fatty may not have known *Miles*, but he sure as hell knew Pee Chee."

And Destiny knew exactly what that meant.

Pee Chee and Miles.

Miles and Pee Chee.

It was impossible to say where one of them stopped, and the other began.

Destiny picked up her cell phone, punched in a number, waited a minute.

"Hey." She grabbed one of the pillows, clutched it to her chest. "I know. Me, too. How y'all been doing?" She glanced at me, then stepped out of the room.

While she was gone, I checked my phone. Two calls from Lieutenant Hepworth, but no message.

Destiny was back a couple of minutes later.

"Blood isn't exactly thicker than water," she said.

"Excuse me?"

"That was Floyd Sims I was talking to."

Floyd da Gangsta. Fatty's cousin. They recorded together as Cuz Til Death, not that it worked out that way. "I thought he and Fatty hated each other."

"They do," Destiny said. "Why else do you think he told me where Fatty was?" She handed me a piece of paper with an address on it. "Don't make me regret this."

As I left, Tootie leapt at me from inside her cage, rage rolling off her in waves so strong you could smell them.

I tried not to take it personally.

Chapter 37

BY THE TIME I returned Cat had Lisa Chen eating out of her hand.

"I love your wife!" the latter told me. "Have a great evening! See you soon!"

We got back into the car. "She seems to have recovered quite nicely from losing a $7,350,000 sale."

Cat said, "Let's just say Lisa Chen has layers."

As it turned out, the middle-aged woman had led a wildly misspent youth in the San Gabriel Valley, one sorry vestige of which was a half-finished lace garter tattoo that Cat would be filling in this Sunday at 9 a.m. sharp, leaving our now ex-broker just enough time to set up for an open house later that afternoon.

I told you.

Some people have a gift.

"Did your mother actually sleep with Prince?" Cat asked.

"I'm not allowed to comment. She signed a non-disclosure agreement."

"She needs to write her memoir," said Cat.

"What do you have on for tomorrow?" I asked.

"Wednesday?" Cat flipped down the mirror and touched up her eyeliner. "Nothing special. Work."

"What do you think about taking a little road trip?"

She pulled out a pot of gloss. "Just you and me?"

"Yeah." I got into the turn lane. "I was thinking we'd pack a picnic and I have that nice blanket and we can stop and look at the scenery, maybe take a hike."

"You have the arrow," Cat said.

I took the left.

"Listen, it sounds awesome." She smacked her lips, flipped the mirror back up. "But it's going to be a busy day. I have two hips back to back, which I try not to do because I hate being hunched in the same position for hours at a time. And then this Snapchat exec who wants to get me into bed even though I've made it perfectly clear I loathe facial hair is coming in for an old school hula girl. Can it wait until Monday?"

Unfortunately, it couldn't.

Which is why I hit the road by myself the following morning.

It was clear and sunny in Venice, but before the day was out I'd be at an elevation of five thousand feet, so I deposited my beanie, my puffer, and my white goat hair après-ski boots into the trunk. Not that I anticipated a pleasant afternoon of sipping hot toddies by the fire. But it's good to be prepared. In any case, I had an important stop to make before getting to my final destination. And that one was at an even higher elevation.

The freeway was backed up from downtown to El Monte, but once I hit the 210, it was wide open. Not much to look at as you venture into the Inland Empire, aside from the San Bernardino Mountains rising to the north, and a vast expanse of tract homes where there used to be orange groves and chicken ranches. And what looked like a gargantuan six-pack of Miller Lite parked on the side of the freeway, which turned out to be the tanks at the MillerCoors brewery. They offered tours, but only on weekends.

Just past Fontana, where the Hell's Angels was founded in the 1940s, I stopped to get gas. Then I headed up into the mountains. Ten minutes later, the windows were fogged. I put on the defogger, which rattles. I turned on the music to drown out the defogger, but I couldn't get any stations because of the static. And I was freezing. I cranked the heat, then checked the thermometer. Two degrees below zero, which was impossible. One more thing to fix.

By the time I'd approached the junction to the 138, I was deep into the forest, majestic trees surrounding me on all sides, sunlight streaming through the branches, then hiding behind the clouds. Instead of going east, however, I veered west, toward Wrightwood, a tiny community nestled in the San Gabriels at the edge of the Angeles National Forest, which is where the bodies get dumped. Google it.

Day-old snow lined the side of the road as I drove through the sweet little town, with its one coffee house, still draped in Christmas lights; one needlepoint shop, with its teddy bear–themed window; and one traffic light. No one was around except for a pair of stray dogs digging through a trash can, but maybe they were coyotes. Dotting the hills were vintage log cabins, as well as newer homes with unique personalities: Bavarian ski chalet meets Clan of the Cave Bear, neo-Victorian manse with hacienda vibe, modernist A-frame/bomb shelter. Southern California is all about choice.

At Pine Canyon, I took a sharp left. The trees were now so dense you couldn't see sky. I slowed at a dirt road marked by a jumble of signs: "Private Road," "Private Property," "No Trespassing," "Road Closed." Someone had already removed the chain and left it hanging, which I took as an invitation. As I bumped along, I saw the burned-out remains of somebody's vacation getaway. A quarter of a mile further, a pick-up truck abandoned in the snow. And then, on my left, nearly hidden behind the towering pines, cedars, and oaks, a one-story cabin from the thirties with a shingled roof and a shallow front porch.

I pulled up in front and studied the place. The curtains were drawn and the lights were off. At the foot of the steps were two wooden statues: a six-foot cigar-store Indian, and a leaping dolphin. Didn't seem like Ray's taste, but people are complicated.

That's right.

This was Uncle Ray's cabin.

He'd bought it cheap years ago, in the bad old days when he was part of the CRASH unit, and the Rampart Division cops were just another gang. It was someplace he could lay low, away from the gangbangers, not to mention colleagues with divided loyalties. And no one knew it existed. Not even Gram.

Ray told me about it during the worst time of my life, right after Luke Cutt and I had split up. The paparazzi were camped out on my doorstep, desperate to get a shot of me crying or drinking to excess or sleeping around. Mea culpa. After watching me act out for a solid two weeks, Ray came over and handed me a key. He swore me to secrecy, then told me I could come here whenever I needed to. But I'd never needed to. Until now.

I cut the motor and stepped outside, breathing into my hands to warm them up, then popped the trunk and pulled out my jacket.

It was quiet. The birds had all gone home. The squirrels playing in the brush took one look at me and scampered away. But maybe it was the wind, which was whipping up the leaves with brutal efficiency. This was the kind of blustery day that makes you want to hole up with someone you love, not that I had such a person in my life. But today wasn't about me. It was about Gram and Ray. They belonged together. But that wasn't going to happen until Ray's name was cleared, which is why I was here.

No footprints or tire tread in the driveway. I took the steps up to the house two at a time. No footprints on the porch either. I reached into the pocket of my jeans, pulled out the key, and let myself in.

"Hello?" I called out.

No one was there.

And from the looks of it, hadn't been in some time.

The living room was kind of on the austere side, with a La-Z-Boy recliner in cracked tan pleather and a corduroy couch to match. Draped over the back of the couch was a Pendleton blanket, which looked itchy. No T.V. No jigsaw puzzle or checkers board. No books or magazines. A blue rag rug where the coffee table should have been.

I checked the kitchen. The cupboards were neatly stacked with plain white dishes. The sink was empty, as was the dishwasher. I lifted the lid of the coffeemaker. Clean and dry. Ray's a caffeine addict, like me. If he'd been here, he'd have made coffee.

The bedroom was down the hall. The bed didn't look particularly inviting. I pulled up the blue velveteen spread. Hospital corners. Ray had learned in the army, and taught me when I was a kid. It looks tricky, but all it takes is practice.

The washer and dryer were tucked into the utility closet in the hallway. I opened the door, checked both of them. Empty. Nothing in the lint trap either. I picked up the mop. Dry as a bone. Ditto the bucket. Looked like this pit stop was a bust.

The bathroom had the feel of a Holiday Inn Express, with some wrapped soaps and a little emergency kit. I grabbed a couple of sheets of toilet paper and blew my nose, tossed the paper into the trash. Then I stopped short. Sitting at the bottom of the can was a cup from Starbucks. I bent down, and picked it up.

There was a name scrawled on the side in black Sharpie.

"Ray" was what it said.

So he *had* been here.

Unfortunately, I had no way of knowing when, or why he'd left the cup behind when the place was otherwise so immaculate. I marched back outside, and checked the garbage cans.

The black one was empty. The blue one was empty. The green one was full of wet leaves.

He'd been here, but not long enough to generate any garbage.

Odd.

I stood there for a minute, shivering, then went back inside and took a seat on the La-Z-Boy. I closed my eyes, leaned all the way back, nearly fell over, then popped back up. I couldn't think in here. It was too cold. I reached over to grab the Pendleton blanket, and as I shook it out, something flew through the air and landed on the rug.

Something yellow.

A mini legal pad.

I got up, picked it up, turned to the front page.

And there was Lizeth Pimentel's name and number, scrawled in red ink.

Okay.

This was clearly the pad Destiny had seen in the back of the Miles's black stretch Bentley. Had Ray broken in and taken it? He could easily have tracked down the car. I'd given him the license plate number myself. But why would he have thought to do that?

And if he had thought to do that, why would he have left something so potentially explosive just lying around for anyone to find?

He wouldn't have.

Ray is not a careless person.

Which meant that it wasn't Ray who'd been here.

Someone else had been here.

Someone who knew this place existed.

Someone who knew how to cover his tracks.

Someone who knew that if the pad were found here, along with the coffee cup, Ray would be in so deep he'd never be able to get out.

It was kind of brilliant, really. This person had covered every angle. I mean, he must've realized it was kind of shady that my uncle even owned this place. And here was the final nail in the coffin. This person had tipped off Lieutenant Hepworth. That was why the latter was calling me so frantically. He was probably already on his way.

I grabbed the legal pad and shoved it into my basket, then grabbed the Starbucks cup and shoved it in there, too. And noticed, as I did, that there was an order scrawled on it.

2 CH/S/L.

Double Chai soy latte.

That wasn't my uncle's drink.

Ray liked coffee, and he took it black, as God intended it.

That was Miles McCoy's drink.

Chapter 38

THIS TIME OF year, the sun sets close to five, which didn't leave me much time. After locking up the cabin, I hopped back into the car and retraced my steps to the 15, periodically checking the mirror for cars that might be following a bit too closely. Such as Lieutenant Hepworth's, for example. I wondered if he'd left the department vehicle at home and taken his own ride, like Will Smith in *Bad Boys II* (Ferrari) or Danny Glover in *Lethal Weapon II* (wife's station wagon). Although maybe with that eye he didn't drive. Such things can affect depth perception. In any case, I'm happy to report that no one was following me. Sort of happy. Because now there was no excuse not to continue east, toward Lake Arrowhead.

Lake Arrowhead was where I was going to find Big Fatty.

First, though, I had to navigate the Rim of the World.

The Rim of the World Highway traverses the crest of the San Bernardinos, offering panoramic views of the verdant valley below. It is also the place where buses filled with hapless tourists regularly plunge over the edge during storms. Thus, the rapid-fire series of signs reading, "Carry Chains," "4-W Drive with Snow

Tires OK," and "No Exceptions." Unfortunately, I hadn't come prepared for the elements. At the first hairpin turn, my head started to swim. At the second, I broke out in a cold sweat. White-knuckling the steering wheel, I scanned the horizon for a fixed point, but we were rapidly gaining elevation, and there wasn't one. I turned off the radio, and for the next eight miles drove in silence, eyes squinting, back hunched, up until the very moment I passed a "Chains Required" sign—to which someone had added, "Whips Optional"—and I actually laughed out loud. Two minutes later, I hit the turnoff for Lake Arrowhead.

At the first traffic light, I loosened my death grip and took a look around. I saw green trees. A brilliant blue sky. Snow-dusted rooftops sparkling in the sun. A father and a son in matching flannel shirts loading fishing rods into the back of a shiny red pick-up. It was straight out of Norman Rockwell. What could possibly go wrong?

Big Fatty's house was on the east side of the lake, between Orchard and Emerald Bay. I'd looked it up on Trulia. Nothing but the best for Fatty. After getting out of jail, he'd retired to a 1929 lakefront classic that had been remodeled into a five-bedroom, six-bathroom "luxe meets lodge," which included a Shrek-scaled stone fireplace, vaulted ceilings, and an unholy profusion of mahogany paneling. The pièce de résistance was the rooster-themed kitchen, which featured two refrigerators, two dishwashers, and half a dozen barstools made of Châteauneuf-du-Pape wine barrels. The house also came with its own dock and a double slip so Fatty could have his choice of vessels when he was in the mood for some recreational boating.

I parked my car at a discreet distance, then strolled down the densely wooded street, stopping directly opposite the house, which backed onto the lake. There was a flat private driveway in front, as well as a footbridge with a lily pond below. Then there were the gates. That would be the ten-foot gates with the nasty-looking metal spikes on top. There were also signs. One read: "WARNING: PRIVATE PROPERTY." Another read: "NO TRESPASSING." And then, for unwelcome visitors who didn't speak English, there was a sign with a drawing of a guard dog. The specks of saliva on his massive jaw added to the verisimilitude.

For want of a better idea, I started snapping pictures, and that's when the security car cruised by. Forgot about those guys. In neighborhoods like these, there are not only security cars cruising at regular intervals, there are cameras—mounted inside light fixtures, camouflaged by bushes, affixed to the undersides of pilasters. If I lingered too long in any one spot some nosy neighbor was going to call it in to the authorities. Consequences would ensue. This was the crucial moment. I needed to ring Big Fatty's bell, or get a move on.

I rang Big Fatty's bell.

"*Si?*" came a voice over the intercom.

"Is Mr. Sims at home? I'm an old friend. He's expecting me." And if he wasn't, maybe he should've been. There's no escaping Destiny—D-Low, that is.

The voice came back. "Sorry, miss. Nobody home."

"Do you know when he'll be back? Hello? Hello?"

I rang the bell again, but she wasn't particularly receptive. I had several options left.

I could pretend to be a lawyer representing someone who'd left Fatty a bequest.

I could pretend to be the UPS guy.

I could pretend to have an aneurysm.

I could go down to the dock via the public access road and peek inside the house from the other side.

It was sort of a no-brainer.

I descended the steep pathway, grabbing at random branches to steady myself as the dirt shifted under my feet. The goat hair après-ski boots turned out to be somewhat impractical. No tread. Plus, they weren't waterproof, so by the time I'd skidded my way down to the lake my feet were soaked. The boots weren't my only problem. Unless I was prepared to whack my way across a wooded slope without a machete, then scale a fifty-foot vertical retaining wall without a harness or ropes, I wasn't getting anywhere near Fatty's house.

The dock, however, was unsecured. All I had to do was lift a latch and I was in. Kind of foolish actually, considering there was a fancy powerboat parked in the double slip that somebody who knew what they were doing could totally make off with. I couldn't read the boat's name because it was obscured by some plastic sheeting. I crouched down to get a better look, but I never did figure it out. Or get to admire the spectacular view. Because by that point I was distracted by something I saw in the water. Admittedly, I'd just read Chandler's *Lady in the Lake*, but it looked an awful lot like a dead body.

I found a skinny branch, then parked myself at the edge of the water and poked gingerly, then more aggressively, at the thing that looked like a dead body. It had no heft. That was a good sign. Dead bodies have heft, especially water-logged ones. I poked at it a couple more times and then, all of a sudden, the thing that looked like a dead body shot out of the water and landed with a splat on the dock.

It was an inflatable sex doll.

Now seemed like a good time to regroup.

The hunt for the elusive Big Fatty was not going particularly well. I was out of ideas. Getting a headache. Feeling cranky. Hoping to boost my morale and blood sugar, I repaired to the Ye Olde Shopping Plaza (not its real name). After putting my name down at the waffle house, I took a stroll around, past a variety of tchotchke shops, a Wells Fargo, and a Jockey outlet store, in case a person lacked an internet connection and wanted to load up on men's underpants. Then I checked my phone. One text from Cat, who'd decided she was going to sleep with the Snapchat exec with the facial hair, as an experiment. She'd report back in the morning. Hurray for love. No, really.

I grabbed copies of the *L.A. Times* and the *Mountain News* as the hostess finally escorted me to my table. There were seventeen types of waffles to choose from. I decided on the Peanutty Belgian, which combined healthy fat, protein, and an anti-oxidant (chocolate). Then I paged through the newspapers. The *Times* was full of the usual fare: political corruption, real estate chicanery, morning fog clearing by midday. The *Mountain News* was a more exotic beast. The top story was the evacuation of the local Von's due to a broken sprinkler head, which had leaked onto the wiring and set off the smoke alarms. I also enjoyed the headline reading, "Local high school's septic system takes a dump." Who said journalism is dead? Then I turned to the page with the classifieds. And something caught my eye.

I grabbed my phone, did some quick Googling.

Oh, yes.

A waffle can change everything.

I knew *exactly* where Fatty was going to be at 9 p.m. tonight.

And I was going to be waiting.

Chapter 39

THE DOOR TO the quaint Tudor-style inn swung open.

Bracken Fern Manor.

The front desk clerk, who looked like he'd wandered in off the set of *Twilight: Breaking Dawn*, gave me a supercilious look.

"Excuse me," I said. "I was wondering if you had a room available?"

"We're fully committed." A small black cat jumped up onto his paperwork. "Hello, pretty," he murmured.

I propped my elbows on the desk, leaned in. "Listen, all I need is a broom closet."

"Sorry." He scratched the cat behind the ears. "Destination wedding."

I'd surmised. The small lobby was festooned with pink and white balloons, pink and white honeycombed bells, and a glittery banner strung across the fireplace that read, "Sheena and Alasdair Forever." However, I needed a nap before I faced Big Fatty tonight, and I'd tried every other motel and B&B in town. Plus, this place happened to be the most geographically desirable.

"Oh, man," I said. "I've been out of the country, and didn't have a chance to mail in my R.S.V.P., and now"—I mumbled something incoherent that could have been John, Jason, or Josh, having once read that a disproportionate number of names start with J—".is going to be *sooo* disappointed."

"Excuse me?" Sitting by the fireplace was a young woman who looked like Courtney Love circa Hole. "Sorry to eavesdrop, but did you say *Jim?*"

Worked like a charm.

I spun around, smiled. "That's exactly what I said."

The woman leapt to her feet. "I can't believe it! You're the famous *Ellie!*"

She said it. I didn't.

"I've heard so much about you from my brother!" She ran over and enveloped me in a hug. "We didn't think you could come! And with him out of phone contact in that village in Borneo."

Borneo.

"Do not say another word." She put her hands on my shoulders and gave me a little squeeze. "What you two lovebirds have been doing is amazing. Providing access to clean water and sanitation." She blinked back a tear. "I'm like in awe."

"Awe" was a big word.

She smiled coyly. "And I haven't even had a chance to congratulate you on *your* engagement!"

"No worries," I said wanly.

"Where's your ring?" she asked.

I looked at the empty place on the fourth finger of my left hand. "There was no time."

"Of course not," she said. "You guys are saving the world!"

The woman—whom I now believed to be the bride, Sheena—

turned to the front desk clerk, who was brushing large flakes of dandruff from the lapels of his Edwardian frock coat. "My brides-maids will double up. You can give Ellie one of their rooms."

"So happy to be able to accommodate you." The clerk narrowed his dark-lidded gaze. *Ellie.*

I gathered up my things, and promised Sheena I'd try to make it to the wine tasting before everyone headed across the street for the big show at nine. Sheena also reminded me that immediate family—which now included me, her future sister-in-law—would be seated in the front.

On the way up to the second floor, the clerk gave me a potted history of Bracken Fern Manor. It was part of a large resort built in the 1920s by Bugsy Siegel, who created it as an escape for Hollywood stars looking for a place to indulge their vices unobserved. We were standing on the site of the former brothel. The wine cave around back was where they used to store the moonshine. Tudor House across the street—now a dinner theater—was the casino. All were connected by a network of long-defunct underground tunnels.

"Voilà." The clerk opened the door to my room.

It was modest in scale, almost spartan. It reminded me of a college dorm, only for working girls. Like in that Tori Spelling movie.

"This room used to belong to Violet, who broke house rules by sleeping with the maintenance man." The clerk wagged his finger. "Bugsy wasn't happy so he had one of his goons toss the guy out the window. Violet was so upset she killed herself. And now she haunts the place."

"Naturally," I said.

"I'm detecting some skepticism," the clerk said. "But there's no denying the evidence. A few months ago we had a small flood and closed for the day. When I came back, there was a violet-scented candle mysteriously burning in here. Who do you suppose lit it? And how did it stay lit for so long?"

Sounded like the miracle of Hannukah, but I kept my mouth shut.

Several hours later, there was a knock at my door.

"Ellie. It's me."

I roused myself from bed and opened the door. Sheena was standing there, trembling.

"Come in. You look like you've seen a ghost." Not that I believed in them.

She sat down on the bed next to me, plucking nervously at the hem of her blue satin baby doll dress.

I rubbed the sleep out of my eyes. "Everything okay?"

"I guess."

"You can tell me."

"It's probably just cold feet. I'm so afraid, you know?"

I totally knew.

She started pacing. "I mean, can we ever really know another person? For example, Alasdair. I thought he was over his ex-girlfriend, but then I find a text from her on his phone."

"What did it say?"

She chewed on her lip. "She said that she was happy he was happy with me."

"That's it?"

"Yeah."

"I don't think that's much to worry about." This sister-in-law thing wasn't so hard.

"That isn't all. I always thought Alasdair was frugal, and I'm fine with that. I'm frugal, too. I mean, we're lucky if we can make our bills. But then he goes and does this super-extravagant thing I told him not to."

"What's that?"

She walked over to the mirror and fussed with her hair. "He went behind my back and ordered a car to take us to the church tomorrow morning. And of all things, a black stretch Bentley. God knows how expensive that's gonna be."

A black stretch Bentley.

What was *Miles* doing here?

I guess the answer was pretty obvious.

"When did you see it?" I asked her.

"Like two hours ago. When I went downstairs to get an ice bucket."

I rushed over to the window and peered out. "Where was it parked?"

"Right across the street." She came and stood next to me, looked outside. "Huh. It's gone. Maybe it wasn't Alasdair after all." She laughed. "Well, now I'm disappointed. Like, am I not worth it?"

"Listen, Sheena, I kind of wanted to . . ." I pushed her toward the door.

"I get it. No problem. I'm going."

She opened the door, then turned around. "You know, I can't believe my brother never told me how much you look like that girl from the song."

"Dreama," I said. "I get that all the time."

Sheena laughed. "How embarrassing. I mean, that song is so cheesy."

This girl was starting to irritate me. "Totally."

After she left, I put on my jacket and hat and slipped down to the lobby. It was a cozy scene. There were grayish cookies on a tray, the player piano was plinking out the theme song from *The Exorcist*, and the cat was writhing frenetically in what I hoped was catnip.

"Just getting some stuff from my car," I said breezily.

The clerk tucked some greasy strands behind his ears and shrugged.

It was dark outside. There were no streetlamps, and the crescent moon was shrouded in mist. I walked down the steps, careful not to slip on the wet asphalt, and took a quick look around. There were three or four compact cars in the lot, plus one van (not white) parked at the rear. No black stretch Bentley. I wrapped my coat tighter around my body and dashed across the street.

The Tudor House, like Bracken Fern, was calculated to ingratiate, with its cutesy half-timbers and dormer windows. The parking lot had more handicapped spots than I'd ever seen in one place. Maybe they got an older clientele. Aside from one blue truck, however, the lot was empty.

I turned on the flashlight on my phone, then climbed a short flight of steps. When I got to the top, the door swung open and out came a workman carrying a ladder.

"We open in another hour, miss," he said.

"Were you in there setting up?"

"Fixing the lights," he said. "Is there something I can do for you?"

I gave him a smile. "Just looking for my ride."

"What kind of car?"

"A black stretch Bentley," I said. "Seen it around here?"

He shook his head. "Flashy car like that I'd have noticed. Not too much going on around here."

I was hoping it would stay that way.

There was still an hour to go before the show. I supposed I had no choice but to drop in on Sheena and Alasdair's wine tasting. Whatever. After everything that had happened I probably deserved a free glass of Chardonnay.

The door to the wine cave was closed. I knocked a couple of times, then pushed it open.

It was dark in there. I couldn't see a thing. I felt around for a light switch, but couldn't find one.

"Where is everybody?" I called out.

I half expected the lights to go on and my friends and family to pop out of the woodwork, but my birthday was months away, not to mention nobody I knew had the vaguest inkling I was here in Lake Arrowhead, which was kind of a problem, now that I'd thought about it. Anyway, I'd obviously missed the wine tasting. Oh, well. Maybe there was some sherry in the lobby.

I turned to go, and then, all at once, I felt a rush of air, I tripped over something, I fell onto the stone floor, and something very heavy, very wet, and very sharp came crashing down on top of me.

After that, all I saw was stars.

Chapter 40

"ELLIE! WAKE UP!" a voice pleaded.

Who was Ellie? I wondered.

"Just do it," said another voice.

Suddenly, I felt a stinging sensation. My eyes blinked open and my hand flew up to my cheek.

"Sorry, Ellie." Sheena was crouched beside me, her brows knit in concern. "It was either slap you, or dump cold water on you."

I turned my head, looked around. "Where am I? What happened?"

"Can you sit up?" She put her arm around my shoulder.

As I sat up, a shower of glass rained down onto my lap.

"Oh, my god," she said. "You're lucky you're not dead."

I looked down at my clothes. "Is that . . . *blood*?"

"Cabernet Sauvignon," said the bespectacled young man standing with Sheena, whom I was presuming to be Alasdair, the fiancé. "We're in the wine cave. A shelf fell over. It was filled with dozens of bottles."

"*Expensive* bottles," the clerk added, his pale face slick with sweat. "Pinot Noirs. Syrahs. Malbecs."

"No whites?" I asked.

The clerk fixed his gaze on me. "*Somebody's* got to pay for them."

Alasdair and Sheena exchanged worried glances.

This vampire had a lot of chutzpah. I picked a couple of shards of glass off my legs, then struggled to my feet. My head was pounding, and I had a small cut on my hand, but aside from that, I appeared to be fine.

"Isn't that what insurance is for?" I asked him. "To cover property damage, yes, but also in case an unsecured piece of furniture falls over and someone gets hurt, then takes you for everything you're worth, leaving your small business in shambles?"

That shut him up.

Alisdair said, "I think maybe you tripped. Simple accident. No one's to blame."

Sheena pointed mutely to a pink and white noisemaker on the floor.

So I'd tripped on a plastic party favor, then tumbled headlong into a massive piece of wood cabinetry twenty feet away, causing it to topple to the ground, missing me by mere inches? I'm no Einstein, but I didn't think the physics was going to pencil out.

Sheena said, "C'mon, everybody. All's well that ends well." She looked at her watch, then at me. "The show's going to start in half an hour. We should get you cleaned up. Your clothes are ruined."

"I don't have anything to change into." All I had in the back of my car were my wet boots and my Bunny Lebowski bikini, and the latter wasn't going to cut it in temperatures well below freezing.

"What are sisters for?" asked Sheena.

Twenty minutes later, I was posing for pictures with the happy couple's nearest and dearest, decked out in a wrinkled white slip dress, Mary Jane pumps, and a rhinestone tiara on loan from Sheena's seemingly vast archive of kinderwhore classics. I looked like I'd been beamed down from 1994.

"Can I get everybody in front of the fireplace for one last shot?" asked the photographer.

We were gathered in the front half of the former casino, which had been transformed into a supper club, with vaulted ceilings, a stage on one end, and against the near wall a seventy-ton rock fireplace that wouldn't have been out of place in a medieval castle. Above it was a mural depicting the local flora and fauna—a bear, an elk, a wolf, and an eagle soaring over a lake with a wintry little cabin. Which looked exactly like my uncle Ray's.

It was important to remember why I'd taken this road trip.

People were dead, relationships had been broken, lives destroyed.

And it wasn't over.

"Here's the head table," Sheena said. "Let's sit. I'm so excited about the show."

"Last month, we saw True Willie here," said Alasdair. "They're a Willie Nelson tribute band."

"My parents heard the real Willie Nelson once," Sheena said. "Not so great."

"We do, however, support his marijuana entrepreneurialism," said Alasdair. "What Paul Newman did for salad dressing, Willie Nelson's going to do for weed."

I was more interested in tonight's headliner.

Wilby Goodrich.

The name had jumped out at me when I was at the waffle house, flipping through the *Mountain News*, and I'd stumbled upon Tudor House's calendar of events. I'd typed the name into Google. The singer Wilby Goodrich did not have a website. But several other things had popped up.

A Wilby Goodrich who worked in P.R. in New Mexico.

A Wilby Goodrich who'd won a golf tournament in Greenwich, Connecticut.

Several BFGoodrich tire dealers.

But none of those was what I was after so I searched alternate spellings.

Nothing came up for Willby Goodrich with two *ls*. Nothing for Wil*bur* Goodrich either. Finally, I tried Will B. Goodrich. And that was when I hit pay dirt.

Will B. Goodrich was the alias taken by the disgraced silent film actor Roscoe "Fatty" Arbuckle.

How clever he was.

I'm not talking about Fatty Arbuckle.

I'm talking about Big Fatty.

He'd taken the exact same alias.

But here's the interesting part.

In 1921, Fatty Arbuckle was accused of raping and killing starlet Virginia Rappe after a two-day bacchanal at a hotel in San Francisco. It destroyed his career. He was shamed by the press, heckled in the street, blacklisted by the studio, bled dry by the lawyers. But after two mistrials, he was found innocent of all crimes. In fact, the jury went so far as to offer an apology for besmirching his good name.

That's right.

It was a smear job.

Fatty Arbuckle hadn't raped anyone.

Was Big Fatty trying to let the world know he hadn't raped anyone either?

And was Miles here to stop him?

Chapter 41

I'D NEVER HAVE recognized him.

The man who swaggered onto the Tudor House stage, grinning behind his dark-tinted aviators, bore no resemblance whatsoever to the pictures I'd seen of Big Fatty.

This man was in phenomenal shape, and not particularly modest about it. He was wearing a black, form-fitting T-shirt that showed off his well-developed pecs, and dark denims that were baggy enough to be street, but not so baggy they weren't sexy. "Sexy" was the operative word.

"Good evening." His voice was low, equal parts gravel and cream. "Y'all ready to have a good time?"

They were. Especially the ladies. I looked over at Sheena and her bridesmaids and they were slack-jawed. He had them eating out of his hand before he sang a single note.

And then there was the music.

Big Fatty—Wilby Goodrich, I mean—had not only transformed his body, he'd swapped gangster rap for uptown funk. I'm talking R&B-

inspired, gospel-infused, get a room and make a baby music. Think the Reverend Al Green. Think Marvin Gaye. Then throw in some T.I. and R. Kelly to make it clear that this wasn't your mother's slow jam.

I enjoyed the show. Really I did.

It was professional, slick, and—lineage aside—completely and utterly soulless.

Whatever else he was, Big Fatty was a visionary.

But Wilby Goodrich was a hack.

By the time I came back from the bathroom, he'd performed his encore. The night, however, was far from over. The audience was chanting his name, and tossing flowers from the vases on their tables. He couldn't get enough. The man had lost two hundred pounds, but he was still hungry.

"Sweet Jesus." He gave the audience a wicked grin. "What do y'all think? That I can go all night?"

More cheers.

"I see we've got a wedding party here." The "Bridezilla" sash Sheena was wearing must've given it away. "How about a request from the bride-to-be?"

One of Sheena's bridesmaids whispered, "'Just the Way You Are,' by Bruno Mars?"

The other one whispered, "'What You Need,' by The Weeknd?"

Sheena turned to me. "What do you think?"

I downed some liquid courage, then looked up at the former Big Fatty, and said, "I want to hear the Velvet Underground's 'I'll Be Your Mirror.' Can you do that for me?"

I saw the confusion register on his face. But only for a second. Then he bared his big, white teeth. "That ain't the only thing I can do for you, sweetheart."

When he was done singing, he shook a few hands, took a few pictures, and signed a few autographs. Then he crooked his finger at me, summoning me to the other side of the red velvet curtain.

That's the thing about us groupies.

We know how to get backstage.

Chapter 42

"HAVE A SEAT." Fatty whipped a sheet off of a tapestried ottoman. "I'll be right back."

Before I could object, he'd disappeared down a spiral staircase.

One minute, then I was going after him.

I took a quick look around. Not much to see backstage except wedding paraphernalia: wicker trellises, papier maché cupids, iced branches wrapped in tulle. Some of it was haphazardly covered in sheets, the rest was blanketed in dust. Backstage looked like the place love went to die.

But if I closed my eyes I could imagine it in Bugsy Siegel's day, a vast open space crammed with movie stars in evening dress, smoking, drinking, and losing money at the roulette wheel or the craps table. Then it was off to the brothel for more good, clean fun.

Fatty's grace period was up.

There was no railing, and the staircase was steep and rickety. Down below was the basement, a rabbit warren of rooms lit up by some bulbs dangling from cords, all snaking into a single power strip. Talk about a fire hazard. At the far end I could see a couple of stacks of cardboard boxes, and a pile of dirt blocking off a corridor. Must've been one of the old tunnels.

"That you, sweetheart?"

A door swung open, banging against the wall. The sound echoed through the dank space. I followed it into a makeshift dressing room. Fatty was seated on a folding chair, his back to me.

"It's cold down here," I said.

Fatty pulled on a clean T-shirt, then slapped some cologne on his freshly shaven face. "Relax. Daddy'll warm you right up."

"I don't think so."

"Yeah. I had a feeling." He caught my eye in the mirror. "How'd you find me?"

"I asked around," I said.

"No such thing as privacy these days. And you should know. Tabloids ate you up and spit you out, didn't they?"

So he knew who I was. I guess that made us even.

"I'm still standing," I said.

"No surprise there. You got looks, money, family. Most of us don't have it so easy."

"Spare me," I said.

He spun around in his chair. "Who do you think you're talking to?" Then he stood up. "I think you'd better stop playing and tell me why you're here." He came closer. "I know I look good, but I don't think it's 'cause you want to fuck me."

The mask was slipping.

I hadn't expected it to happen so fast.

"I'm here because people have been hurt." I backed away.

"You scared of me?" he asked.

"A little," I answered truthfully.

"I'm not gonna lay a finger on you. Beer?"

"No, thanks."

He popped open a bottle and took a slug.

"Please stop," I said. "Maybe you didn't hear me. Lives have been ruined. Somebody is *dead*. You can help make it right."

"Why me?"

I waited a beat. "Because of Carmen Luz."

"'Forget the former things,'" he said. "'Do not dwell on the past.'"

"Excuse me?"

"Isaiah 43:18–19. 'See, I am doing a new thing! Now it springs up; do you not perceive it?'"

"Are you asking me a question?"

He slapped his hand on the table, hard enough to send his beer crashing to the floor. "Fuck, no! I'm a Christian! I left the bad shit behind when I got out of prison. I renewed my body and I renewed my soul. I walk with the Lord now. That's why I call myself Wilby Goodrich. *Will B. Good*. Do you not understand?"

"I get it. Fatty Arbuckle. It's pretty interesting your taking his alias."

"We have a lot in common," he said carefully.

"You see yourself as a martyr."

"*Jesus* was a martyr. I don't compare myself to the Lord. I'm grateful for his forgiveness and love."

"You can stop now. I know you didn't rape Carmen Luz."

He looked surprised that I was willing to come out and say it. But I was getting impatient.

"Say something," I said.

He shook his head. "You're some kind of crazy, aren't you? Yeah, I raped her. But I've paid my debt to society. That shit is over."

"The evidence was compromised. And I'll bet I know just who messed with it."

"D.N.A. doesn't lie."

"Sure it does," I said.

D.N.A. lies.

Cops lie.

People lie.

"Dreama, little Dreama." He stood right in front of me. I could feel his breath on my face. Then he leaned forward and whispered in my ear, "You're so goddamn smart, then tell me. If I didn't rape her, who did?"

He was daring me to say it.

So I did.

"Miles McCoy," I said. "He told me everything."

Now Fatty was the one backing away. "I'm leaving. I got people waiting for me."

I ignored him. "Miles raped his girlfriend Carmen Luz, and then he had you take the fall for him."

Fatty put his head in his hands. "Shut up."

"And as payment," I pressed on, "he bought you a big house to live in."

When I'd looked up Fatty's house, I'd found the owner of record. Dixon Steele, LLC. Dixon Steele was the name of the down-on-his-luck screenwriter played by Humphrey Bogart in Nicholas Ray's noir masterpiece *In A Lonely Place*. Miles couldn't resist an inside joke. Well, that's what I'd thought at first. Then I'd realized that he'd been waiting for someone to figure it out. And that on some level he wanted to be caught.

"Was it worth it, Freddy?" I asked.

"I told you to shut up."

"I don't even know what to call you. Freddy? Fatty? Wilby? You keep changing your name, but you can't run away from what you did. You let a rapist go free."

Fatty sank down into his chair. He was exhausted. Exhausted after spending two years in prison for something he didn't do. Exhausted after covering it up for years after that.

"It isn't so simple," he finally said.

"Then why don't you explain? I want to understand."

He had his back to me. He was staring at himself in the mirror. Maybe he was finally ready to see who he was.

"I'd been out partying that night with a couple of buddies," he said. "Carmen was there, too. Girl liked to have a good time, you know what I'm saying? No harm in that. We were all adults."

Carmen had been all of twenty-one at the time.

"We wound up at her place. We were messed up on molly, coke, tequila, you name it. But everybody was chill. Having a good time, you know? Then her sugar daddy shows up. Miles McCoy. I knew him only by reputation. Pretentious asshole who thinks his shit doesn't smell. Anyway, he isn't exactly happy to see her all *shit-faced*, with a bunch of strangers. I don't need any trouble so I leave. A couple hours later, the phone rings. Two in the fucking morning."

He didn't have to tell me that it was Pee Chee Lowenstein. The mastermind behind his thwarted comeback.

"We go back a ways, me and Pee Chee," he said. "She wrote about me when she was at *Spin*. I remember the day that article came out." He snorted out a laugh. "I thought I'd hit the jackpot. I didn't know *shit* about this business, turns out. It isn't for folks like me, with tender hearts."

I wasn't about to deny him his illusions. Not when I still needed him.

"Long and short of it," he said, "I didn't become who I was sup-posed to become. Things got a little out of hand. I wound up going inside. It was hard that first time. Even for a gangsta like me. When I got out, nobody was there for me, except for Pee Chee. She'd just been fired from her magazine job and we got together. We under-stood each other. We had plans. We were going to put an album together. We were going to show everybody." He shook his head. "Another fucking disaster."

He was losing focus. "What exactly did Pee Chee say when she called?"

"That she needed me. That I was the only one who could help. She'd found Miles on the floor. He'd gone through a couple of bottles of bourbon, and blacked out. When he woke up, he didn't remember what he'd done to his girlfriend. Which was beat her ass and rape her and leave her to die."

Jesus.

He was telling me what I already knew, but that didn't make it any easier to hear.

"At first," Fatty said, "I didn't get why Pee Chee was telling me. She started going on about my career, how it was over, how I wasn't getting another shot, how I had to face reality. I had no fucking idea why this woman was pouring salt in the wound. Then she started in on wouldn't I like to get away from all the vultures in L.A.? Wouldn't I like to have some peace and quiet? Wouldn't I like to finally get clean?"

"All you had to do," I supplied, "was spend a little time in prison."

He sighed. "She said Miles couldn't survive prison, but I'd done it before and I could do it again. And if I did this one, lousy favor for them I could have everything I ever wanted. I could have a car,

I could have a boat, I could have a beautiful house on a beautiful fucking lake."

"You'd just been at Carmen's that night. Your D.N.A. was all over. It was the perfect setup."

"Until now," Fatty turned around. "Until you showed up here."

"No," I replied. "Until Maya figured it out."

"Maya Duran?"

"Miles's fiancée."

"I know her from way back. She was a dancer."

"She worked with you on 'I'll Be Your Mirror,'" I said. "I saw footage from that night. It was amazing."

He nodded. "Damn shame the girl tried to kill herself."

"She didn't. Miles tried to kill her. I think so, at least. He couldn't trust her to stay quiet."

Poor Sleeping Beauty.

Disney may have given her a storybook ending, but in the original version, the prince doesn't save the princess.

He rapes her while she's sleeping.

"And then there was the third girl," I said. "Lizeth Pimentel."

Fatty closed his eyes. "Carmen, Maya, and Lizeth. All of them sweet enough to make your teeth ache." He looked at me. "What happened to Lizeth?"

"She's dead."

He said, "Fucking Miles McCoy."

All of a sudden, the bulbs out in the corridor started flickering, then went out.

And Big Fatty and I were left there, alone in the dark.

Chapter 43

"Must be the wind," Fatty said. "Got a match?"

I rifled through my basket, but couldn't find one.

"Never mind," he said. "Come with me."

We stumbled out into the pitch-black corridor. Fatty made his way over to the cardboard boxes, and dug around in the top one until he found a flashlight. Then he flicked it on.

Standing there, illuminated by a beam of light, was Pee Chee Lowenstein.

With a gun in her hand.

I froze as the bulbs overhead sputtered back to life.

"Nice tiara," she said to me.

Fatty handed her the flashlight, stretched his arms behind his head, yawned.

Pee Chee tucked the flashlight into the belt of her neon yellow jumpsuit. She'd obviously dressed for the occasion.

"It's been a long time, Freddy." Her eyes ran up and down his newly sculpted body. "I've got to hand it to you. It takes a lot of self-discipline to do what you did. Too bad you couldn't keep your mouth shut when it really mattered."

Fatty cocked his head at me. "You talking about her? She's not a problem."

Pee Chee tightened her grip on her gun. "No, you're the problem. We had a deal."

"I held up my end," he said. "I could've come back for more. I could've bled you fuckers dry. Lucky for you my vice is lust, not greed."

Lust, not greed.

Oh, my god.

I'd gotten the whole thing wrong.

I'd listened to the lies Fatty was spewing without questioning why he was so eager to spew them.

It wasn't *Miles* who'd raped Carmen.

It had been *Fatty* all along.

I looked at him, and he could see in my eyes that I knew the truth.

"Bitch wanted it," he said with a shrug.

Pee Chee shook her head. "This is *exactly* why you keep fucking up, Freddy."

"I served my time," he said. "I don't have to pretend anymore."

She said, "The problem is your lack of discretion. It's like Miles always says. Discretion is the one thing that can't be taught."

"Miles, Miles, Miles." Fatty rolled his eyes. "All this time and you can't shut up about the man. You're fucking pathetic."

Pee Chee raised an eyebrow. "I believe you're the one who's fucking pathetic. As I remember, it wasn't me who made a phone call at two in the morning with blood on my hands. It was you."

Fatty spat out, "Don't act like you did *me* some kind of favor. I was the one who did *you* a favor."

Suddenly, the last piece of the puzzle clicked into place.

Fatty calls Pee Chee at 2 a.m. He tells her what he did to Carmen. He needs her help. She's a fixer, after all. Pee Chee tells him to calm down. That he's come to the right person. Pee Chee Lowenstein is indeed the right person. Because she knows an opportunity when she sees one.

The woman can't believe her luck. She can't bear seeing Miles and Carmen in love, and now, by a quirk of fate, Fatty has given her a way to tear them apart. Pee Chee is going to tell Miles he's the culprit. He's a hopeless drunk, after all. He blacks out, does things he doesn't remember. Things he isn't proud of. Miles must have given Carmen that black eye. He'd have felt guilty about it. And Pee Chee decides to use his guilt against him.

That night she convinces Fatty that she can massage the evidence. That he will serve a minimal sentence. And that when he gets out of prison, Miles will compensate him generously for his trouble. After Fatty agrees to her scheme, she wakes Miles up and makes him face up to what he's done. She tells him he'd not only beaten the woman he loved, he'd raped her and left her to die. But if he knows what's good for him, he'll let Fatty take the blame. Carmen had been unconscious through the whole ordeal. She couldn't know who was responsible. Could Miles bear for her to know the truth? Pee Chee knew he couldn't. She knew he was weak. Oh, Pee Chee. Did you feel triumphant as you watched the shame eat away at Miles's soul?

"I can see the wheels in your little pea brain turning." Pee Chee stared at me down the barrel of her gun. "You think you know something. But you don't have the slightest idea who I am or what I want."

"I know you're in love with Miles," I said.

"Give the bitch a gold star," said Fatty.

"Shut up." Pee Chee ran a hand through her wild red hair. "I'm going to deal with you next."

"Don't fucking threaten me," said Fatty.

Pee Chee waved her gun at him. "You. Move. I want you next to Dreama."

Fatty came over to where I was standing. He gave me a sidelong glance, which I made a point of ignoring. It was hardly like I could trust him. I had to think for myself now.

"Any more insights, Dreama?" Pee Chee asked. "Your arrogance amuses me."

"You like to be in control," I said.

"Somebody has to be," she said.

"But you're never going to find what you want," I said, "if you're not willing to let down your guard."

Pee Chee shifted her weight a little. She was getting antsy. I had no idea what that meant for me, or for Fatty. "Wow. That's some nerve you've got, lecturing me on love. From what I hear you're no expert."

"I don't claim to be," I said. "I'm just trying to learn from my mistakes."

"You didn't know Carmen," Pee Chee said. "She wasn't good for Miles. She didn't understand him."

"I guess Maya didn't understand him either," I said.

"Oh, Maya understood him just fine. I made damn sure of that." She stopped short, as if she'd suddenly realized she'd said too much. And then Fatty jumped in.

"Dreama." He turned to me. "You blind, or what? You saw a clip of Maya that night at the dance club. You saw all that pretty blond hair. Who do you think fucking *paid her* to dye it black? This bitch right here."

He'd just handed me the shovel I was going to bury Pee Chee with. Assuming she didn't kill me first.

"There you go again, Freddy," said Pee Chee. "Men are so simple, aren't they, Dreama?"

Too bad I hadn't seen it earlier.

I'd known Pee Chee was single-minded.

But I hadn't dreamed of the lengths to which she'd go.

Tricking Miles into believing he'd raped Carmen was only the start of it. Convincing Miles to let Fatty take the blame, that must've been a challenge, too. Keeping Miles apart from Carmen afterward, another brilliant manipulation. But the real genius move was selecting Carmen's replacement, someone Pee Chee could own, body and soul.

Enter Maya Duran.

She was young and beautiful. She was talented and ambitious. She'd spent time with Carmen, so she was familiar with her mannerisms and personality. All Pee Chee had to do was cut off Maya's long, blond hair, dye it black, buy her the right clothes, and take her to see Clayton Key, who'd tricked her out with a replica of Carmen's lotus flower tattoo. It was that easy. Pee Chee said it herself. Men are simple. They like what they like. They have *types*. Miles was a sucker for smooth, shiny girls, hard-boiled and loaded with sin. He'd see Maya as his second chance at Carmen. Only this time, he'd do everything right. Poor fool.

"I'm tired of standing around. What are you going to do?" Fatty taunted. "Shoot us?"

Pee Chee said, "Not yet."

Maya must've gotten restless. Maybe she didn't like being under

Pee Chee's thumb. Maybe she wanted out. Pee Chee couldn't allow that. So she'd "helped" Maya by finding her a gun to use in her act, then visited her backstage the night of her show and swapped out a bullet for a blank. Maya had taken care of the rest.

"You can't pull the trigger. You don't have the balls." Fatty shot me another glance. He wanted me to do something. Say something. But I wasn't about to play a guessing game.

"Pee Chee doesn't do her own dirty work," I finally said. "Why don't you tell us who you're waiting for, Pee Chee?"

She smiled. "You know who I'm waiting for. And exactly what's going to happen to him."

"You're a monster," I said. Then I looked at Fatty. "You're both monsters."

Fatty gritted his teeth. "You're gonna let her talk to you like that?"

"First things first," Pee Chee said. Then she pointed the gun at Fatty and shot him. The sound was deafening. Like a jackhammer. A race car. A fighter jet. And then Fatty crumpled to the ground.

"What have you *done*?" I dropped to my knees and felt for a pulse.

"Get up, Dreama!" Pee Chee ordered.

No pulse. Fatty was dead.

Pee Chee waved her gun. "Are you *high*? I told you to get up!"

As I got up, I bumped against the wall, exerting just enough pressure to dislodge the overloaded power strip from the socket. The bulbs flickered once, then went out.

"What the *fuck*?" cried Pee Chee.

I stayed silent while she fumbled for the flashlight.

"Don't even think about it!" Pee Chee cautioned. "It may be

dark, but I've still got my gun on you. And you've seen what I'm capable of."

I'd already known what she was capable of.

Which was why, when she finally turned the flashlight on me, Pee Chee saw me pointing a .38 special at her.

Maya's .38 special.

I'd put it in my basket this morning before I'd left town. In case of emergency. And I was pretty confident this counted.

"Recognize it?" I asked her. "You should. You got it from Lucius Ramsay." Who got it from Omar G. Patterson, the hairy marble.

"Put the gun down," said Pee Chee. "It's not a prop."

"Too bad Maya didn't know that. What's the matter?" I asked. "You don't look very good. Your hand is shaking."

"We're playing chicken now?" Pee Chee asked.

Not exactly. There were no bullets in the gun. But she didn't know that.

"It's over," I said. "I know everything. What you did to Carmen and Miles, what you did to Maya, what you did to Lizeth." Who'd had the misfortune of showing up at the hospital that day to check up on Maya. Lizeth was collateral damage. Just like I was. Just like Uncle Ray was.

"You thought you were safe," I went on. "Fatty was in Lake Arrowhead. You knew how to take care of Maya. But then Fatty's old friend Lucius showed up on your doorstep and your world came crashing down. Fatty told Lucius everything, didn't he? Meaning Lucius was in a position to demand favors. And he wasn't exactly shy about it. He needed you to make the gun charge go away. It was his third strike. He was going to prison, and they were throwing away the key. You would've loved to have gotten rid of him, but

Lucius scared you. He was violent. Unpredictable. So you did some digging. Found out that the cop who was slated to testify against him was my uncle. And then you came up with the perfect idea. A wedding present for Maya." I shook my head. "The whole noir tour was just a ruse to destroy my uncle's credibility."

Pee Chee said, "Well, you're not exactly worth $40,000 now, are you?"

That stung.

She smiled. "Like I said, Dreama, you're just so fucking arrogant. Maybe if you'd had a little *humility* you'd have questioned that five-figure sum. Saved yourself a lot of aggravation."

"I was trusting," I said. "Like Miles was. Don't you get it, Pee Chee? He *trusted* you. You wanted him to love you? He *did*. You just didn't recognize it."

"I'm done talking," she said. "And so are you, Dreama."

And suddenly everything felt like it was moving in slow motion. I heard Pee Chee cock her gun, and instinctually, I squeezed my trigger finger. After that I heard a sound, a *pfft*, as soft as a kitten jumping onto a pillow. It wasn't until I saw something red spreading across the front of Pee Chee's yellow jumpsuit that I understood what had happened.

Teddy had been wrong when he'd said the gun wasn't loaded.

There had obviously been one more bullet in that .38.

Pee Chee looked down at herself. "You bitch. You shot me." Her voice was so faint I could barely hear it.

I dropped the gun. I couldn't breathe. I couldn't think. What had I done? "I—"

"Dreama didn't shoot you," said another voice coming from somewhere behind me. "I did."

I saw something happen to Pee Chee then.

I saw her eyes go wide, her mouth fall open, and her heart break in two.

Then I spun around.

And saw Miles McCoy, at the mouth of the tunnel, holding a smoking gun.

Chapter 44

"HOW LONG HAVE you been standing there?" I asked.

"Long enough." He looked unutterably sad.

"Miles—"

"Stop. Is this loaded?" He pointed to the .38 special.

I shook my head.

"Then put it away." I put it back into my basket.

"Take this." He bent down to pick up Pee Chee's gun, then handed it to me. "Keep it on her. Mookie's outside. We're going to get help."

"I'm sorry," I said.

"You? What the fuck do you have to be sorry for?" Miles asked.

"I misjudged you." This bear of a man was just a human being, as fragile and vulnerable as the rest of us.

"I'm far from innocent," Miles answered. "But now's not the time."

I knelt down and grabbed Pee Chee's hand. It was warm. I could see the pulse throbbing in her wrist. "She's still alive."

"Keep her talking," he said. "I'll be back."

I didn't let go of Pee Chee's hand. It felt so small in mine. Like it belonged to someone else. Not the ferocious, pitiless woman I'd come to know.

"Where's Miles?" Pee Chee whispered.

"He's getting help," I said. "Hold on."

I put the gun down and used both hands to rip off the bottom of my flimsy slip dress. Then I balled up the length of white satin, and pressed it to Pee Chee's chest. Within seconds, it was soaked through with blood. Pee Chee's pupils were now fixed and dilated. I knew that wasn't a good sign. But her chest was still moving up and down.

"Please stay with me," I said in a strangled voice.

She didn't answer.

"It's going to be okay." I knew she didn't have much time.

And then I heard footsteps coming from the staircase leading down from backstage. I turned my head. "Miles?"

But it wasn't Miles.

It was a small African-American man wearing a sharp green suit. The same man I'd followed out of the courtroom the other day and to Grand Central Market, only to lose him as he drove off with the woman who now lay at my feet, dying.

Before I had a chance to collect my thoughts, much less collect Pee Chee's gun from the floor, Lucius Ramsay said, "Let's put Pee Chee out of her misery, shall we?" And then he shot her right between the eyes.

Pee Chee's body jerked once, then lay still. I watched the blood run down her face and puddle on the ground, a small crimson flood. When I looked up, Lucius was bouncing back and forth on the balls of his feet, mouth twitching, eyes sparkling.

"Get up." He pointed his gun at me.

"We can't just leave her here," I said.

"Maybe you didn't hear me." Lucius tapped his foot. "I said *get up.*"

I struggled to my feet.

He picked up a length of rope from the top of one of the cardboard boxes, and tucked it under his arm. "Now walk toward the stairs."

He stuck the gun in the small of my back and edged me forward.

"You don't have to do this," I said.

"Shut up and keep walking."

My head was pounding and my legs were trembling. I don't know how I managed to stay standing, much less walk up the spiral staircase. When I got to the top, I searched the cavernous space for some way out of this situation. But there was nowhere to hide. Nowhere to run. There was only one small door leading outside, and it was on the other side of the stage.

Where the hell was Miles?

"This way." Lucius nudged me along, kicking wedding decorations out of his way: dewdrop garlands, woodland box planters, looking-glass lanterns.

"Where are we going?" I asked.

"Stop asking so many questions," he said.

With his free hand, he pulled open the red velvet curtain, then shoved me through it. We were in the main room. The tables had been cleared. The floors had been swept. They'd locked up hours before. It was just me and Lucius now. Maybe I could pretend to stumble on one of the chairs as we wound our way to the front door. Maybe he'd lose his balance and I could grab his gun. Maybe pigs could fly.

"We're almost there." I could feel his hot breath on the back of my neck.

"Then what?"

He reached over my shoulder and pushed open the door to the outside. A blast of cold mountain air rushed up the remains of my tattered dress.

"We're going to take a ride," he said. "And I'm going to let you drive."

"Where are we going?"

"Somewhere nice and scenic. You ever heard of Angeles National Forest?"

The place where a convicted swindler's headless body was found in a shallow grave deep in the woods? And where a baby beaten to death by her half-sister was shoved into a garbage bag and tossed to the bottom of a hill? And a teenager accused by two friends of sleeping with their boyfriends was found under a log in a creek? And a strangled model was dumped into a remote canyon by a photographer who couldn't take no for an answer? I told you to Google it.

"Pick up the pace." Lucius kicked me in the ankle. "You don't want to piss me off."

We walked through the parking lot to the back of the Tudor House, stopping beside Miles's black stretch Bentley, which was parked sideways on the crest of a snow-covered hill.

"What did you do with Miles and Mookie?" I asked.

By way of an answer, Lucius popped the trunk.

Miles and Mookie were inside, bound and gagged.

Lucius tossed the length of rope he'd been holding next to them, and slammed the trunk closed.

"Get into the car," he said to me.

My uncle taught me to never get into the car.

If you get into the car, you will not escape.

If you get into the car, you will not be rescued.

When they tell you to get in the car, that's when you make a run for it.

A predator will only hit a running target four in one hundred times. And even then, it will most likely not be a vital organ.

Now was the time.

When Lucius opened the driver's side door, I took a half-step toward the car, and as he relaxed his hold on me, I leaned back sharply against his chest and stomped down on his instep with the heel of the Mary Jane pumps Sheena had loaned me. As he doubled over, I sprang to the side and started sprinting across the parking lot.

"You're *dead*!" cried Lucius, taking off after me.

Then I heard a shot ring out. Then another. Then a third. After that, I heard the sound of something hitting the pavement with a thud. And that something wasn't me.

I stopped short, slowly turned around.

Lucius was on the ground, clutching his ass and cursing a blue streak.

Standing over him was my uncle Ray.

"Third strike," Ray said with a smile.

Then he came over to where I was standing, put his arm around my shoulder, and pulled me close.

And at that moment I knew that nothing was ever going to be the same, and also, that everything was going to be fine.

Chapter 45

TWO WEEKS LATER, everybody showed up at my house for my annual Grammy viewing party. Okay, my *second* annual Grammy viewing party. Assuming my mother doesn't make a habit of re-enacting Robin Thicke's "Blurred Lines" video, it may well become a family tradition. But that remains to be seen.

The house was spotless. I'd laid out pillows and throw blankets. I'd stocked the bar. Because it's important to be accommodating, there were lentil crisps and my grandmother's Jackson Five Layer Bean Dip, which is 100 percent vegan. But it's also important not to hide your true feelings. To that end, I'd put out Reese's Peanut Butter Cups and a plastic tub of Red Vines.

Gram and Ray were the first to arrive. Gram was resplendent in a black-on-black velvet burnout dress with fishnet fringe, lace granny boots, and a white orchid tucked behind her ear. Ray looked like he was on cloud nine. First of all, he had my grandmother on his arm. Secondly, he'd gotten his long-awaited promotion. And no one deserved it more than he did.

Turns out Ray had made Lucius Ramsay his own special project for months, ever since he'd first encountered the gun-toting two-time felon by chance that night at the dive bar. One of the things Ray had learned was that Lucius was a former confidential informant who still had friends in high places. That was why Ray had had to go under the radar. But when it was all over, my uncle had managed to tie him not only to Lizeth's murder, but to two other unsolved murders, not to mention a money-laundering operation. Which was, by the way, how Lucius had been able to get his hands on the marked bills—handily traceable to a drug dealer under federal investigation—that he'd slipped into a manila envelope and dropped off on my stoop. Pee Chee had been kind enough to loan him Miles's black stretch Bentley for that particular errand. Of course, it doesn't necessarily pay to accept a favor from a woman like Pee Chee.

Next to arrive was my mother and her new lover, the C.E.O. of Cowboys4Angels, who was quite the silver fox. He'd met her when she'd tagged along on my *American Gigolo* tour, having promised to keep a low profile, which to her mind apparently meant interrupting my spiel at regular intervals to drop tantalizing bits of libelous gossip about *American Gigolo*'s original lead, John Travolta. The C.E.O. was inexplicably charmed. He'd demonstrated his commitment by buying himself an annual pass to her bi-weekly CrossFit class.

Tigertail and Rory came with their beautiful ten-pound baby girl, whom I kept wanting to call Sprite, even though they'd decided at the last minute to name her Kate. Who would have guessed that two punkabilly diehards would have a soft spot for the commoner who'd stolen Prince William's heart?

Cat showed up soon afterward with the Snapchat executive. One night with my best friend, and the poor guy had not only shaved off his facial hair, he'd waxed his entire body. Cat was still wavering. She walked him over to the bar and told him to fix himself a cocktail, then she took me into the bedroom.

"How have you been?" she asked.

"Fine," I said.

She rolled her eyes. "Tell me."

"I'm still numb," I said. "It was the strangest night of my life."

After my uncle had untied Miles and Mookie, four cop cars had come screeching into the lot, sirens blaring. Lieutenant Hepworth had hitched a ride in one of them. He took my uncle aside and they talked for a long time. In the interim, the coroner's van had showed up. It was too late for Pee Chee and Fatty. But Lucius was going to make it. After the ambulance took him away, there were lots of questions. Miles waived his right to an attorney, but the situation was pretty clear-cut. Miles had saved my life. As for me, the police made me promise not to leave Southern California until everything was sorted out. That wasn't going to be a problem. All I wanted was my own bed.

It was 5 a.m. when I finally made it home. I couldn't sleep, so I spent the next hour just walking the streets of Venice. As I wandered with no particular destination in mind I was struck by the beauty of the place where I lived. The ruby red trumpet vines climbing a graffitied wall, the Moroccan lanterns strung across a canopy of olive trees in the courtyard of a closed café, the extravagant spills of pink and orange bougainvillea. I stopped and watched a hummingbird sticking its little beak into a cactus flower. I breathed in the sweet scent of orange blossom. Then I took Washington to the sand, and sat down at the edge of the water to watch the sun rise.

Some things still confused me.

One of them was the whereabouts of Maya Duran. Maya had made a miraculous recovery, and the day the doctor had okayed her release, she hadn't just left the hospital. She'd also taken all her new clothes and left town. Miles said she was the sort who needed her freedom. Sounded to me more like she'd had a fit of conscience. Or maybe she was afraid of Pee Chee. Given everything that had happened, Maya was probably lucky to have escaped with her life.

Another thing I never found out was who Pee Chee was waiting for when we were down in that basement. Lucius? Uncle Ray? Miles? And what exactly she was planning to do to him when he showed up. I think she knew that things had gone too far. That she was stuck between a rock and a hard place. That it was either keep killing to protect her secret, or face Miles with the truth of what she'd done, and neither was a viable option.

"Dreama!" my mother called from the living room.

"Please tell me she isn't getting ready to strip down to her flesh-colored G-string again," Cat whispered.

"It's Luke." My mother pointed to the T.V. "He's on the red carpet with that *insanely gorgeous* young woman."

Cat and I walked back into the living room just in time to see the Victoria's Secret supermodel flashing her brand-new 8.5 carat engagement ring.

"Don't worry, Dreama," my mother said. "One day it'll be your turn. Or not," she added cheerfully.

Gram leaned in to me. "Did you tell her you and Teddy have started talking again?"

I shook my head. "I don't want to jinx it." Which I didn't. Maybe Teddy and I would get it right this time. Maybe we wouldn't. All I knew was I wasn't going to hold back. I was done with being afraid.

"Are there any *real* chips around here?" Uncle Ray called out from the kitchen.

Rory dove into his tartan plaid satchel and extracted a party-sized bag of Tostitos. "I always keep an emergency stash."

Speaking of emergency stashes, Ray finally came clean about having taken the $40,000 from under my mattress. He'd thought he was protecting me, and that everything would be resolved before I'd even noticed the money was missing. When I'd asked him what he'd done with it, since he was hardly about to return it to Lucius or the drug dealer Lucius had stolen it from, Ray told me it was in a safety deposit box with my name on it at the Wells Fargo in Lake Arrowhead. That money was my Plan B. It was there in case everything went to hell. Chances are that wouldn't happen, but life is unpredictable. In any case, Ray said, I'd earned it. That last point was hard to argue.

Gram patted the couch, and I took a seat next to her just in time to catch Destiny D-Low waltzing down the red carpet in a hooded yellow silk robe that looked like it had come straight out of Rocky Balboa's closet. "Oil Slick" was widely expected to win for Best Song, but Destiny obviously still thought of herself as an underdog.

"Look who's coming up behind Destiny," said my mother. "*Someone* looks like he's been dipping into the honeypot."

She was talking about my former employer, Miles McCoy.

Remember how he'd saved my life?

Well, I was lucky enough to have been able to reciprocate.

A few days after getting back from Arrowhead, Miles and I took a road trip of our own. Mookie drove. Miles talked. And I listened, which is something I'm not always good at. I've been told that I lack humility. That I'm impetuous, and occasionally thoughtless. I'm trying. Like most people, I'm a work in progress.

Miles and I had more in common than either of us would've guessed. Like me, he was raised by two strong women. He and his grandmother had been especially close. She was a girl from a small town in Michigan who came out to Hollywood in the forties to make it in pictures. Her second day in town she got a job as a coat check girl at Lucey's, the bar directly across the street from Paramount. One of the people she'd gotten to know there was Raymond Chandler, who frequented the place while he was under contract to Paramount to adapt *Double Indemnity*. He was a true gentleman, Miles's grandmother said, who never failed to have a kind word for her. But he was also a troubled soul who didn't have the stomach for the movie business. Hollywood, he once wrote, was the kind of town where they stuck a knife in your back, then arrested you for carrying a concealed weapon. Miles's grandmother didn't have the stomach for Hollywood either. After a couple of years, she went back home, and found her happiness there.

She'd passed on her love of noir to her grandson, however, and it had stuck. Miles had particularly admired Chandler's detective, Philip Marlowe. But Marlowe was a cautionary tale. Chandler often said that Marlowe would never marry. That he'd always have a shabby office, a lonely house, affairs, but not lasting connections. Miles had finally figured out that he didn't want to be that person. That he wanted love, and was willing to sacrifice his pride to get it. Pride was another thing Miles and I had in common. And it was the reason we were taking this drive down south.

We were going to find Carmen Luz.

Miles had never stopped loving her.

She'd never stopped loving him either.

He'd realized that only after I'd given him the stack of letters I'd found the day I'd hidden in Maya's closet. After the rape, Carmen had written to Miles every week for three years, asking him if he could ever forget about what Fatty had done to her, if he could ever forgive her for allowing it to happen, if he could ever find a way to be with her again.

Miles had never seen a single one of those letters.

Pee Chee had intercepted them all.

Miles had thought about reaching out to Carmen—not once, but countless times. But each of those times Pee Chee had stopped him. She'd said that it would be selfish. That Carmen was healing. That the last thing she needed was to be bullied by the man who'd raped her. Poor Miles. All of those years obsessed with noir, and he hadn't recognized the femme fatale standing right in front of him.

Three hours after leaving Los Angeles, Miles and I pulled up in front of a small house in a quiet neighborhood just across the border.

And out came Carmen Luz.

Her smile was the most beautiful thing I'd ever seen.

Tonight, as she walked the red carpet with Miles, it looked even more so.

"Carmen's dress is amazing." Cat grabbed the remote and hit pause. "And if I do say so myself, I did a damn good job on her lotus flower tattoo." Then she turned to me. "She paid us what she owed us, by the way. And she's coming in this weekend to move ahead with her sleeve. She specifically asked if Rory could work on the dharma wheel."

Rory stroked his mustache, which had evolved nicely into a half horseshoe. "What can I say? The ladies love me."

Tigertail looked up from nursing baby Kate. "The validation is helping Rory's post-partum depression."

Just then the doorbell rang. Strange. I wasn't expecting anyone else.

By the time I got to the door whoever it was had already left.

I looked down.

And saw a manila envelope on the stoop.

Impossible.

I shut my eyes for a second, then opened them again.

The envelope was still there.

I picked it up, took it into my bedroom, closed the door, ripped it open.

There was $40,000 in cash inside.

This time, there was also a note.

Dear Dreama,

Okay, so maybe I did slash your tires and steal the money from your car. What can I say? I'm an angry person. And a starving artist with bills to pay. Also, you pissed me off when you called me Chick. Nonetheless, you did something really kind for Carmen. She came by yesterday and told me about it. And both of us appreciate it. I also remembered that it's wrong to steal. This is your money. I hope you don't feel guilty or anything and try to give it back to me just because I desperately need it.

> *Best wishes,*
> *Charlie Churchill*

No worries, Chick.

Guilt isn't particularly my issue.

So here's the thing.

I seemed to be up $80,000, which was quite a handsome sum to have made off of a film noir tour that had never happened. But that was hardly my fault, was it? I'd done a lot of work. And learned some life lessons. Plus, I was never going to touch that first $40,000. Well, maybe years from now. If I *absolutely* needed to. And only one bill at a time. To be spent in far-flung locations. I was starting to think of it as hazard pay, actually.

After slipping the manila envelope under my mattress, I went over to the mirror, and touched up my bangs, which weren't looking half-bad tonight. Then I went back out to my party.

"Drink this immediately." Cat handed me a tequila shot. "Your ex Luke Cutt just won for Best Song of the Year."

I downed the shot.

Then Cat and I both started laughing.

Yeah, that's the thing about us groupies.

We never say no.

Dreama Black's Noir L.A.

GET READY TO plunge into the noir underbelly of the City of the Angels. This tour requires a car, five to six hours (with two optional side trips), and a tolerance for bourbon and blood . . .

1. Mildred Pierce House, 1147 N. Jackson Street, Glendale, CA

You can't go wrong starting with *Mildred Pierce*, written in 1941 by the poet laureate of hard-boiled fiction, James M. Cain. This house is one of the filming locations for the 1945 film starring the inimitable Joan Crawford, who won an Academy Award for the role. Rumor has it she faked an illness to get out of the ceremony, certain she'd lose to Ingrid Bergman in *The Bells of St. Mary's*. After she won, she slipped into a negligée with padded shoulders, painted on her eyebrows, and invited members of the press to chat with her as she accepted her Oscar in bed. Screen the movie first, and then marvel at the fact that very little has changed on Jackson Street in the intervening years. Besides, of course, the real estate values.

2. **Glendale Train Station, 400 W. Cerritos Avenue, Glendale, CA**

For years, it was taken as gospel that the filming location where the ball-busting Phyllis Dietrichson and the pussy-whipped Walter Neff conspire to commit murder in the film version of Cain's *Double Indemnity* (with a screenplay by Raymond Chandler and director Billy Wilder) was this magnificent Spanish Revival structure with sculpted terra cotta, a faux second story, and elaborately carved wooden doors. Too bad the Glendale station wasn't actually where the scene was shot in 1944. That honor goes to the far less ornate Mission-style depot in Burbank. You can't go there, however, because it was knocked down almost two decades ago— because it was old, and because that's the way we do it in L.A.

3. **Union Station, 800 N. Alameda Street, Los Angeles, CA**

As well as being the largest railroad passenger terminal in the western U.S., Union Station is one of L.A.'s most famous architectural sites. Designed by John and Donald B. Parkinson, the 1939 structure brilliantly cross-pollinates the Art Deco, Mission Revival and Streamline Moderne idioms. I especially like the trompe l'oeil–esque ceiling in the waiting room, which looks like wood, but is made of steel. Union Station has been used as a location in countless noirs, among them *Criss Cross*, *Cry Danger*, *The Bigamist*, and *Union Station*, which, ironically, was based on a story set in New York City, but filmed entirely in L.A.

4. **Far East Building, 347 E. 1st Street, Little Tokyo, CA**

This building in Little Tokyo was home to the prototypical Depression-era Chinese joint (known alternately as the Far East Café and the Chop Suey Café) immortalized in Raymond

Chandler's *Farewell, My Lovely* as the meeting place between the hulking client, Moose Malloy, and the reluctant detective, Philip Marlowe, the latter of whose lunch was interrupted when "a dark shadow fell over my chop suey." Currently a hipster bar, the private booths with red curtains add period flavor.

5.   The Varnish, 118 E. 6th Street, Los Angeles, CA

First, order a French dip at Cole's, which is a wonderful sandwich, if not as superlative as the French dip at Philippe's. However, Philippe's does not have an old storage room in the back, marked solely by the etching of a cocktail on the door, which leads onto the veritable epicenter of the craft cocktail universe. Welcome to the Varnish. For as long as it takes you to finish your gin gimlet or old-fashioned, you can pretend you are in a Prohibition-era speakeasy. Oh, and they chip ice from a single block. With an ice pick.

6.   Eastern Columbia Building, 849 S. Broadway, Los Angeles, CA

Yes, Johnny Depp once owned six units in this thirteen-story turquoise, blue, and gold Art Deco icon. If you can get up to the rooftop pool, god bless. Otherwise, marvel at the details from the street—the sunbursts, the chevrons, the zigzags, the flying buttresses surmounting the spectacular four-sided clock tower. Originally built in 1930 after only nine months of construction, the steel-reinforced concrete structure had fallen into complete disrepair when it was snapped up by the Kor Group and transformed into luxury condos. Be sure to check out the movie palaces surrounding it down Broadway, in particular the Beaux-Arts Orpheum and the Spanish Gothic United Artists.

7. **MacArthur Park, 2230 W. 6th Street, Los Angeles, CA**

Originally called Westlake Park, it was established in the 1880s with the idea of beautifying the rough and tumble new city. Featured in the Donna Summer song, as well as many film noirs, including *Too Late for Tears*, *Down Three Dark Streets*, and *The Bigamist*. You probably don't want to linger. After taking pictures and posting them, head straight over to Langer's Deli for a #19, which is pastrami, coleslaw, and Swiss on rye.

8. **Black Dahlia Death Site, 3825 S. Norton Avenue, Leimert Park, CA**

Elizabeth Short was a beautiful, twenty-two-year-old girl from Boston, last seen on the night of January 9, 1947, walking south on Olive Street, after having been dropped at the Biltmore Hotel by a married traveling salesman. Six days later, her naked, mutilated body was found on this site—now an ordinary-looking house, then a trash-strewn empty lot. In short order, Beth Short became the Black Dahlia and ascended to the status of myth. People have confessed, books have been written, theories have been proposed, police files have been reopened, but this iconic, real-life L.A. murder remains unsolved.

9. **Sowden House, 5121 Franklin Avenue, Los Angeles, CA**

One of the most intriguing suspects in the Black Dahlia case is Dr. George Hodel, the man who owned this extraordinary 1926 residence in Los Feliz from 1945–1951. Built by Lloyd Wright (eldest son of Frank Lloyd Wright) to resemble a Mayan Revival–style fortress, the sharp ridges of the house's façade are often likened to the gaping jaws of a vicious shark. Enter Dr. Hodel, whose day job was running a VD clinic catering to the rich and famous, and whose evening activities allegedly included beating his sons in the basement, throwing orgies in his gold bedroom, and raping his daughter Tamar. After his death, his son, a retired L.A.P.D. detective named Steve Hodel, came across a photo in his father's effects that he claimed was of Elizabeth Short. Steve Hodel embarked upon an investigation, soon becoming convinced that his father had not only killed Short, but had also been responsible for several other brutal murders that took place in the 1940s, at least some of them in the basement of the Sowden House. Read Steve Hodel's *Black Dahlia Avenger* for a provocative addition to the Black Dahlia franchise.

10. Philip Marlowe Office, 6385 Hollywood Blvd., Hollywood, CA

Unlike that other iconic detective, Sam Spade, Philip Marlowe didn't have a secretary. Marlowe worked alone, in a decidedly unglamorous two rooms on the sixth floor of the fictional Cahuenga Building—the former Security Trust and Savings Bank Building on Hollywood and Cahuenga. A six-story structure built in 1921 by the Parkinsons, who also designed Union Station (see above), City Hall and the exquisite Bullock's Wilshire, this was once the tallest building on Hollywood. Yes, it's seen better days and is in need of some TLC, but be careful about what you wish for. Word is there are plans to turn the building into a boutique hotel.

11. Musso and Frank, 6667 Hollywood Blvd., Hollywood, CA

Legendary Hollywood watering hole, first opened in 1919, with worn leather booths and a stunning mahogany bar, where old school bartenders mix the driest martinis in town. With the Screenwriters' Guild just across the street, literary greats like Fitzgerald, Faulkner, and Chandler—in town just long enough to eke some extra dollars out of the movie studios—dropped in regularly for liquid refreshment. Chandler, in fact, is rumored to have written several chapters of *The Big Sleep* while downing bottles of Kentucky bourbon in the Back Room. The menu still features classic dishes such as Welsh rarebit, lobster thermidor, and mushrooms on toast. You can never go wrong, however, with the sand dabs.

12. Alto Nido Apartments, 1851 Ivar Avenue, Los Angeles, CA

This modest Spanish Revival building, with its red tile roof and iron balconies, was home to the unemployed screenwriter Joe Gillis (played by William Holden) before he sold his soul and moved in with the aging silent film actress Norma Desmond (an unforgettable Gloria Swanson) in Billy Wilder's *Sunset Boulevard*. Once in a while there's actually a vacancy, but who's kidding whom? These days, no struggling screenwriter could afford to live in this 1929 charmer, a mere block northwest of the legendary intersection, Hollywood and Vine. Sidebar: In 1948, Lila Leeds, who played a bit part in *Lady in the Lake*, adapted from the Chandler novel of the same name, survived an overdose of sleeping pills at the Alto Nido only to be arrested with Robert Mitchum for marijuana possession a few months later.

13. Crossroads of the World, 6671 Sunset Blvd., Los Angeles, CA

Located at the corner of Sunset and Las Palmas in Hollywood, Crossroads of the World is often described as America's first outdoor shopping mall. Designed in 1936 by Robert V. Derrah in the Streamline Moderne style, with idiosyncratic cruise ship, lighthouse, and minaret details, it served as the headquarters of the tabloid *Hush-Hush* in the magisterial noir throwback *L.A. Confidential*, based on the book of the same title by James Ellroy.

14. High Tower Court, 2181 Broadview Terrace, Hollywood, CA

At the end of a steep hill not far from the Hollywood Bowl is a small complex of homes and apartment buildings designed by architect Carl Lay between 1935 and 1956, whose original walk street layout was meant to evoke Positano, Italy. None of the residences is accessible by car. Instead, there are garages at the base of the hill. After parking your car, you can puzzle your way through the labyrinth of stairs, walkways, and bridges hidden behind shady trees and climbing vines, or you can talk your way into the five-story private elevator concealed inside a campanile that Kay built when his wife got sick of taking the stairs. High Tower Court is where Elliott Gould's laid-back Philip Marlowe lives in Robert Altman's fantastic 1973 *The Long Goodbye*, which deftly pushes against the noir genre, while embracing its subterranean romanticism.

15. The Dietrichson Residence, 6301 Quebec Drive, Hollywood Hills, CA

You know the story. Poor Walter Neff was just making a house call, to one of those California Spanish houses that everybody was nuts about ten or fifteen years earlier. Must've cost Mr. Dietrichson $30,000, if he was finished paying for it, that is. Anyway, the guy's car insurance was about to lapse and Neff made his living getting people to renew. Inside, Neff catches one glimpse of the wife, Phyllis Dietrichson, in a towel, slippers with pom-poms, and that honey of an anklet, and boom, he's a goner. Actually, it's Mr. Dietrichson who's the goner. That, in a nutshell, is *Double*

Indemnity, everybody's favorite film noir. Though the Dietrichson residence is supposed to be in Los Feliz, the shooting location was actually in Beachwood Canyon, and is virtually unchanged since 1944. Better hurry, though.

16. Formosa Cafe, 7156 Santa Monica Blvd., West Hollywood, CA

Bugsy Siegel kept a safe under his favorite booth of this legendary cocktail lounge. Is there anything else to say? Oh, yeah. The safe was sealed after he was gunned down by rivals in 1947, but in 2000, it was drilled open. What was inside? "Rust, lots and lots of rust, not even a paper clip," according to the grandson of the man who'd installed it. The Formosa has been featured in countless films, including the unforgettable "a hooker cut to look like Lana Turner is still just a hooker" scene in *L.A. Confidential.*

17. Villa Primavera, 1300–1308 Harper Avenue, West Hollywood, CA

The earliest surviving example of the eight courtyard complexes designed by the husband-and-wife team of Arthur and Nina Zwebell, Villa Primavera (1923) has been home to many stars including Katherine Hepburn and James Dean, as well as director Nicholas Ray. The latter liked the Spanish Revival ambience so much that he had a replica built on a Columbia Studios backlot to be used as the set for his 1950 noir, *In a Lonely Place*, starring Humphrey Bogart and Ray's wife at the time, Gloria Grahame. Now it gets weird. Halfway through the shoot, Ray's marriage blew up when the director caught Grahame in bed with his thirteen-year-old son from a previous marriage. After that, the director packed his bags and moved onto the set—a simulacrum of his own bachelor apartment—for the duration of shooting.

18. Greystone Mansion, 905 Loma Vista, Beverly Hills, CA

A fifty-five-room Tudor Revival mansion designed by architect Gordon Kaufmann and completed in 1928 as a gift from oil tycoon Edward Doheny to his son, Ned. Widely thought to have been ex–oil man Raymond Chandler's model for the palatial Sternwood Manor, which Philip Marlowe visits in the opening pages of *The Big Sleep*: "I was neat, clean, shaved and sober, and I didn't care who knew it. I was everything the well-dressed detective ought to be. I was calling on four million dollars." If only money bought happiness. When he gets hired by Colonel Sternwood, Marlowe enters a maelstrom of jealousy, blackmail, and murder. The Dohenys would have known something about that. Four months after Ned, his wife, and their five children moved into Greystone, Ned died in a guest bedroom in a murder-suicide with his secretary, Hugh Plunket. The official story, that Hugh did the shooting, didn't exactly jibe with the fact that Ned's gun was the weapon. But what do I know?

19. Sheats-Goldstein House, 10104 Angelo View Drive, Los Angeles, CA

With its slippery glass walkways and no railings around the patios and outdoor hallways, this landmark John Lautner house is perhaps not the best place to tie one on. An example of American organic architecture, it was built in 1961 directly into the sandstone of the hillside and intended to mimic a cave, which might explain why it was chosen by the Coen Brothers to be the party house of pornographer Jackie Treehorn in their noir throwback *The Big Lebowski*. Recently donated to the Los Angeles County Museum of Art, the house is currently being restored.

If you're game for more things noir, here are two side trips:

1. **Mount Hope Cemetery, 3751 Market Street, San Diego, CA**
Fifty years after their deaths, Raymond Chandler and his wife were finally reunited here. Cissy Chandler died at eighty-four, after thirty years of marriage. Her much-younger husband, who died five alcohol-soaked years later, had wanted to be buried next to the woman who'd inspired him to write. But he'd never completed the documents. So her ashes remained at a nearby mausoleum, while he was interred at Mount Hope. A few years ago, some Chandler fans began a campaign to have the oversight corrected. They convinced a judge, and Cissy's ashes were transferred to her husband's grave in 2011, on Valentine's Day. When you visit, bring roses, and read aloud from Chandler's letters. "Everything I've ever done," he once wrote about Cissy, "was just a fire for her to warm her hands at."

2. **Bracken Fern Manor, 815 Arrowhead Villa Road, Lake Arrowhead, CA**
Bracken Fern was originally part of a sprawling private resort which was comprised of three buildings housing a gambling club, a brothel, a speakeasy, luxury guest quarters, tennis courts, an Olympic-sized pool, a barbershop, a private gas station, a ski lift, horse stables, and that Depression-era all-essential: a supply of artesian well water, used in the making of moonshine. The property

cost $1.3 million to construct in 1929, so one can only imagine how lavish it must have been. Nothing but the best for Bugsy Siegel. It's haunted, too. Don't take my word for it. Check out Violet's room. Or better yet, Episode 12, Season 2, of the Travel Channel's *Ghost Adventures*, in which paranormal investigator Zak Bagans and his team uncover the secret tunnels below Bracken Fern. You know. The ones where the demons are lurking.

cost $1.3 million to construct in 1825, so one can only imagine how lavish it must have been. Nothing but the best for Bugsy Siegel. It's haunted, too. Don't take my word for it. Check out Violet's room. Or better yet, Episode 12, Season 2, of the Travel Channel's Ghost Adventures, in which paranormal investigator Zak Bagans and his team uncover the secret tunnels below Bracken Fern. You know. The ones where the demons are lurking.

About the Author

An Agatha, Edgar, and SCIBA nominee, **SUSAN KANDEL** is the author of the nationally bestselling and critically acclaimed Cece Caruso series, the most recent of which, *Dial H for Hitchcock* (Morrow), was named by NPR as one of the five best mysteries of the year. A Los Angeles native, she was trained as an art historian, taught at NYU and UCLA, and spent a decade as an art critic at the *Los Angeles Times*. When not writing, she volunteers as a court-appointed advocate for foster children, and loves to explore secret, forgotten, and kitschy L.A. She lives with her husband in West Hollywood.

Discover great authors, exclusive offers, and more at hc.com.